心斋集

王 勣◎编著

上海交通大学出版社
SHANGHAI JIAO TONG UNIVERSITY PRESS

内容提要

本书为作者个人翻译精选集，包含汉译英、英译汉两个部分，既有小说、散文、诗歌、词话等等的翻译，也涉及了少量的翻译研究，为翻译爱好者学习翻译实用技巧，从事翻译实践工作提供了素材。

图书在版编目(CIP)数据

译心斋集 / 王勲编著. —上海：上海交通大学出版社，2019

ISBN 978-7-313-22842-0

Ⅰ.①译… Ⅱ.①王… Ⅲ.①诗集-世界 Ⅳ.①I12

中国版本图书馆 CIP 数据核字(2019)第 296453 号

译心斋集

YI XIN ZHAI JI

编　　著：王　勲

出版发行：上海交通大学出版社　　地　　址：上海市番禺路 951 号

邮政编码：200030　　电　　话：021-64071208

印　　刷：当纳利(上海)信息技术有限公司　　经　　销：全国新华书店

开　　本：710mm×1000mm　1/16　　印　　张：13.5

字　　数：225 千字

版　　次：2019 年 12 月第 1 版　　印　　次：2019 年 12 月第 1 次印刷

书　　号：ISBN 978-7-313-22842-0

定　　价：78.00 元

序　言

龚　刚

（澳门大学南国人文研究中心副主任，澳门文艺评论家协会副主席）

文学翻译是一项艰巨而孤独的事业，而且报酬与付出往往不成比例。王勳老师长年坚守在文学翻译的前线，如果没有对文学翻译由衷的热爱，以及不为功名利禄所沾染的纯净心灵，恐怕很难做得到。一旦心灵凭借对文学的热爱摆脱了世俗的羁绊，挣断了与世俗相连的一线游丝，它就能够逍遥于文学的天空，体会到文学世界的自由的快乐。文学翻译进一步打破了不同语言对心灵的阻隔，打通了不同语言的文学世界，为心灵的驰骋开拓出更广袤瑰丽的空间。文学翻译是翻译事业，是文学事业，也是心灵的事业。

文学翻译事业如同其他事业一样，需要获得心力的滋养，才能茁壮成长，实现自身的发展。王勳老师长年的坚守，滋养着她历久弥新的文学翻译花园，在这个超越季节和地域的花园里，她不断超越着时间和空间的限制，与一众古今中外文学名家进行着心灵上的交流。这部《译心斋集》就是这种天马行空的交流的记录，从中读者不仅可以体会到文学之美，文学翻译之美，也能体会到不问功名的纯粹的文学心灵之美。

王勳老师不仅拥有深厚的英语文学功底，在中国古典文学研究领域也极有心得。钱钟书先生提出“打通”说，文学翻译也是“打通”的途径和成果之一，而要达到“打通”的状态，臻于“妙合”之境，译者必须同时精通译出语和译入语，并能感受到两种语言各自的美和相通的美。王勳老师主持的“A Moon Over Fountains”（名作经典赏析栏目）旨在向读者介绍英文文学的原文之美以及翻译成中文后的译文之美。这些蕴含着思想的鉴赏文字令人百读不厌。尤其是她对于曼斯菲尔德的小说以及儿童文学的细腻感触，令人读之“口角噙香”。书中收录的她对于《一帧画页》《小红马》和《纸镇》等等翻译作品的鉴赏都是突出的例了。

正由于王[illegible]老师对于文本有着深邃独到的洞察力，她的翻译能把握住原作的精髓和风格，有许多闪光之处。例如，她翻译的曼斯菲尔德的小说《一帧画页》中的一句话：

His heart fell out of the side window of his studio, and down to the balcony of the house opposite — buried itself in the pot of daffodils under the half-opened buds and spears of green...

（王勋老师译文：他的心儿跌出画室的侧窗，落到对屋的阳台上——埋在种着水仙花的花盆里，埋在半开的花蕾和娇绿的嫩茎下……）

这一句话的原文写得生动传神，却又委婉柔美，不知不觉中牵动着读者的心，令人如临其境，如感其情。王勋老师把 heart 翻译成“心儿”，把 fell out 译成“跌出”，spears of green 译成“娇绿的嫩茎”，清新流丽，情感涌动，而且整句译文流畅忠实，完整而真切地传达出了原文的神采，翻译得非常成功。又如她翻译的安东尼·特罗洛普的《归家》中的这段话：

...the clouds soon gathered and poured forth their collected waters as though it had not rained for months among those mountains. Not that it came in big drops, or with the violence which wind can give it, beating hither and thither, breaking branches from the trees, and rising up again as it pattered against the ground. There was no violence in the rain. It fell softly in a long, continuous, noiseless stream, sinking into everything that it touched, converting the deep rich earth on all sides into mud. Not a word was said by any of them as it came on. The Indian covered the baby with her blanket, closer than she was covered before, and the guide who walked by Mrs. Arkwright's side drew her cloak around her knees. But such efforts were in vain.

（王勋老师译文：很快乌云密布，聚集的雨水倾倒下来，好似山地这一带数月没下过雨。其实雨点不大，没有夹杂在狂风里四下胡乱抽打一气，也没有折树断枝敲落地面后飞溅。雨下得一点儿也不猛烈。它轻柔地落下，悄无声息地汇成源源不断的长流，渗进所到之处，把四方肥沃的地下土壤变成泥浆。下雨时，他们当中没有一个人开口说话。印第安人用毛毯裹住婴儿，裹得比先前更紧了，走在阿克赖特夫人身旁的向导拿她的披风盖住她的膝盖。但这样做是徒劳的。）

“乌云密布”“没有……胡乱抽打”“也没有……飞溅”“四方”等译文不仅准确地传达出原文意思，还通过中文特有的修饰方式，突出了当时的晦暗压抑的气氛和旅行者焦灼不安的心情。而且，译者的这种处理方式减弱了“翻译腔”，使译文读来更为自然顺畅。此外，译者对于英文长句的处理也非常娴熟，译文中几乎见不到佶屈聱牙的长句，消除了中文和英文之间的语法隔阂，为读者呈现出极高水准的译文，减低阅读障碍，并通过翻译帮助读者更深入地了解和赏析原文。

王[illegible]老师非常擅长英译汉，同时在汉译英上也造诣深厚。她在前人的翻译基础上重译《人间词话》，展示出过人的勇气和强大的自信心。《人间词话》的翻译是非常困难的，其核心概念“境界”一词的翻译就争议重重。王勣老师重译《人间词话》并非刻意要超越前人，而是为了帮助中国文化“走出去”，通过翻译将中国古代的经典作品及其蕴含的博大思想传播至英语世界。从译文的细致程度可以看出她作为知识分子的文化责任心。

现代人生活在物质文明高度发达的城市中，容易成为技术的奴隶，也常常受到流行文化、消费主义、金钱逻辑等等的干扰，很难常保心灵的纯净和澄明。阅读优美的文学翻译作品，有利于帮助人们排除这些干扰，重新思考存在的意义。经典的文学翻译作品能够成为我们灵魂安顿之所，在某种程度上化解我们的“哲性乡愁”。如果各位读者静下心来慢慢品读王勣老师的《译心斋集》，也许能够在繁忙的工作和生活中获得片刻的安宁，而对于青少年读者来说，就更加多了一层陶冶性情、开拓视野的作用。

前　言

有人说翻译是一门技艺，也有人说翻译是一门学问，我始终认为翻译是一种心境，是一种**以天合天、以心译心、以心感心**的审美情愫。《译心斋集》正是一本精心撰写的翻译赏析集，书名源于一个中国古代的故事。

庄子《达生》篇里有一个叫梓庆的鲁国木匠的故事：他"削木为鐻"，把一种乐器做成了"见者惊为鬼神"，乐器上面的猛虎被雕刻得栩栩如生。于是梓庆声名远播，鲁侯召见他，问他怎么能够雕刻得这么像？梓庆很谦虚，对鲁侯说："我准备做这个鐻的时候，一定要斋戒静心，让自己的内心真正安静下来，毫无杂念。三天之后，我就可以忘记'庆赏爵禄'了，也就是说，我成功以后，可以得到的封功赏赐啊，升官发财啊，这些东西都可以扔掉了，也就是说忘记利益了。斋戒到第五天，我就可以忘记'非誉巧拙'了，也就是说，我已经不在乎别人对自己是毁是誉、是是非非，是好也罢，是坏也罢，我都已经不在乎了，也就是说忘记名声了。到第七天的时候，我可以忘却我这个人的'四肢形体'，也就是说，我忘记自己有四肢五官了，达到忘我之境。这个时候，我就进山了。进山以后，静下心来，寻找好的木材，观察木材的质地，看到形态合适的，就砍回来，顺手一加工，就能雕刻成现在的样子。我做事情只是'以天合天'，这就是我的奥秘。"

鲁国木匠的故事给了我在翻译方面这样的启示：翻译的时候，一定要有一个好的心态，超越功利，静心忘我，细致研读原文，体味原文的行文风格、用字特色、感情色彩，才能做到"以天合天"。好的译者要有极强的领悟心与审美力，能够把握各种体裁的原文，把原作品里的镜中花、空中月、山之形、云之状采撷回来，把对原作的心灵感悟诉诸笔端，自然幻化为至臻至善、生机盎然的译文作品。

笔者担任大学英语系教职以来，曾经陆续在各个主要的英语报刊和诗歌会上发表翻译作品。在教授大学英汉、汉英翻译时，无论是在课堂内，还是在课堂外，总有好学的学生向我请教翻译的秘诀，他们孜孜不倦的求学态度是我撰写本书的动力与热情。翻译开阔了学生们的视野，让他们体味到不同的语言与文化之间也有相通之处。翻译也是信息传递的桥梁，是情感沟通的纽带，翻译者一定要守住心斋，才能把优秀精美的原文作品，用不同的语言雕刻出译文作品。

一是**用译者的一颗心去揣摩体味原文作者的一颗心**。本书简述了翻译的基本概念与实用技巧，结合翻译的充足实例，以天合天，以心译心，力图在翻译理论探索与翻译实践应用上有所突破。本书精选了笔者在全国优秀英语杂志《海外英语》主持的翻译专栏"月听清泉"里的文章，还精选了笔者在全国其他优秀英语报刊《英语世界》《新东方英语》《大学英语》《英语沙龙》《英语知识》《英语辅导报》上发表的译文。《人间词话》译文注解，格言隽语，秀草幽花，心灯意蕊，片金碎玉，则为之点缀。翻译实例还涉及考古美学等专业术语。

二是**用译者自己的一颗心去感染打动读者的一颗心**。苏联著名教育学家苏霍姆林斯基说过："我一千次相信：没有一条富有诗意的、感情的和审美的清泉，就不可能有学生全面的智力的发展。富有诗意的创造开始于美的幻想，美使知觉更加敏锐，唤醒创造的思维。"本书不拘囿于枯燥的翻译理论说教，而是努力引导读者体味好的翻译作品的艺术魅力，这些作品有的字字珠玑，有的博大深沉，有的感心动耳，有的立意隽永，让读者体味到翻译之妙，翻译之美，翻译之巧，翻译之用，努力使读者对语言的本质与转换兼具理性与感性认识，从而提高他们的语言素养，陶冶他们的审美意识，培养他们的鉴赏能力，提升他们的人生品位。

好的译文，"外之能喻于人，内之能慊诸己"；好的译者，"遂于作者，又老于作者"；译道，"一名之立，旬日踟蹰"。

《译心斋集》原文作品都是近现代大家的作品，风格流派各具特点，各擅其美，译文努力传达出原作的各具形态的美感。

有关雄壮的：

His life was in his hand, and he was prepared to throw it away in that attempt. Having succeeded in placing himself a little above the large tree, he turned his face towards the bottom of the river, and dived down among the branches. And he also, after that, was never again seen with the life-blood flowing round his heart.

他竭尽全力，准备舍己救人。他成功地游到那棵大树偏上的位置，接着面朝河底，俯冲进树枝丛中。那以后，他生命的血液在心脏里再也没有流动。

有关平淡的：

...the one idea that gives salt to life is the idea of home. On some day, however distant it may be, they will once more turn their faces towards the little northern island, and then all will be well with them.

生活的滋味是对家的思念。某一日，无论相距多么遥远，他们的目光会再次转向北方小岛，那时那刻，一切就会好起来。

有关绮丽的：

It wasn't real night yet but the blinds were down in the dining-room and the lights turned on-and all the lights were red roses. Red ribbons and bunches of roses tied up the table at the corners. In the middle was a lake with rose petals floating on it... Two silver lions with wings had fruit on their backs, and the salt cellars were tiny birds drinking out of basins. And all the winking glasses and shining plates and sparking knives and forks...

天还没有完全黑，但是宴会厅的窗帘已经落下。华灯四落，散发出玫瑰色的光。餐桌的四角绑着红色彩带和玫瑰花束。桌子的中央是漂浮着玫瑰花瓣的水池。……两头带翼的银狮，背上驮着水果，池边喝水的小鸟原来是一个个装盐的瓶子。还有好多好多亮晶晶的玻璃杯、盘子和亮锃锃的刀叉……

有关凄美的：

The sky is the colour of jade. There are a great many stars; an enormous white moon hangs over the garden. Far away lightning flutters — flutters like a wing — flutters like a broken bird that tries to fly and sinks again and again struggles.

冷翡翠色的天空里，繁星万点，一轮硕大苍白的月悬在花园上空。远处的闪电忽明忽暗——扑哧扑哧像一只翅膀——像折翅的鸟儿挣扎着飞起来，跌下去，飞起又跌落。

有关清奇的：

In the day-time you felt that you had got high up, near to the sun, but the early mornings and evenings were limpid and restful, and the nights were cold.

白天里，你登高望远，似乎太阳也触手可及；拂晓或傍晚却来得清，来得静；到了夜间还有些许寒意。

有关肃穆的：

But in the midst of the long row there hangs a canvas which differs from the others. The frame of it is as fine and as heavy as any, and as proudly as any carries the golden plate with the royal crown. But on this one plate no name is inscribed, and the linen within the frame is snow-white from corner to comer, a blank page.

在这一长排正中间却悬挂着一块与众不同的亚麻布，它同样有精美厚重的画框，和带供放皇冠的金色托盘的画框一样，傲然挂立，但是它的托盘没刻上名字，画框里的亚麻布，竟然整块雪白雪白的，是一幅空白页。

有关典雅的：

Again the same softness of intimacy came over her, as she stood before a tumbling heap of pink petals. Then she wondered over the white rose, that was greenish, like ice, in the centre. So, slowly, like a white, pathetic butterfly, she drifted down the path, coming at last to a tiny terrace all full of roses. They seemed to fill the place, a sunny, gay throng. She was shy of them; they were so many and so bright. They seemed to be conversing and laughing. She felt herself in a strange crowd. It exhilarated her, carried her out of herself. She flushed with excitement. The air was pure scent.

当她站在层层叠叠、颤颤巍巍的粉色花瓣面前时，心中又会涌起亲密的柔情。她还惊讶地发现白色玫瑰，花心如冰，泛出淡淡的绿色。就这样，好似一只结着愁怨的白色蝴蝶，她轻挪着步子沿小路来到一个开满玫瑰花的小阳台。那儿似乎填满了玫瑰花，团团簇簇，灿烂欢快。在它们中间，她感到羞涩，它们是如此繁多，如此亮丽，它们似乎在畅谈，在大笑，她觉得自己身处一群陌生人当中，这让她激动不已，神魂颠倒。她兴奋得脸颊泛红。空气中弥漫着纯纯的花香味道。

有关悲慨的：

The sun was going down over the chestnut ridge. A lark was singing. It was late for a lark to sing. The red evening clouds floated above the pine trees on our pasture hill. My father stood beside the path. His black hair was moved by the wind. His face was red in the blue wind of day. His eyes looked toward the sinking sun.

太阳缓缓沉落到棕褐色山岭后。天色已晚，云雀仍在嘤唱。殷红的落霞飘浮在牧场山头、松树林间，父亲站在小路旁，任风儿吹动他的黑发，凛冽寒风中，他满脸通红，遥望西下的斜阳。

有关洗练的：

He had come in the night, under the roof of stars, as the moon shed rays of light on the quivering clouds of green.

他循着夜色而来，苍穹之间，繁星点点，明月相照，碧云漾漾。

有关质朴的：

Two people, vastly different, separated by language and culture and a whole lot else, yet giving and giving back the best they had to offer, their own humanity, their cartoons, their pickles. He gratefully accepted the pink plastic bag with its soggy lump, this beautiful token of universal friendship. It was incredible, so warming to the heart. He would keep it forever...

两个不同国度的人，语言不通，文化迥异，还有其他许多差异，但是仍然相互馈赠彼此最美好的东西，他们的博爱，他们的绘画，甚至是他们的咸菜。他感激地接过装有泡菜的粉色塑料袋，这是世界友谊的美好象征，这份礼物棒极了，情暖人心，他将永远珍藏它……

本译集的付梓要特别感谢武汉大学外国语学院翻译系前副主任胡孝申教授、澳门大学中文系博士生导师龚刚副教授、浙江大学外国语言文化与国际交流学院何辉斌教授的鼓励，父母的谆谆教诲与默默支持，我的挚友渭南师范学院陈平安、闫媛媛夫妇绘制了精美插图、我的学生伦敦政治经济学院研究生万琪珑、应用英语专业 1603 班陈红霞、豆玲、张启嵘、杨秋檀、王丽丽，师范英语专业 1901 班刘维嘉、1902 班张楚睿等的协助。

王[illegible]

戊戌年畅月

于湖师青山湖畔

目　录

英译汉

汉译英

英译汉

成长篇

成长的隐喻——《纸镇》片段选译及赏析

约翰·格林(John Green, 1977~),美国小说家、教育家,曾任美国国家公共电台(NPR)节目讲评人,并曾在《纽约时报》等媒体上发表书评。2005年,格林的处女作《寻找阿拉斯加》(*Looking for Alaska*)问世。该作品使他一举获得了2006年普林茨奖(Printz Award)。此后,格林还发表了《多面的凯瑟琳》(*An Abundance of Katherines*)、《星运里的错》(*The Fault in Our Stars*)、《纸镇》(*Paper Towns*)等多部小说。其中,《星运里的错》曾夺得《纽约时报》畅销书排行榜第一名,并于2014年被拍成同名电影。2015年,其小说《纸镇》也被搬上了银幕,在国外青少年中引起巨大反响。

《纸镇》主要围绕少年昆汀(Quentin)与邻家女孩玛戈(Margo)这两个性格迥异的高中生展开。高中毕业前的某天深夜,玛戈带着昆汀参与了自己的一系列针对曾在高中时伤害过自己的人的报复行动,第二天便离奇失踪。昆汀顺着玛戈留下的一条条线索与好友本(Ben)、拉达尔(Radar)以及玛戈的闺蜜莱西(Lacey)一同踏上了寻找玛戈的旅程。

下文节选自本书第三部分最后一节,讲述了昆汀最终找到玛戈,与玛戈一起向过去告别的故事。

When I wake up, the dying light of the day makes everything seem to matter. I roll onto my side and see Margo on her hands and knees a few feet from me. It takes me a moment to realize that she is digging. I crawl over to her and start to dig beside her. She smiles at me. My heart beats at the speed of sound.

"What are we digging to?" I ask her.

"That's not the right question," she says. "The question is, Who are we digging for?"

"Okay, then. Who are we digging for?"

"We are digging graves for Little Margo and Little Quentin and puppy Myrna① and poor dead

Robert Joyner②," she says.

"I can get behind③ those burials, I think," I say. We dig our bare hands into the ground over and over again, each fistful of earth accompanied by a little cloud of dust. The sleeve of my shirt gets dusty when I wipe the sweat from my cheek. Margo's cheeks are reddening.

"I never really thought of him as a real person," she says.

When she speaks, I take the opportunity to take a break, and sit back on my haunches④. "Who, Robert Joyner?"

She keeps digging. "Yeah. I mean, he was something that happened to me, you know? But before he was this minor figure in the drama of my life, he was—you know, the central figure in the drama of his own life."

I have never really thought of him as a person, either. A guy whose strings were broken, who didn't feel the root of his leaf of grass connected to the field, a guy who was cracked. Like me. "Yeah," I say after a while as I return to digging. "He was always just a body to me."

"I wish we could have done something," she says. "I wish we could have proven how heroic we were."

"Yeah," I say. "It would have been nice to tell him that, whatever it was, that it didn't have to be the end of the world."

---

① 默纳，是玛戈小时候养的小狗。

② 罗伯特·乔伊纳，住在昆汀和玛戈所在的社区。昆汀和玛戈在公园里玩耍时无意中看到了自杀身亡的罗伯特。

③ get behind 通过赞同与支持来帮助(某人或某事)

④ haunch /hɔːntʃ/ *n.* (人的)胯部，臀部

"Yeah, although in the end something kills you."

I shrug. "Yeah, I know. I'm not saying that everything is survivable. Just that everything except the last thing is." I have never spoken this many words in a row to Margo, but here it is, my last play for her.

"When I've thought about him dying, I always thought of it like you said, that all the strings inside him broke. But there are a thousand ways to look at it: maybe the strings break, or maybe our ships sink, or maybe we're grass—our roots so interdependent that no one is dead as long as someone is still alive. We don't suffer from a shortage of metaphors, is what I mean. But you have to be careful which metaphor you choose, because it matters. If you choose the strings, then you're imagining a world in which you can become irreparably① broken. If you choose the grass, you're saying that we are all infinitely interconnected, that we can use these root systems not only to understand one another but to become one another. The metaphors have implications. Do you know what I mean?"

She nods.

"I like the strings. I always have. Because that's how it feels. But the strings make pain seem more fatal than it is, I think. We're not as frail as the strings would make us believe. And I like the grass, too. The grass got me to you, helped me to imagine you as an actual person. But we're not different sprouts from the same plant. I can't be you. You can't be me. You can imagine another well—but never quite perfectly, you know?"

"Maybe it's more like you said before, all of us being cracked open. Like, each of us starts out as a watertight② vessel. And these things happen—these people leave us, or don't love us, or don't get③ us, or we don't get them, and we lose and fail and hurt one another. And the vessel starts to crack open in places. And I mean, yeah, once the vessel cracks open, the end becomes

① irreparably /ɪˈrepərəblɪ/ *adv*. 不能修复地,无可挽救地

② watertight /ˈwɔːtətaɪt/ *adj*. 防水的,不透水的

③ get /get/ *vt*.〈口〉理解

inevitable. But there is all this time between when the cracks start to open up and when we finally fall apart. And it's only in that time that we can see one another, because we see out of ourselves through our cracks and into others through theirs. When did we see each other face-to-face? Not until you saw into my cracks and I saw into yours. Before that, we were just looking at ideas of each other, like looking at your window shade but never seeing inside. But once the vessel cracks, the light can get in. The light can get out."

我醒来时已是傍晚时分，暮光让一切看上去都有了意义。我翻了个身，发现玛戈趴在离我几英尺[①]远的地上。我怔了一会儿才意识到她在挖土。我朝她爬过去，开始在她身旁挖起来。她冲我笑了笑，我心跳的速度都赶上了音速。

“我们在挖什么？”我问她。

“这样问不对。”她说，“应该问，我们在为谁挖？”

“好吧。那我们在为谁挖？”

“我们在为小玛戈、小昆汀、小狗默纳和死去的可怜人罗伯特·乔伊纳挖坟墓。”她说。

“我想，这样的葬礼我可以帮忙。”我说。我们赤手空拳，不停地在地里挖，每挖出一把土，就扬起一小片尘土。在我擦去脸颊上的汗水时，我衬衫的袖口上也沾满了尘土。玛戈的脸颊变得通红。

“我以前从没真正认为他是一个真实的人。”她说。

在她说话的工夫，我一屁股向后坐了下来，抓住机会歇了会儿。“谁？罗伯特·乔伊纳？”

她一边继续挖一边说：“是的。我是说，他是发生在我身上的一件事，你知道吗？但是在他成为我人生戏剧里的配角之前，他是——你知道——他自己人生戏剧里的主角。”

我也从来没有真正认为他是一个真实的人。他是一个内心的弦全都断了的人，是一个感受不到自己草叶的根与大地相连的人，是一个支离破碎的人。就像我。“是啊，”过了一会儿我一边接着挖土一边说道，“对于我来说，他以前一直就只

① 1英尺＝0.3048米

是一具尸体而已。”

“我多想我们那时能做点什么，”她说，“我多希望我们可以证明自己是多么英勇。”

“是的，”我说，“如果有人曾经这样告诉他就好了。不管发生什么，那都绝不会是世界末日。”

“是啊，只不过最后你还是会被某些事置于死地。”

我耸了耸肩。“这个我知道。我不是说人能挺过所有困难。我只是想说，除了最后致命的困难，其他的都能熬过来。”我从未对玛戈说过这样长的一番话，但是此时此刻，这是我对她最后的劝说。

“每当我想到他的死，我总会按照你说的去看待它——他内心的所有弦都断了。但是，这件事情我们可以用1000种方式去看待：也许是那些弦断了，或者可能是我们的船沉没了，抑或是我们可能是草——我们根与根相连，相互依赖，只要有人仍然活着，就不会有人死去。我们的人生并不缺乏隐喻，这是我想表达的。但是你必须慎重选择你的隐喻，因为这至关重要。如果你选择‘弦’，那么你所想象的就是一个会让你变得彻底崩溃的世界。如果你选择‘草’，你在传达的就是我们所有人永远相连，我们不仅可以用我们的根系理解彼此，而且还可以成为彼此。这些隐喻都有其暗含的意义。你明白我的意思吗？”她点点头。

“我喜欢弦的说法，一直都喜欢，因为我的感觉就是那样。但是我认为弦会让痛苦看起来比其本身更加致命，让人以为自己如同弦一样脆弱，但我们并不是这样。我也喜欢草的说法。草曾让我找到了你，帮助我把你想象成一个真实的人。但是我们不是同一株植物上萌发出的不同枝芽。我无法成为你，你也不可能成为我。你可以把别人想象得很美好，但你知道吗？你永远不能把别人想象得那么完美。”

“或许更像你以前说过的，我们所有人都支离破碎了。就好像，我们每个人出发时都是一艘密不漏水的船。接着这些事情发生了：有些人离开了我们，或是不爱我们了；他们不理解我们，或者我们不理解他们；我们失去了彼此，让彼此失望、受到伤害。随后，船的某些地方就开始破裂。我是说，是的，一旦船开裂，死亡就变得不可避免。但是，在船开始破裂到我们最终沉没之间，还有这么一整段时间。只有在那时，我们才能够看清楚彼此，因为我们透过自身的裂缝认清了自己，也透过对方的裂缝认清了对方。我们是什么时候见到了彼此的真容呢？是在我们透过彼此的裂缝看到对方时才见到的。在这之前，我们一直在看的只是想象中的彼此，就像看着彼此的窗帘，却看不到窗帘里面是什么。但是一旦船裂开，外面的光就可以射进来，而里面的光才能透出去。”

赏析

成长是什么？是不自暴自弃，是懂得关怀他人，是学会勇敢、执着和坚强，是努力向前走，是追寻真善美，是破茧成蝶。成长如同一盏明灯，让我们在黑暗中摇曳出光芒，照亮自己，也照亮别人。《纸镇》讲述的正是一个关于成长的青春故事。故事的主人公是正值花季的少年昆汀和女孩玛戈，他们在交织着美与丑、善与恶的现实生活中，在情感与死亡的困扰下，踏上了一段追寻真我和友谊的旅程。

昆汀和玛戈是从小一起长大的邻居，就读于同一所中学。玛戈活泼外向，喜欢冒险，在学校里光彩夺目。昆汀自小胆小怕事，做事缺少勇气和魄力。性格迥异的两人渐行渐远，但对昆汀来说，玛戈一直是他十分仰慕的朋友。高中毕业的日子临近，玛戈发现好友贾森和闺蜜贝卡背叛了她，于是深夜去找昆汀，让他协助自己进行了一系列刺激而又冒险的报复行动。昆汀驾车载着玛戈一夜狂奔，帮助玛戈了了心愿。他本以为就此可以与玛戈重新拉近距离，孰料翌日玛戈却不辞而别，只留下了一些零碎的线索：美国诗人惠特曼的诗集中的诗句，夹在昆汀屋门上的纸条，藏在墙壁白漆里的留言……昆汀凭借这些蛛丝马迹般的线索，与好友本、拉达尔等一同踏上了一段不离不弃、驱车 21 小时寻找玛戈的旅程。在不断寻找玛戈，不断接近其藏身之地“纸镇”阿格罗（Agloc）的过程中，昆汀渐渐改变了对玛戈出走的认识和理解。最后，昆汀一行人终于在阿格罗的一座废弃谷仓里找到了玛戈。昆汀极力劝说玛戈回家，却被玛戈拒绝了。两人漫步在谷仓外的田野上，回忆过去，谈及未来。这是他们第一次心与心的交流，也是在这一刻，昆汀和玛戈完成了对人生意义以及人与人之间社会联系的思考，懂得了只有不断认识自我、完善自我才能成长，才能逐步走向成熟。

弦、草、船是小说的三个子标题，也是贯穿小说的三个隐喻，如同昆汀千里追寻谜一般的玛戈的过程，紧紧攥住读者的心。“弦”代表了人遭遇坎坷和挫折后内心的挣扎。在小说开头，九岁的玛戈和昆汀在公园玩耍时发现了一具死尸，年幼的玛戈敢于冒险，在经过一番调查后，当晚就跑到昆汀的窗外，告诉了他事情的真相：公园里的那具死尸是他们社区的罗伯特先生，他遭遇了情感的背叛，选择了自杀，或许是因为他内心的弦断了。与罗伯特先生一样，成年后的玛戈也是因为自己内心的弦断了，无法在故乡生活下去，才选择逃离到“纸镇”。“纸镇”本是地图绘制者为了版权绘制出的虚构城镇，目的是使这份地图独一无二、不可仿造。可是当玛戈带着昆汀爬上故乡的高楼，从高处俯瞰这座城镇时，在玛戈眼里，这座真实存在的城镇却成了虚无的“纸镇”。她生于斯，长于斯，爱于斯，是什么让她对故乡心生了厌恶呢？原来是好友贾森与闺蜜贝卡的欺骗和背叛。残酷的真相让玛戈变得心灰意冷，深陷情感泥沼的她觉得自己和罗伯特先生一样，内心紧绷的弦也几乎要断了。在她看来，原本美好的故乡变得虚伪浅薄，没有灵魂，缺乏关爱，这里的一切薄脆如纸，不堪一击。于是，当她觉得生命中有不可承受的丑与恶时，她选择了逃离，选择了孤独，一个人奔赴地图上存在而现实中可能并不存在的“纸镇”，选择去做个心灵脆弱的“纸人”。

玛戈离家出走后，给昆汀留下了美国诗人惠特曼的诗集《草叶集》，这成为昆汀寻找玛戈最为重要的线索。“草”代表着人与人之间的信任和关爱，代表着勇敢面对挫折和困难的韧性。玛戈在《草叶集》中的许多诗句下都做了标记，其中有几句为：“我化为泥土，然后从我心爱的草叶中生长出来，倘若你想再见到我，就请在你的鞋底下寻找……一时找不到我，请继续勇敢点，一处找不到，去到另一处，我会在某处永远等着你。”在反复读过这些诗句后，昆汀以为遭受感情创伤的玛戈会像罗伯特先生一样选择了自杀，心生疑惑的他去向老师请教这些诗句的含义。老师告诉他，这几句诗可以解读为人与人之间像草一样，根连着根，相互有着联系，并不一定代表着消极、绝望甚至是死亡。昆汀从小就害怕面对死亡，与玛戈在公园发现死尸的事情曾把他吓得魂飞魄散，但是在坚持不懈地找寻玛戈的过程中，惠特曼的《草叶集》不断给他暗示：要像草一样顽强、勇敢，彼此相守相伴，只有经受种种磨难的洗礼，才能成长。在小说结尾，当昆汀终于找到玛戈时，他表露了自己的真实想法，对草也有了大彻大悟的理解。他们举行了告别脆弱过去的仪式，在玛戈的日记本上各自洒了一抔土，并且祝福彼此：“一路走好，年轻英勇的昆汀。一路走好，无畏的奥兰多女孩玛戈。”他们将代表自己过去的日记本用土掩埋，踩实，希望草再长回来。

小说中的第三个隐喻“船”则代表从挫折中汲取光和力量，不断向人生目标迈进。在经历了寻找玛戈的旅程后，昆汀对死亡、对成长、对人生都有了深刻的认识。当他看到玛戈还沉浸在过往，对人生不抱什么希望时，昆汀决定要帮助玛戈，他将自己对弦、草和船的理解告诉玛戈，希望她可以重拾希望。节选片段描述的正是昆汀对玛戈的劝说。正如昆汀所言，人生是一艘行进的船，可能会碰壁、触礁、开裂，但正是在人生之船遇到危险的时候，正是这些开裂的地方，才能更好地帮助我们成长，才能让我们更了解真实的自我，才能让我们看见从彼此裂缝中照射出的光，感受到彼此的爱。如果昆汀没有坚持不懈地寻找玛戈，他或许不知道自己原来可以如此勇敢；如果玛戈没有留下线索，并对生活依然眷顾，她或许体会不到昆汀这群朋友原来对自己会有这么深的情谊。成长让他们懂得了相互鼓励、相互关怀、不离不弃，也让他们拥有了爱与希望。拥有了这些，即便今后的人生再漫长，他们又何所畏惧呢？

每个人都要经历成长，面对成长过程中遇到的种种挫折，你是选择成为孤立脆弱的“弦”，放大痛苦，独自吞咽苦果？还是选择成为彼此根根相连的“草”，一起用勇气和韧性战胜挫折、克服困难，用爱心融化隔阂和冷漠？抑或你会选择成为扬帆起航、不惧沉没的“船”，虽不能避免船开裂甚至是沉没，但能够借助友谊之光，向更远大的人生目标多开进一步呢？

成长的礼物——《小红马》片段选译及赏析

约翰·斯坦贝克(John Steinbeck，1902～1968)，20世纪美国最具影响力的作家之一。他的许多作品都是以社会底层人物为主人公，展现他们善良、质朴的品格，创造出了"斯坦贝克式的英雄"形象，对后来的美国文学，尤其是西部文学的发展产生了重大影响。其代表作有中篇小说《小红马》(*The Red Pony*)、《人鼠之间》(*Of Mice and Men*)以及长篇小说《愤怒的葡萄》(*The Grapes of Wrath*)、《月亮下去了》(*The Moon Is Down*)等。

《小红马》是斯坦贝克的儿童文学名著，书中共包含了四个独立的故事，每个故事都围绕住在加利福尼亚农场的蒂福林一家(the Tiflins)展开。这四个故事分别讲述了小男孩乔迪·蒂福林(Jody Tiflin)与小红马、老人、母马以及外祖父之间发生的故事。

下文节选自本书第三个故事"The Promise"，主要讲述了蒂福林先生决定让乔迪再养一匹小马驹的故事。

"Ma'am, ma'am, there's a catalog①."

Mrs. Tiflin was in the kitchen spooning clabbered milk② into a cotton bag. She put down her work and rinsed③ her hands under the tap. "Here in the kitchen, Jody. Here I am."

He ran in and clattered④ his lunch pail⑤ on the sink. "Here it is. Can I open the catalog, ma'am?"

Mrs. Tiflin took up the spoon again and went back to her cottage cheese⑥.

---

① catalog /ˈkætəlɒg/ *n*. 商品目录；邮购目录

② clabbered milk：凝乳

③ rinse /rɪns/ *vt*. 用清水冲洗

④ clatter /ˈklætə(r)/ *vt*. 使发出连续而清脆的撞击声

⑤ pail /peɪl/ *n*. 桶，提桶

⑥ cottage cheese：农家鲜干酪(一种用乳酸制成的白色软干酪)

"Don't lose it, Jody. Your father will want to see it." She scraped[1] the last of the milk into the bag. "Oh, Jody, your father wants to see you before you go to do your chores."

The boy laid the catalog gently on the sink board. "Do you—is it something I did?"

Mrs. Tiflin laughed. "Always a bad conscience[2]. What did you do?"

"Nothing, ma'am," he said lamely[3].

His mother hung the full bag on a nail where it could drip into the sink. "He just said he wanted to see you when you got home. He's somewhere down by the barn."

Jody turned and went out the back door. Hearing his mother open the lunch pail and then gasp with rage, a memory stabbed him and he trotted[4] away toward the barn, conscientiously[5] not hearing the angry voice that called him from the house.

Carl Tiflin and Billy Buck, the ranch-hand, stood against the lower pasture fence. They were talking slowly and aimlessly. In the pasture half a dozen horses nibbled[6] contentedly at the sweet grass[7]. The mare, Nellie, stood backed up against the gate, rubbing her buttocks[8] on the heavy post.

Jody sidled[9] uneasily near. He dragged one foot to give an impression of great innocence and nonchalance[10].

The two men glanced sideways at him.

"I wanted to see you," Carl said in the stern tone he reserved for children

---

① scrape /skreɪp/ *vt.* 刮;刮净

② a bad conscience 内疚

③ lamely /ˈleɪmli/ *adv.* (尤指借口或论据)站不住脚地,无说服力地

④ trot /trɒt/ *vi.* 慢跑;快步走

⑤ conscientiously /ˌkɒnʃɪˈenʃəsli/ *adv.* 非常努力地,小心翼翼地

⑥ nibble /ˈnɪbl/ *vi.* 轻轻地咬(at)

⑦ sweet grass: 甜味草(常用作饲料)

⑧ buttock /ˈbʌtək/ *n.* (鸟兽的)臀尾部

⑨ sidle /ˈsaɪdl/ *vi.* (好像生怕别人注意到似的)迟迟疑疑地走,小心翼翼地走

⑩ nonchalance /ˈnɒnʃələns/ *n.* 若无其事;漠不关心

and animals.

“Yes, sir,” said Jody guiltily.

“Billy, here, says you took good care of the pony before it died.”

No punishment was in the air. Jody grew bolder. “Yes, sir, I did.”

“Billy says you have a good patient hand with horses.”

Jody felt a sudden warm friendliness for the ranch-hand.

Billy put in, “He trained that pony as good as anybody I ever seen.”

Then Carl Tiflin came gradually to the point.“If you could have another horse would you work for it?”

Jody shivered. “Yes, sir.”

“Well, look here, then. Billy says the best way for you to be a good hand with horses is to raise a colt.”

“It's the only good way,” Billy interrupted.

“Now, look here, Jody,” continued Carl. “Jess Taylor, up to the ridge ranch, has a fair stallion, but it'll cost five dollars. I'll put up the money, but you'll have to work it out all summer. Will you do that?”

Jody felt that his insides were shriveling. “Yes, sir,” he said softly.

“And no complaining? And no forgetting when you're told to do something?”

“Yes, sir.”

“Well, all right, then. Tomorrow morning you take Nellie up to the ridge ranch and get her bred. You'll have to take care of her, too, till she throws the colt.”

“Yes, sir.”

“You better get to the chickens and the wood now.”

Jody slid away. His shoulders swayed a little with maturity and importance.

He went to his work with unprecedented seriousness. This night he did not dump the can of grain to the chickens so that they had to leap over each other and struggle to get it. No, he spread the wheat so far and so carefully that the hens couldn't find some of it at all. And in the house, after listening to his mother's despair over boys who filled their lunch pails with slimy, suffocated reptiles, and bugs, he promised never to do it again. Indeed, Jody felt that all such foolishness was lost in the past. He was far too grown up ever to put toads in his lunch pail any more. He carried in so much wood and built such a high structure with it that his mother walked in fear of an avalanche of oak. When he was done, when he had gathered eggs that had remained hidden for weeks, Jody walked down again past the cypress tree, and past the bunkhouse toward the pasture. A fat toad that looked out at him from under the watering trough had no emotional effect on him at all.

"妈,妈,有一本产品册子。"

厨房里,蒂福林太太将凝乳一勺勺舀进棉布袋。她放下手中的活儿,在水龙头下面洗了洗手。"在厨房这儿,乔迪。我在这里。"

他跑了进去,哐啷一声把他的午饭桶扔进了水槽。"就是这本。妈,我可以打开看看吗?"

蒂福林太太又拿起勺子,继续做她的农家鲜干酪。"别把它弄丢了,乔迪。你爸爸还要看的。"她把最后一点儿凝乳刮进袋子里。"对啦。乔迪,去干活之前,你爸爸想见见你。"

乔迪把册子轻轻地放在水槽板上。"您……是我做错什么了吗?"

蒂福林太太笑了。"又心虚了吧。你做了什么吗?"

"没做什么呀,妈。"他的回答毫无说服力。

他妈妈把满满一袋子凝乳挂在钉子上,这样袋子里的水就可以滴进水槽中。"他刚才只说让你回家后去见他。他在下面的牲口棚附近。"

乔迪转身从后门出去了。他听见妈妈打开午饭桶,紧接着气得直喘,这让他猛地想起了自己干的事,于是他赶紧朝牲口棚小跑过去,尽量不去听屋里传来的那叫他的怒喊声。

卡尔·蒂福林和农场帮工比利·巴克背靠低矮的牧场围栏站着。他们不紧不慢、不着边际地聊着天。牧场上六匹马在啃咬着甜味草,一副心满意足的样子。母马内莉则倚靠着大门站着,不停地在笨重的柱子上蹭着自己的后臀。

乔迪提心吊胆、小心翼翼地走到旁边。他拖着一只脚,装出一副清白无辜、若无其事的样子。

这两个男人瞟了他一眼。

“我正要找你。”卡尔用一种对孩子和牲畜惯用的严厉口吻说道。

“好的，爸爸。”乔迪心虚地说。

“比利说那只小马死之前你照料得还不错。”

不是惩罚的语气。乔迪变得大胆了一些。“是的，爸爸，我是那样做的。”

“比利说你照看马时很用心也很有耐心。”

乔迪突然觉得这位农场帮工的友好格外暖心。

比利插话说：“他对那只小马的训练不比我见过的任何人差。”

这时卡尔·蒂福林渐渐进入正题。“要是你可以再有一匹马，你会好好伺候它吗？”

乔迪颤抖着。“会的，爸爸。”

“好，那么听我说。比利说让你成为养马能手的最好办法是从养小马驹开始。”

“这是唯一的好办法。”比利打断道。

“现在听我说，乔迪。”卡尔继续说，“山上牧场的杰斯·泰勒有一匹漂亮的种马，不过得花五美元才能配种。钱我先垫上，但是你必须干一夏天的活。你愿意这么做吗？”

乔迪感到心头一紧。“愿意，爸爸。”他轻声说道。

“不会抱怨？也不会忘记交代给你的事情？”

“不会的，爸爸。”

“嗯，那就这样说好了。明天一大早，你把内莉牵到山上的牧场，给它配种。你还必须照料好它，一直等到它生出小马驹来。”

“好的，爸爸。”

“你现在最好去喂鸡、拾柴火吧。”

乔迪一溜烟跑了，双肩稍稍有些抖动。一副长大了、了不得的样子。

他从未这样认真地干过活。这天晚上，他没有把整桶谷物倒进鸡群里，让它们不得不踩着彼此蹦来跳去地争食吃。他没有这样做，而是极为小心地把小麦撒得远远的，以至于有些麦粒母鸡们根本都找不到。回屋后，听妈妈说完对男孩们往午饭桶里塞那些令人窒息的、黏糊糊的爬虫和臭虫感到很失望后，他保证再也不搞这种恶作剧了。乔迪甚至觉得所有这些傻事都遗失在过去了。现在他长大了，不会再把癞蛤蟆放进自己的午饭桶里。他拾了很多柴火，把它们堆成高高的柴火堆，害得他妈妈路过时都担心橡木柴火堆会塌下来。在干完这些活儿，又捡完好几周都没发现的那些鸡蛋后，乔迪穿过那棵柏树，走过那间农舍，又一路朝牧场走去。一只胖乎乎的癞蛤蟆从牲口的饮水槽底下看着他，可他根本没有兴趣去抓它。

赏析

没有一种成长是一帆风顺的，也没有一种成长不伴随痛苦。在成长的道路上，亲情的冲突，友谊的考验，死亡的残酷，是一颗又一颗让人不断走向成熟的磨砺石。

美国作家约翰·斯坦贝克的中篇小说《小红马》讲述的就是一个小男孩在经历了一件件令人痛苦甚至可以说受到伤害的事情后逐渐成长、变得成熟的故事。《小红马》包含了四个故事，在第一个故事中，我们遇到了小说主人公乔迪，他才十岁，还没有进入青春期。和大部分农家小男孩一样，他虽然有服从父母管教的一面，但同时也有调皮好动的一面。他有时会忘记干杂活，有时会逗逗野鸟，甚至偶尔还会踩烂一只发青的甜瓜，再用泥土将其掩埋。从男孩成为男人，需要付出什么样的代价，具备什么样的品质呢？乔迪认为男人比男孩更多的应该是责任心，他的父母则认为自立自强才会帮助成长，而在艰难困顿的农村生活尤其需要自律的精神。为了考验和培养乔迪，让他逐渐成为一个勇于担当、有责任心的成熟男人，乔迪的父母送给他一件成长的礼物——一匹属于他自己的小马驹，让他去喂养它、照顾它、驯服它，而不再只是干些诸如喂养小鸡、拾捡柴火的简单农活。

这是一只红色的小马驹，是乔迪的父亲从一个破产的马戏团买回来的。红色在西方文化中代表着残酷和血腥，这似乎暗示了小马驹成长道路的坎坷与曲折。乔迪竭尽全力想照料好这匹小红马，因为他把它视为生命的一部分。在小红马出现之前，乔迪只是一个腼腆、怯弱的小男生，但是在和小红马相处的日子里，乔迪变得越来越勇敢，还常常幻想着自己是英姿飒爽的骑士。父亲的严肃、刻板让乔迪更喜欢与粗犷、热情的农场帮工比利待在一起，比利教他如何照料和训练小马驹，如何给小马驹带上马笼头、装好马鞍，还教他正确的骑马姿势。乔迪精心驯养小红马，喂它胡萝卜，帮它梳理马鬃，陪它散步。冬日的一天，艳阳高照，乔迪上学之前决定让小马驹留在露天的马厩里晒晒太阳，比利也说这么好的天气不会下雨。在比利的一再保证下，乔迪安心去上学了。可是大人也有失算的时候，一场突如其来的暴雨使小马驹淋了雨、生了病。乔迪在照料小马驹的过程中表现出强烈的责任心:他不仅用酒精给它擦身体来降温,用蒸汽给它进行药物治疗,还亲自帮它开刀,日夜守护着它,想尽各种办法救治它。可是,即便有养马能手比利的悉心治疗,小红马还是撞开围栏跑到山上死掉了,最后被秃鹫残忍叼食。这是乔迪第一次直面死亡的残酷和大人们在死亡面前的无助,也正是从那时起,他成长了,有了自己的想法,不再盲从大人们的判断与经验。

从生到死,在希望中播种未来,在失望中收获成长。在《小红马》的另一个故事中,为了让乔迪从小红马死亡的阴影和痛苦中摆脱出来,并且尽快成长为农场的养马好手,他的父亲准备再给他一匹小马驹。节选片段讲述的正是这个故事。这一次,小马驹不再是礼物,因为乔迪不仅要干活赚取给母马配种的钱,还要负责接生,只有这样他才能获得小马驹。这样的体验让乔迪成长得更快,一方面,他懂得了劳动的艰辛、赚钱的不易和肩上担负的责任;而另一方面,在接生小马驹的过程中,他见证了一个新生命的诞生,也目睹了母马用汗水、血泪甚至是生命来换取小马驹的存活。这是一堂生动的课,也是一堂有关生命起源与价值的课。在母马难产之时,面对保住母马还是保住小马驹这个生命取舍的难题,比利迫于无奈的选择又一次让乔迪感受到生命的沉痛。尽管他曾精心照料母马,曾无比耐心地等待接生,尽管他最终又获得了一匹小马驹,但他却不得不面对母马的死亡,面对生命的脆弱和现实的残酷。这次经历给他心灵上带来的震撼比他失去小红马时的还要大,他不再玩弄小动物、搞恶作剧,干农活也比以前更加细心认真。经此一事,他懂得珍惜生命,懂得自立与自律,他获得了成长,也变得成熟了。

让乔迪日渐成熟的还有另外两个故事里的两位老人。其中一位名叫吉达诺(Gitano),他出生在乔迪家附近的牧场,如今叶落归根,回到故地,想在这里做些零活,慢慢老去。乔迪的父亲非常不乐意收留这位老人,他不愿养活不中用的老人,更不愿意他死在自己的家里,所以只答应让他留宿一晚。乔迪的父亲用家里只能吃但活不长的老马挖苦老人,乔迪则十分同情老人尴尬的处境,还安慰他说父亲的挖苦并无恶意。次日一大早,有着强烈自尊心的老人悄悄骑上那匹行将就木的老马,消失在神秘的大山里,平静而从容地走向死亡。遥望巍巍群山,想到孤寂的老人被遗弃,乔迪心里涌动着不可名状的悲哀。另一位老人则是乔迪的外祖父,他曾经带领马车队横跨广阔的西部平原,对于这段经历始终念念不忘。乔迪的父母厌烦老人总是絮叨过去的辉煌,只有乔迪是其最忠实的听众,并对外祖父的壮举打心眼里崇拜。在外祖父讲完故事后,他还会体贴地给外祖父调一杯柠檬水喝,却没想着给自己也来一杯。在需要他人关心的年龄，乔迪却已然懂得去关心、尊重老者和弱者，懂得接受与包容他人，他不仅打开了心灵之门，更获得了心灵的成长。

《小红马》是一份向成长致敬的珍贵礼物，牧场发生的四个小故事让乔迪在目睹生老病死、历经成长的痛苦后不断走向成熟，也让阅读这些故事的我们在忙忙碌碌的现实中静下心来，去反思自我的成长，学会在人生跋山涉水的征程中体味爱，感受爱，付出爱，从而收获更好的成长。

成长的善与爱——《诺福镇的奇幻夏天》片段选译及赏析

杰克·甘托斯(Jack Gantos, 1951～),美国作家,其创作领域十分广泛,包括儿童绘本、青少年小说,以及成年人小说。上小学时,甘托斯就意识到日常故事是构成优秀文学作品的基础,因此便开始收集逸闻轶事。六年级时读了姐姐的日记之后,他认为自己可以比姐姐写得更好,就此在心中播下了从事写作的种子。其代表作有《红猫拉尔夫》(*Rotten Ralph*)系列绘本,小说《失去控制的乔伊》(*Joey Pigza Loses Control*)和《诺福镇的奇幻夏天》等。

《诺福镇的奇幻夏天》2011 年出版,次年便获得了纽伯瑞儿童文学奖金奖(Newbery Medal),被认为是"2011 年为美国儿童文学所做的最为杰出的贡献"。此外,该书还获得了 2012 年的司各特·奥台尔历史小说奖(Scott O'Dell Award for Historical Fiction),该奖项每年都会从为儿童创作的历史小说中评选出一本最佳作品。

这是一本自传体式的小说,书中的小主人公和作者同名。小说讲述了 12 岁的小男孩杰克·甘托斯在诺福镇的成长故事。因为闯了祸,杰克被妈妈惩罚整个暑假都要在家关禁闭,唯一可以出门的机会就是帮助小镇的首席法医、年迈的沃尔克小姐(Miss Volker)把她口述的讣告打出来,然后交由当地报社刊发。随着一篇篇讣告,杰克了解到小镇上死去的每一位第一代居民的人生故事以及小镇的历史变迁,踏上了一段悬念迭起的奇幻旅程……下文节选自小说第二章,讲述了杰克第一次见到沃尔克小姐时发生的有趣故事。

When I came to[①], I was alive and stretched out on Miss Volker's kitchen floor. I was covered with blood but I didn't know if it was nose blood[②] or blood

① come to 苏醒;清醒

② 杰克非常容易流鼻血,一旦受到惊吓或是太过兴奋,又或者无缘无故因为什么小事而感到害怕,他就会流鼻血。上文中,沃尔克小姐请杰克来帮自己写讣告,当杰克到她家时,她正在一个滚烫的锅里煮自己的双手,这让杰克感到惊恐不已,开始流鼻血。他以为沃尔克小姐是一个煮自己的肉来吃的神经病,还以为她马上要来吃自己的肉。紧接着,杰克便昏死过去了。

from after she started eating me. I lifted my head and turned it left and right to check if she had eaten through my neck. I was fine but she was standing above me and pulling long, rotten strips of flesh off her arms and hands as if peeling a rotten banana. She wadded[①] them all up, leaned to one side, and dropped a ball into the large pot on the stove.

"Am I dead?" I asked. I felt dead.

"You fainted[②]," she replied. "And I fixed your nose."

"You touched me?" I asked fearfully, and reached for my nose to see if it was still on my face.

"Yes," she said. "After I got the wax off my fingers they were working okay so I folded some tissues into a wad and shoved[③] them up between your upper lip and gum[④]. That's what stops a nosebleed."

"You have fingers?" I asked, confused. I had seen them melt off like the Inca gold being melted down[⑤].

"Yes," she said. "I'm human and I have fingers. They don't work well because of my arthritis[⑥] so I have to heat them up in a pot of hot paraffin[⑦] in order to get them working for about fifteen minutes."

"Hot what?"

"Hot wax," she repeated impatiently. "You saw me doing it when you came in. Did that smack[⑧] on your head when you hit the floor give you amnesia[⑨]?"

I sat up and rubbed the lump[⑩] on the back of my head. "I thought you were melting your fingers into gold," I said. "I thought you had gone crazy."

---

① wad /wɒd/ *vt*. 将……揉成团

② faint /feɪnt/ *vi*. 昏厥；晕倒

③ shove /ʃʌv/ *vt*. 塞入；乱塞

④ gum /gʌm/ *n*. 牙龈；牙床

⑤ 杰克最近在读有关弗朗西斯科・皮萨罗(Francisco Pizarro，约 1471 或 1476～1541)的书。皮萨罗是征服印加帝国的西班牙殖民者。

⑥ arthritis /ɑːˈθraɪtɪs/ *n*. 关节炎

⑦ paraffin /ˈpærəfɪn/ *n*. 石蜡

⑧ smack /smæk/ *n*. 拍击，碰击

⑨ amnesia /æmˈniːzɪə/ *n*. 记忆缺失；健忘(症)

⑩ lump /lʌmp/ *n*. 隆起；肿块

"I think you've gone crazy," she replied. "You're delusional①. Now let's not waste any more time. I have a deadline."

"What are we doing?" I asked.

"Writing an obituary②," she revealed.

"Mine?"

"No! You are fine—you're a spineless③ jellyfish④, but not dead enough to bury. Now take a look at these hands," she ordered, and thrust⑤ them in front of me. They were still bright red from the hot wax and curled over like the talons⑥ of a hawk perched⑦ on a fence. "I can't write with them anymore," she explained, "or do anything that requires fine motor⑧ skills. My twin sister used to write out the obituaries for me but her jug-headed⑨ idiot husband moved her to Florida last month. I was hoping he'd just have a spasm⑩ and drop dead and she would move in with me—but it didn't work out that way. So you are now my official scribe⑪. I got the idea from reading about President John Quincy Adams⑫. He had arthritis too and when his hands gave out ⑬he had a young scribe who wrote for him. I'll talk and you'll write. You got that?"

"Sure," I said, and then she caught me sneaking a peek at the glowing kitchen clock which was in the shape of a giant Bayer aspirin⑭. It was six-thirty in the morning.

"That," she said proudly, and aimed her chin at the clock, "was given to

---

① delusional /dɪˈluːʒənl/ *adj*. 妄想的；错觉的

② obituary /əˈbɪtʃuərɪ/ *n*. 讣告；讣文。下文中的 obit 是其口语缩略形式。

③ spineless /ˈspaɪnləs/ *adj*. 没有骨气的；软弱的

④ jellyfish /ˈdʒelɪfɪʃ/ *n*. 软弱无用的人

⑤ thrust /θrʌst/ *vt*. (用力)推

⑥ talon /ˈtælən/ *n*. (某些鸟类，尤指猛禽的)爪

⑦ perch /pɜːtʃ/ *vt*. 栖息；停留

⑧ motor /ˈməʊtə(r)/ *adj*. 肌肉运动的；运动神经的

⑨ jug-headed /ˈdʒʌghedɪd/ *adj*. 愚蠢的；呆头呆脑的

⑩ spasm /ˈspæzəm/ *n*. 痉挛；抽搐

⑪ scribe /skraɪb/ *n*. (尤指印刷术未发明之前的)抄写员

⑫ 约翰·昆西·亚当斯(1767～1848)，美国第六任总统，是美国历史上著名的外交家。

⑬ give out 停止运转

⑭ aspirin /ˈæsprɪn/ *n*. 阿司匹林(阵痛解热消炎药)

me by the Bayer Pharmaceutical① Company after I gave out over a quarter million of their aspirin tablets to coal miners here in western Pennsylvania who suffered with back pain and splitting headaches②."

"That is a lot of pills," I remarked, not knowing what else to say but the obvious.

"In nursing school," she said, "I was taught by the doctors that the role of medical science is to relieve all human suffering, and I've lived by that motto all my life."

"What about your hands?" I said, pointing up at them.

"Someday science will solve that. But for now, get up off the floor," she ordered. "We've got to get this obit to the newspaper in an hour so Mr. Greene can print③ it for tomorrow morning's edition."

I stood all the way up and staggered④ into the living room.

"There's your office," she said, and pointed a shiny red hand toward an old school desk and matching chair. "Lift the top."

I did. There were several pads of lined paper and a bundle of sharpened pencils held together with a rubber band⑤.

"I'll talk, and you write," she explained, setting the rules. "If I talk too quickly then you just tell me and I'll slow down. You got it?"

"Yeah," I said. I was really ready to do anything that would clear my head from thinking about this old lady melting her flesh in a kitchen pot.

Miss Volker stood by the fireplace mantel⑥ and took a breath so deep it straightened out her curved spine.

当我醒过来时，我还活着，四仰八叉地躺在沃尔克小姐家厨房的地板上。我浑

---

① pharmaceutical /ˌfɑːməˈsuːtɪkl/ *adj*. 制药的，配药的

② splitting headache 头痛欲裂

③ print /prɪnt/ *vt*. 登载；刊登；发表

④ stagger /ˈstæɡə(r)/ *vi*. 摇摇晃晃地走；蹒跚

⑤ rubber band 橡皮筋

⑥ mantel /ˈmæntl/ *n*. 壁炉架

身是血，但我不知道那是鼻血还是她开始吃我之后我身上流的血。我抬起头左右转动，想检查一下她有没有把我的脖子咬断。我还好好的，但她正站在我的上方，从她的双臂和两只手上扯下长长的、腐烂的肉条，就好像在剥一根腐烂的香蕉似的。她把它们揉成一团，侧身把一个肉球扔进了炉子上的那口大锅里。

“我死了吗？”我问。我感觉自己已经死了。

“你昏过去了，”她回答道，“我给你的鼻子止了血。”

“你碰过我？”我边惊恐地问，边伸手去摸自己的鼻子，想看看它是否还在我的脸上。

“是啊，”她说，“我剥下手指上的蜡之后，手指就灵活了，于是我把一些纸巾折叠成一个团，塞在你的上唇和牙龈之间，就这样止住了你的鼻血。”

“你还有手指？”我疑惑地问。我刚才看见它们熔化了，就像印加人的黄金被熔化了那样。

“是呀，”她说，“我是人，当然有手指啦。因为关节炎，我的手指不太灵活，所以我不得不用一锅热石蜡给手指加加热，好让指头能灵活动上大概那么15分钟。”

“热什么？”

“热蜡，”她不耐烦地重复了一遍，“你进来的时候看见我这么做的。你倒地时撞到了脑袋，难道那让你失去记忆了？”

我坐了起来，揉了揉后脑勺上的那个大包。“我当时还以为你要把手指熔化成黄金呢，”我说，“我以为你已经疯了。”

“我才以为你已经疯了呢，”她回答说，“你出现错觉了吧。好了，我们不要再浪费时间了，马上要截稿了。”

“我们要做什么？”我问。

“写一篇讣告。”她透露说。

“关于我的讣告？”

“不是啊！你活得好好的——你就是个没骨头的怂包，不过还没到入土的地步。好了，来瞧瞧这双手。”她边说边把手硬伸到我面前。它们刚从热蜡里出来，还是红通通的，手指蜷曲着，就像落在篱笆上的一只老鹰的爪子。“我无法再用手写字了，”她解释道，“也无法再做任何需要灵活的手指才能做的事情了。我的孪生姐姐过去常常帮我写讣告，可是上个月她那呆头呆脑的傻丈夫让她搬到佛罗里达州去住了。我那会儿真希望他会抽搐，倒地身亡，这样我姐姐就可以搬回来和我同住了——不过事情并没有像我想的那样发生。因此你现在就是我的正式抄写员了。我是通过读约翰·昆西亚·亚当斯总统的故事想到这个主意的。他也患有关节炎，当他的两只手不好使时，他就让一位年轻的抄写员来帮他写。到时我来说，你来写。明白了吗？”

“没问题。”我说，接着她就发现我在偷瞄厨房里那座铿亮的钟，它的形状像是一颗硕大的拜耳牌阿司匹林药片，指针指向早上6:30。

“那个，”她骄傲地说，用下巴指了指那座钟，“是拜耳医药公司送给我的，此前我给咱们宾夕法尼亚州西部这儿的煤矿工人分发了超过25万粒他们公司生产的阿司匹林药片，这些工人饱受背疼和剧烈的头痛之苦。”

“那可是很多药片呢。”我说道，除了这个明显的事实，我不知道还能说点什么。

“在护士学校里，”她说，“医生们教导我医学的任务就是减轻人的痛苦，而我这一辈子都在践行这句格言。”

“那你自己的两只手怎么办呢？”我指着它们说。

“总有一天，医学会攻克这个问题的。不过眼下，从地上站起来吧，”她命令道，“我们要在一个小时之内把这条讣告送到报社，这样格林先生就能把它刊登在明天的晨报上了。”

我完全站直了身子，摇摇晃晃地走进了客厅。

“你的办公室在那边，”她用红得发亮的手指着一张旧课桌以及和它配套的椅子说，“把桌盖儿掀起来。”

我照办了。桌子里面有几本横格纸和一捆用橡皮筋绑着的削好的铅笔。

“我来说，你来写。”她解释道，定下了规矩。“要是我说得太快，你就只管告诉我，我就说得慢一点儿，明白了吗？”

“明白了。”我说。我真的已经准备好去做任何事了，只要能让我的脑子不再去想这位老太太在做饭的锅里熔化自己的肉这件事儿就可以。

沃尔克小姐站在壁炉架旁，深深地吸了一口气，都把她那弯曲的脊柱给撑直了。

赏析

美国诗人沃尔特·惠特曼（Walt Whitman）写过一首名叫《有一个孩子向前走去》（“There Was a Child Went Forth”）的诗，诗的开头是这样说的：“有一个孩子每天向前走去/他最初看到了一个东西,他就变成了那个东西/那东西就变成了他的一部分,在那一天或是那一天的某段时间里/或是在几年的时间里,抑或是延续了好多年”。在小说《诺福镇的奇幻夏天》中,小男孩杰克·甘托斯通过用打字机将沃尔克小姐口述的一篇篇讣告打出来,使小镇第一代居民播下的善与美的种子渐渐在他心中生根发芽,并成为照亮他未来人生路的明灯。

诺福镇是一个有着深远历史背景的小镇,它是在美国经济大萧条时期由美国联邦政府出资建立的新型社区,旨在为那些失业的煤矿工人及其家人提供房屋以及工作机会,提高他们的生活水平。在小镇的建设过程中,美国前总统富兰克林·罗斯福的妻子埃莉诺·罗斯福(Eleanor Roosevelt)做出了很大的贡献,她不顾部分官员的反对,坚持认为应该给这些新建的房屋配备水暖设备,安装电灯、自来水以及其他现代化设施,用一颗关爱、体恤人民的心为当地居民争取了诸多权益。1934年,诺福镇建成,250户家庭在此安了家,他们便是小说中提到的第一代居民(the original Norvelters)。不过,随着时间的流逝和二战之后人们观念的转变,很多人开始外迁,再加上人口老龄化,小镇逐渐开始衰落。小说中的故事正是发生在这样的背景之下。

暑假刚刚拉开帷幕,杰克就因为误开了爸爸的来复枪(这是爸爸在二战中的战利品)差点儿伤了人。为了帮爸爸修建飞机跑道和挖防空洞,杰克在几天之后又铲除了妈妈种的爱心玉米,要知道,那是妈妈特意为穷人和社区中心有需要的老人们种的。因为这两件事儿,杰克被妈妈关了禁闭,整个暑假都不能出门,唯一的出门机会便是帮沃尔克小姐把她口述的讣告用打字机打出来,然后交给当地报社的格林先生刊登。沃尔克小姐此前受到罗斯福夫人的委派,以总护士长的身份照顾小镇的第一代居民,记录他们的健康状况;同时,她又是小镇的首席法医,当每一位第一代居民去世之后,她都会签发他们的死亡报告,并为其撰写讣告。为了完成对罗斯福夫人的承诺,沃尔克小姐甚至终生未嫁。

当杰克第一次来到沃尔克小姐家时,她正在大锅里煮自己的双手,选段所展现的正是这部分内容。这一举动把杰克吓得魂飞魄散,误以为沃尔克小姐患有精神病。后来他才得知,原来,沃尔克小姐患有关节炎,她是在用锅里的热蜡加热双手,好让自己的手指变得灵活起来。尽管自己的双手无法正常打字,但沃尔克小姐还是用心地准备每一篇讣告,虔诚地为每一位逝去的诺福镇第一代居民送别。她教会杰克使用打字机,教导他应当像爱自己一样爱自己的邻居。后来,她又给杰克做了鼻部手术，成功地治好了他爱流鼻血的鼻子，但却分文不收……沃尔克小姐这些充满善与爱的举动都让杰克深受感动。

通过沃尔克小姐口述的讣告，杰克了解到诺福镇第一代居民善待友邻、关爱他人的各种故事。比如，斯莱特太太（Mrs. Slater）曾担任过多年的学校马路守护员，深受孩子们的爱戴。来自黑人家庭的怀特夫人（Mrs. White）写信给罗斯福总统及其夫人埃莉诺·罗斯福，希望在诺福镇拥有一间自己的屋子，在罗斯福夫人的努力下，怀特太太最终如愿。为感谢总统夫人为让镇上居民过上有尊严的生活而做出的努力，她把这位伟大女性名字中的“诺（nor）”和“福（velt）”合在一起，为小镇改名为诺福镇（Norvelt）。

在短短两个月的时间里，诺福镇的老人相继离世。就在这时，报社的格林先生却在报纸上发表了一篇社论，他想知道为什么所有的老太太都会这么快死去，并怀疑沃尔克小姐是否尽心尽力地照顾过她们。这些老人是因为年事已高自然死亡，还是别有隐情？看到这篇社论后，杰克的妈妈哭了，因为她怀疑是自己采了有毒的蘑菇，才致使老人们误食后中毒身亡的。杰克则猜想如果老人们是被毒死的，那就跟 1080 毒药有关，而沃尔克小姐、殡仪馆老板赫佛先生（Mr. Huffer）以及追求了沃尔克小姐 50 年的巡警斯皮兹先生（Mr. Spizz）都买过 1080 毒药，杰克自己还替斯皮兹先生跑腿在店里买过一些，并且登记了自己的名字。

谜底后来揭晓了，原来，是斯皮兹先生投毒害死了诺福镇的老太太们。他认为只有这样做，沃尔克小姐才能尽早完成对罗斯福夫人的承诺，自己才能娶到她，并和她一起远走高飞，离开小镇。真相终于大白。

小说结尾部分，沃尔克小姐和一位位已经逝去的小镇第一代居民在诺福镇播撒的善与爱的种子，在以小男孩杰克为代表的年轻一代的心中生根发芽。杰克意识到自己最初摆弄爸爸的来复枪是一件多么危险的事情，因为这可能会误伤他人；而割掉妈妈的玉米又是一件多么愚蠢的事情，因为这些粮食是为那些吃不饱饭的小镇邻居准备的。此时的杰克已经真正体味到善与爱的美好，他也确信在未来的人生中，这两种美好的品质将与自己如影随形。

童真,最美的梦——《阳儿和月女》片段选译及赏析

新西兰著名女作家凯瑟琳·曼斯菲尔德(Katherine Mansfield, 1888～1923)在短篇小说《阳儿和月女》("*Sun and Moon*")里描绘的那份天真和无邪,令人心驰神往,她用细腻的笔触、传神的语言为读者编织了世间最美的梦。

为了盛大的家庭聚会,一家人上上下下、忙忙碌碌,两个五岁大的小主人公阳儿和月女也沉浸在派对的喜悦之中。懵懵懂懂的他们对真实世界的模糊认知和童言趣语让人忍俊不禁。

IN THE AFTERNOON the chairs came, a whole big cart full of little gold ones with their legs in the air. And then the flowers came. When you stared down from the balcony at the people carrying them the flowerpots looked like funny awfully nice hats nodding up the path.

Moon thought they were hats. She said: "Look. There's a man wearing a palm on his head." But she never knew the difference between real things and not real ones.

And they looked into the refrigerator. Oh! Oh! Oh! It was a little house. It was a little pink house with white snow on the roof and green windows and a brown door and stuck in the door there was a nut for a handle.

...So they all went into the dining-room. Sun and Moon were almost frightened. They wouldn't go up to the table at first; they just stood at the door and made eyes at it.

It wasn't real night yet but the blinds were down in the dining-room and the lights turned on and all the lights were red roses. Red ribbons and bunches of roses tied up the table at the corners. In the middle was a lake with rose petals floating on it.

"That's where the ice pudding is to be," said cook.

Two silver lions with wings had fruit on their backs, and the salt cellars were tiny birds drinking out of basins.

And all the winking glasses and shining plates and sparking knives and forks — and all the food. And the little red table napkins made into roses...

"Are people going to eat the food?" asked Sun.

"I should just think they were," laughed cook, laughing with Nellie. Moon laughed, too; she always did the same as other people. But Sun didn't want to laugh. Round and round he walked with his hands behind his back. Perhaps he never would have stopped if nurse hadn't called suddenly: "Now then, children. It's high time you were washed and dressed." And they were marched off to the nursery.

And so they went back to the beautiful dining-room.

But—oh! oh! What had happened. The ribbons and the roses were all pulled untied. The little red table napkins lay on the floor, all the shining plates were dirty and all the winking glasses. The lovely food that the man had trimmed was all thrown about, and there were bones and bits and fruit peel and shells everywhere. There was even a bottle lying down with stuff coming out of it on to the cloth and nobody stood it up again.

And the little pink house with the snow roof and the green windows was broken—broken—half melted away in the centre of the table.

"Come on, Sun," said father, pretending not to notice.

...But Sun did not move from the door. Suddenly he put up his head and gave a loud wail.

"I think it's horrid—horrid—horrid!" he sobbed.

下午,椅子运到了,一大卡车金黄色的小椅子,个个椅脚朝上。然后一盆盆花也运到了。从阳台上注视那些搬运工手捧花盆,一路上花头攒动,就像一顶顶奇特的漂亮帽子。

月女认为那些盆花儿就是一顶顶帽子。她说:"看啦,那人头上,巴掌儿帽!"可是她从未分清楚真的假的。

他们朝冰箱里看。哇！哇！哇！这是一座小小的房子呀，一座粉色的小房子，白雪覆盖的屋顶，一扇扇绿色的窗户，棕色的房门上还粘着颗坚果做把手。

于是他们一同走进餐厅。阳儿和月女几乎惊呆了。一开始，他们不敢走到桌前，只是在门口站定了，睁大眼睛往里看。

天还没有完全黑，但是宴会厅的窗帘已经落下。华灯四落，散发出玫瑰色的光。餐桌的四角绑着红色彩带和玫瑰花束。桌子的中央是漂浮着玫瑰花瓣的水池。

“冰冻布丁会放在那里。”厨娘说。

两头带翼的银狮，背上驮着水果，池边喝水的小鸟原来是一个个装盐的瓶子。

还有好多好多亮晶晶的玻璃杯、盘子和亮锃锃的刀叉——还有好多好多好吃的。红色的小餐巾叠成了一朵朵玫瑰花……

“大家会把这些都吃掉吗？”阳儿问。

“我想他们会吧！”厨娘笑了，和内莉一起笑了。月女也笑了，她总是别人做什么，她也跟着做什么。但是阳儿不想笑。他背着手，来回走了一圈又一圈。也许他要永远这样踱步下去，要不是保姆突然叫道：“孩子们，现在该洗洗穿衣了”，他们才被护送回儿童室。

于是他们又一起走回那漂亮的宴会厅。

可是，啊！啊！发生什么事啦？彩带啦，玫瑰花啦，全都松开了。一块块红色的小餐巾散落一地，那些亮闪闪的盘子、亮晶晶的玻璃杯变得脏兮兮的。精心雕刻的食物乱扔四处，骨头啦，碎渣啦，果皮啦，果壳啦，到处都是。甚至瓶子碰倒了，瓶子里的酒滴落到桌布上，也没有人去扶正它。

还有那座粉色小屋，白雪覆盖的屋顶，一扇扇绿色的窗子，已经全碎了，全碎了，在餐桌中央化掉了一半。

“来吃点，阳儿！”父亲说，假装什么也没有看见。

可是阳儿没有从门口挪移半步。突然他仰起头，号啕大哭起来。

“我觉得，太可怕——太可怕——太可怕啦！”他呜咽着说。

赏析

孩子眼中的世界是隐喻的，他们天生是才情灵动的诗人。月女对周边事物的朦胧认识，亦真亦幻，生动活泼。翻译时注意儿童娇嗔的语言特点，通过使用语气词和短小句，才能将儿童稚气十足、诗意闪动的语言活灵活现地再现出来。

孩子眼中的世界笼罩着美丽的光晕，一件很小的事物都能让他们产生无限遐想，让他们感到无比快乐。他们瞅见冰箱里的冰冻布丁，立刻就被吸引了。在他们眼中，冰冻布丁不再是宾客席上一道佳肴，而是他们的神殿、他们的乐园。“惊呆了”，“睁大眼睛往里看”，这些都是通过增译法，增用生动夸张的字词，惟妙惟肖地再现出孩子们对周围现实世界强烈的好奇心和旺盛的探究欲望。翻译时还注意表现了宴会厅光色形上的浪漫唯美，在孩童的视角里，宴会厅里布置得就像童话里的仙境。“好多好多好吃的”，这样的翻译更是在模仿孩童的口吻，使用有韵味的叠词来传达情感。

阳儿竟然担心漂亮的冰冻布丁会被吃掉，心事重重地背着手转圈儿踱步，这一动作细节的翻译只有真实细腻，才能让读者体味到世界最美好，最纯净的东西——孩童那颗充盈着纯真善良天性的心。晚餐结束了，阳儿眼中唯美的世界也毁了，他那颗晶莹剔透的童心更碎了。翻译时运用感叹词、语气词、叠词和重复手段，再现了在残酷的现实面前，孩童惊讶、遗憾、失望和伤心的复杂情绪。

阳儿会慢慢地长大。有一天，他或许会像父亲一样，对成人世界乱纷纷的一切释怀淡然。那时，童真，一同和那座冰晶的布丁房子，化掉了，成为昔日最美的梦。

劳动创造美——《愤怒的葡萄》片段选译及赏析

约翰·斯坦贝克(John Steinbeck，1902～1968)被公认为是20世纪美国最出色的作家之一。他的作品关注底层人民的生活疾苦，歌颂劳动人民的淳朴善良，发掘小人物、无产者身上闪耀的光辉与伟大。1940年他的小说《愤怒的葡萄》(*The Grapes of Wrath*)荣获普利策文学奖，1962年他又凭借《鼠与人》(*Of Mice and Men*)等作品荣获诺贝尔文学奖。他对社会有着敏锐的洞察力，运用细腻的写实手法赞扬了劳动人民在一无所有、面临失败时所表现出的伟大精神和仁爱之心。

斯坦贝克的《愤怒的葡萄》第二十二章，讲述了一个感人质朴的故事：寒冷的冬晨，一位饥寒交迫的赶路人，从素不相识的采棉花工人那里，分享到一顿热 气腾腾的早餐。故事虽然没有跌宕起伏的情节，但是热爱劳动、崇善尚美的主题升华了故事意境。

It was very early in the morning. The eastern mountains were blue-black, but behind them the light stood up faintly colored at the mountain rims with a washed red, growing colder, grayer and darker as it went up and overhead until, at a place near the west, it was merged with pure night.

And it was cold, not painfully so, but cold enough so that I rubbed my hands and shoved them deep into my pockets, and I hunched my shoulders up and scuffled my feet in the ground. Down in the valley where I was, the earth was that lavender gray of dawn. I walked along a country road and ahead of me I saw a tent that was only a little lighter gray than the ground. Beside the tent there was a flash of orange fire seeping out of the cracks of an old rusty iron stove. Gray smoke spurted up and out of the stubby stovepipe, spurted up a long way before it spread out and dispersed.

I saw a young woman beside the stove, really a girl. She was dressed in a faded cotton skirt and waist. As I came close I saw that she carried a baby in a crooked arm and the baby was nursing, its head under her waist out of the cold. The mother moved about, poking the fire, shifting the rusty lids of the stove to make a greater draft, opening the oven door; and all the time the baby was nursing, but that didn't interfere with the mother's work, not with the gracefulness of her movements. There was something very precise and practiced about her movements. The orange fire flicked out of the cracks in the stove and threw dancing reflections on the tent... I was close now and I could smell frying bacon and baking bread, the warmest, pleasantest odors I know. From the east the light grew swiftly.

The girl kept to her work, her face averted and her eyes on what she was doing. Her hair was tied back out of her eyes with a string and it hung down her back and swayed as she worked. She set tin cups on a big packing box, set tin plates and knives and forks out too. Then she scooped fried bacon out of the deep grease and laid it on a big tin platter, and the bacon cricked and rustled as it grew crisp. She opened the rusty oven door and took out a square pan full of high big biscuits.

天刚刚破晓,东边山色一片黝蓝。群山背后微微露出一抹晨曦,湿漉漉的红光洇染了山峦的边缘。它一点点升起,越过山头,愈来愈冷,愈来愈淡,逐渐化作黑色,直到接近西边的天际,完全融入漆黑的夜。

天气寒冷,虽然冷得不是那么厉害,但我还是要揉搓双手,将它们深深插入衣服两侧的口袋。我拱肩缩背,双脚蹭在地面上,行走在山谷中。山谷的泥土映照出天破晓时的灰紫色。走在乡间路上,就在前方,我发现了一顶帐篷,帐篷的颜色只比泥地的稍浅。帐篷旁,生锈的旧铁炉缝隙中,闪烁着橘红色火焰。灰白色的浓烟从粗大的火炉烟囱里喷出,扬起长长的一道,飘荡在空中直至消散。

我看见火炉旁有位年轻的妇人,不,是位姑娘。她穿着已经褪色的棉布裙子和背心。我走近后才发现,一个婴儿躺在她的臂弯,正吮吸着奶,脑袋被暖和地裹在她的背心里。这位母亲四处走动,一会儿拨拨炉子的火,一会儿掀开生锈的炉盖通通风,一会儿打开烤炉的门。婴儿一直在吃奶,母亲干活却没有受到影响,她的每个动作轻盈优雅,每个细节都极其准确娴熟。橘红色的火焰从炉子的缝隙中吐出,舞动的倒影投掷在帐篷上。……现在我走得近了，可以闻到煎咸肉和烤面包的味道，这是我所知道的，世界上最温暖人心、最令人愉悦的香味了。就在此刻，东边的天空瞬间放亮了。

姑娘不停地干活，脸侧向一旁，眼睛只盯着她干的活儿。遮住眼睛的头发也被她用头绳扎到脑后。发束垂在她背后，当她干活时，从一侧甩动到另一侧。她在一个大的装货箱子上摆放好几个锡杯，还有几个锡制的盘子和几把刀叉。接着她从油锅里捞出煎好的咸肉片，放在一个锡制的大浅盘子里。油煎的咸肉片一点点变脆时，卷曲起来，沙沙作响。她拉开烤炉生锈的铁门，取出方形的烘烤盘，盘里摆满蓬松的大面包。

赏析

勤劳的主妇，天微微亮时便开始从事烦琐的家务劳动，一面为婴儿哺乳，一面利落地为家人准备丰富的早餐，犹如怀抱圣婴的圣母玛利亚，纯洁、慈爱、美丽，具有伟大的牺牲精神。故事人物写实画面的细腻生动，与恶劣的自然环境、简陋的生活条件形成鲜明对比，洋溢着浪漫主义气息和理想主义美感。翻译时应留意小词翻译的准确性和对一词多义的把握，例如：原文的句子 From the east the light *grew* swiftly 和 The bacon cricked and rustled as it *grew* crisp 中，grew 的不同翻译，顺应了上下文的语境。前一句嗅觉上的香气让视觉的感受性增强，过程极其短暂，食物释放出香气，天空释放出光芒，形成绝妙的互文和通感，体现了劳动驱散黑暗，迎接光明的主题，于是译文变换了原句结构，使原句中的状语变成主语，主语变成宾语；后一句变化上的缓慢，听觉上的持续，更显得食物的美味，所以采取增译法，力求使译文生动贴切。再例如：原文"high big biscuits"也需要通过上下文才能确认它的真实含义，译文"一个个烘烤蓬松的大面包"比"高高的一摞大面饼"更忠实准确。

主妇一家邀请挨饿受冻的路人一同享受丰盛的早餐，并且欣喜地分享好消息：他们采摘了 12 天棉花，领取到新衣裤。至此，故事主题进一步深化：辛勤劳动可以抵御寒冷，创造美好生活。我们进行翻译也同样如此，只有不畏艰辛，斟字酌句，反复推敲，才能收获灿然一新的美好作品。

金玉良言

Humor[1] Them!

By Katherine D. Ortega

One of the requirements of every commencement[2] speaker is that they offer some advice. Well, get ready. It here it comes.

Soon you will be leaving the company[3] of those who think they have all the answers—your professors, instructors and counselors[4]—and going out into what we like to call the real world. In time you will meet up with other people who think they have all the answers. These people are called bosses. My advice is: humor them.

A little later you will meet additional people who think they have all the answers. These are called spouses[5]. My advice is: humor them, too.

And if all goes well, in a few years you will meet still another group of people who think they have all the answers. These are called children. Humor them.

Life will go on, your children will grow up, go to school, and someday they could be taking part in a commencement ceremony just like this one. And who knows, the speaker responsible for handing out good advice might be you. Halfway through your speech, the graduate sitting next to your daughter will lean over and ask, "Who is that woman up there who thinks she has all the answers?"

Well, thanks to the sound advice you are hearing today and that I hope you

---

① humor /hju:mə/ *n*. 迎合，迁就，顺应

② commencement /kə'mensmənt/ *n*. 毕业典礼

③ company /kʌmpənɪ/ *n*./*v*. 交往，陪伴

④ counselor /'kaʊnsələ/ *n*. 辅导员

⑤ spouse /spaʊz/ *n*. 配偶(指夫或妻)

will all pass on, she will be able to say, "That is my mother. Humor her."

毕业典礼上,要求每位发言人都要提出忠告。所以,准备好,下面便是一番肺腑良言。

你们即将离开周围"自以为"能传道解惑的人——你们的教授、导师和辅导员——去闯荡我们喜欢称之为现实的世界。到时候你们会碰到另外一些"自以为"能对付一切的人。这些人是上司。我的忠告是:顺从他们。

稍后你们还会遇到一些"自以为"能出主意的人。他们是你们的配偶。我的忠告是:也听从他们。

如果一切进展顺利的话,几年之后你们又会遇见另外一群"自以为是"的人。他们是孩子。顺从他们。

生命会继续,你们的孩子会长大,上学,某一天也会参加像这样的一个毕业典礼。谁知道呢,在那时的典礼上负责提供忠告的也许就是你。在你讲到一半时,和你女儿坐一块的毕业生会探身打听:"那个自以为无所不知的女士是谁?"

那么,多亏你今天听到的金玉良言,并且如我所盼,你将把它们全部讲给别人,你女儿会说:"那是我母亲,遵从她的劝导吧。"

让爱融化恨意

我们在一生中难免会遇到讨厌我们甚至对我们心怀恨意的人。与其因此气急败坏，进而伺机报复对方以消心头之恨，不如学学美国民谣歌手兼作曲家明迪·格莱德希尔(Mindy Gledhill)的做法，感受一下化"敌"为友之妙。

Three Ways to Love Your Haters

By Mindy Gledhill

Let's be honest: It feels good to be loved. After a performance in Arizona last summer, a young teenage girl waited in a long line of fans to give me a clay heart she had made. Upon receiving it, my own heart melted, as if it were made of the same soft clay.

You don't have to have a performing career to have a following of admirers these days. With the rising of online communities in the last decade such as *YouTube*, *Facebook*, *Twitter*, etc., most of us have had the experience of building our own followings, whether our circle of family and friends or as part of a business or organization that we run. Who doesn't enjoy getting "likes" and reading through the re-affirming comments of others? Indeed, being admired is a validating[①] experience and I don't know many people that don't want to be respected and loved.

But what happens when you are openly and publicly criticized and even hated? Does it knock you off your center? Along with the benefits of these online social communities comes a platform for negative voices that we may not always be able to control. I've had my fair share[②] of haters. Sure you can

---

① validate /ˈvælɪdeɪt/ *vt*. 证实；确证

② fair share 应得的(或应承担的)一份

"block[①]" or "unfriend[②]" anyone who wishes you emotional harm, but once a malicious[③] comment has blindsided[④] you, it can really shake you up[⑤]. Here are a few tips on how to come out of these situations unscathed[⑥] and even more confident than before.

The way we see others tends to be a reflection of how we see ourselves. In other words, if someone is bothered by you or even hating you (or vice versa), that person is only bothered by what they cannot accept about themself. This makes it much easier to stand back[⑦] and make compassions with those who are struggling to find something within themselves to love. Likewise, if someone consistently sees the good in others and in life, they are likely to be confident about who they are as a person and attract like-minded[⑧] personalities[⑨] into their sphere of influence.

Avoid the temptation to fire back to a hater. Respond instead with a disarming[⑩] approach. It will always make things worse to get even[⑪] by firing back and you won't come out on top[⑫], even if you win (I speak from experience!). If you must say something, then I find it extremely effective to say something totally disarming. For example, I once had someone comment on one of my music videos. They said, "Your nose bugs[⑬] me" Not that big of a deal, but still, it's not fun to have your face criticized. I commented back and said something to the effect of[⑭]: "I got my nose from my dad. I love it because

---

① 指在社交网站上屏蔽他人,不让对方看到自己的任何动态消息。
② 指在社交网站上与某人解除好友关系。
③ malicious /məˈlɪʃəs/ *adj*. 恶意的,恶毒的
④ blindside /ˈblaɪndsaɪd/ *vt*. 偷袭,出其不意地打击
⑤ shake up 使不安;使心烦意乱
⑥ unscathed /ʌnˈskeɪðd/ *adj*. 未遭受伤害的;未受损伤的
⑦ stand back 置身事外,退一步(考虑问题)
⑧ like-minded 志趣相投的,想法相同的
⑨ personality /ˌpɜːsəˈnælətɪ/ *n*. 个人
⑩ disarming /dɪsˈɑːmɪŋ/ *adj*. 消除怒气的,宽慰人的
⑪ get even 进行报复,算账
⑫ come out on top 出人头地,获得成功
⑬ bug /bʌg/ *vt*. 使厌烦;使恼怒
⑭ to the effect of 大意是,意思是

it reminds me of him and what an amazing person he is."

On another occasion, I had a commenter criticize me for wearing what she deemed as "an immodest① dress" in one of my music videos and publicly pointed the finger at me for being a bad example. I wrote back and said (paraphrasing), "Whoever you are, wherever you are, I just want you to know that I love you no matter what decisions you make in your life."

She sent me a private apology shortly after that.

It doesn't take much to totally shift the energy of a negative comment into something positive. As a result, you will feel infinitely better too.

In the words of Alison Krauss②: "You say it best, when you say nothing at all." Ask yourself if it's really worth it to spend any energy at all fussing over③ a hater. Most of the time, it's not. So do what you have to do: "Block", "Delete", "Report④", and go on with your day. (Bonus⑤: Send out a prayer, a wish or a good vibration⑥ for the one who tried to hurt you. You'll feel amazing. I promise.)

Sometimes it's easy to forget that there's a real person on the other side of the computer screen. We could all stand to be a little more generous with the positive comments we leave and a lot more cautious about the criticism we make. But when it comes to others leaving waves of negativity in their wake⑦, remember that it's not about you and it never was.

实不相瞒：被爱的感觉真的很好！去年夏天，有一次在亚利桑那州表演完后，一个十来岁的年轻姑娘排在长长的粉丝队伍中，等着要把她用陶土做成的心送给我。拿到手的那一刻，我的心就融化了，仿佛自己的那颗心也是用同样的软泥做成的。

---

① immodest /ɪˈmɒdɪst/ *adj*. 不端庄的，不合礼仪的

② 艾莉森·克劳斯(1971～)，当今美国蓝草音乐(Blue Grass)的领军者，已获得 27 座格莱美奖。

③ fuss over 过分关心

④ 指在社交网站上举报某人。

⑤ bonus /ˈbəʊnəs/ *n*. 额外的赠品(或好处)

⑥ vibration /vaɪˈbreɪʃn/ *n*. (感情上的)感应，共鸣

⑦ in one's wake: (= in the wake of sb.) 在某人身后；随某人之后而来

现如今，你不用非得从事演艺事业，也能拥有一大批仰慕你的人。近十年来，随着诸如YouTube、Facebook和推特等各种网络平台的兴起，我们大多数人都已经有了打造我们自己的追随者的经历，不管是我们的家人、朋友也好，还是我们生意上、团队里的伙伴也罢。谁不喜欢得到别人的“点赞”，谁不喜欢从头到尾地读完别人再三肯定自己的评论？的确，被人仰慕是一种得到认同的体验，我认识的人当中也很少有人不想受到尊敬与爱慕。

但是，如果你遭到公开的批评甚至是憎恨，你会怎样？你会因此失去内心的平衡吗？这些网络社交平台在带来种种好处的同时，也会给网友提供发表各类负面声音的机会，而我们也许并不一定总能掌控这些负面声音。我也免不了有恨我的人。当然，你可以“屏蔽”任何想伤害你感情的人，或者与他们“解除好友关系”。可是，一旦有条恶意言论出其不意地攻击了你。它就真的会让你感到心烦意乱。那么我们如何才能毫发无伤地走出这些困境，甚至做到比以前更加自信呢？下面有几条建议。

我们看待别人的方式往往会反映出我们是如何看待自己的。换句话说，如果有人对你感到厌烦甚至对你心怀怨恨（反之亦然），那么那个人仅仅对其不能接受的关于自身的东西感到厌恶。如果能够这样想，那么置身事外就变得容易得多，也就更容易同情那些正竭力从自身寻找可爱之处的人。同样，如果有人不断发现他人身上和生活中美好的一面，那么他们很可能就会对自己的为人十分自信，从而吸引志趣相投的人到他们的圈子里。

避开诱惑，不去反击仇恨你的人。相反，要心平气和地做出回应。若是为了报复进行反击，永远只会使情况变得更加糟糕，即使你赢了，你也不会成为最后的赢家（我这样说是有亲身经历为依据的！）。如果你非要说些什么，那么我觉得说些能彻底消除敌意的话是非常奏效的。例如，有人曾经这样评价我的一个音乐视频，他们说：“你的鼻子让我觉得很烦！”虽然这没有什么大不了的，但是你的长相被人指摘也不是什么有趣的事情，于是我做了回复，大意是：“我的鼻子随我爸。我喜欢它，因为它让我想起了我爸，想起他是一个多么了不起的人。”

还有一次，有个评论者认为我在某个音乐视频里穿了“一件不合礼仪的裙子”，因而对此颇有微词，而且还公然指责我带了个坏头。我回复道（大致是这样）：“无论你是谁，无论你身在何处，我只是想让你知道我是爱你的，不管你在生活中会做出什么决定。”

在那之后不久，她私下向我道了歉。

没费太多事，负面评论的负能量就完全转化成了正能量。最终，你也会感觉好很多。

用艾莉森·克劳斯的话说："此时无声胜有声。"扪心自问，花费精力去对付一个恨你的人究竟是否真的值得。很多时候，这是不值得的。所以只管做你需要做的就好啦："屏蔽""删除""举报"，继续过自己的日子。(附赠：为那些试图想伤害你的人祈祷、祝福或者说一句让他们有好感的话，我保证，你会感觉棒极了。)

有时，我们很容易忘记电脑屏幕的另一端坐着一个活生生的人。我们若能稍微大方些，多发点儿积极的留言，而在发出批评指责时小心谨慎些，那我们都能从中受益。但若是别人甩下滚滚恶评，请记住，这与你无关，从来都与你无关。

家庭篇

《归家》片段选译及赏析(上)

维多利亚时期是英国历史上的黄金时代。英国在世界范围内迅速扩张殖民地,积聚了巨额的金银财富,经济的迅猛发展推动了文学的空前繁荣。维多利亚时期的文学经典灿若繁星,许多人们耳熟能详、津津乐道的文学佳作横空出世。与狄更斯齐名的大作家,有"小萨克雷"之称的 Anthony Trollope(安东尼·特罗洛普,1815~1882)就曾写下浓墨重彩的一笔,其代表作 *The Barchester Chronicles*(《巴切斯特传》)、*The Way We Live Now*(《如今世道》)广受赞誉,近年来相继改编成 BBC 等频道的影视剧。他用细腻笔法勾画出金钱社会下的人性美丑,闪耀着人文关怀的浓郁光彩,看似平淡却跌宕起伏的情节安排,让人不胜唏嘘。他的短篇小说 *Returning Home*(《归家》)叙述描写的正是维多利亚淘金时代背景下,寄居海外的英国人不远万里归家,在返乡途中发生的凄美故事,字里行间流露出的悲凉无奈,倾注了作者对小人物的怜惜同情。

为了去海外淘金发财,不少英国人背井离乡、跋山涉水,足迹遍及欧、亚、非、美、澳各洲。异国他乡的打拼带给他们的仅仅是金钱物质上的富足,在精神上他们却饱受思家之苦的煎熬。小说一开头,作者以讲故事人的身份的旁白叙述引人入胜。"It is generally supposed that people who live at home—good domestic people, who love tea and their arm-chairs, and who keep the parlour hearth-rug ever warm—it is generally supposed that these are the people who value home the most, and best appreciate all the comforts of that cherished institution. I am inclined to doubt this. It is, I think, to those who live farthest away from home, to those who find the greatest difficulty in visiting home, that the word conveys the sweetest idea.... His home is across the blue waters, in the little northern island, which perhaps he may visit no more; which he has left, at any rate, for half his life; from which circumstances, and the necessity of living, have banished him. His home is still in England, and when he speaks of home his thoughts are there."

(一般认为居家之人——那些迷恋茶点和扶手椅,总让客厅壁炉前地毯保暖的逸居之人——一般认为只有这些人最看重家庭,最为享受那处爱巢的种种舒适。我对此持怀疑态度。在我看来,那些远居他乡、归家艰难的人才能体会到"家"这个字最为甜美的内涵。……他的家在碧蓝大洋的对岸,在他可能不再拜访的北方小岛上。他离开那个小岛,至少半辈子了。为境遇所迫、生计所需,他被放逐,漂泊流离。他的家却始终在英格兰,当他提到"家",让他魂牵梦萦的地方是在那儿。)

作者首先运用 periodic sentences(掉尾句)、repetition(反复):"It is generally supposed that..." 和 parallel sentences(排比句):"people who...",说明了人们认为"家"仅是舒适温暖的家居环境的浅薄理解,紧接着作者笔锋一转,用一个短句"I am inclined to doubt this",引出一组与之形成强烈对比、句式上交相呼应的 parallel sentences(排比句)、emphatic sentences(强调句):"It is... to those who... that...",突现了真正意义上的"家"是浪迹天涯的游子眼里的千里之外、遥不可及的故土。整段话长短句相交错,节奏抑扬顿挫,排比句气势磅礴,反复句余韵悠然,读来感心动耳,回肠荡气。

作者将他们客居异乡的内心痛苦和祈盼娓娓道来:"There are a few Germans and a few Englishmen in the place, who see each other on matters of business during the day; but, sombre as life generally is, they seem to care little for each other's company on any other footing. I know not to what point the aspirations of the Germans may stretch themselves, but to the English the one idea that gives salt to life is the idea of home. On some day, however distant it may be, they will once more turn their faces towards the little northern island, and then all will be well with them."(生活在这里的许多德国人和英国人白天由于生意的事才碰头;平日的生活索然寡味,但是他们似乎很少关注彼此在其他方面的任何交往。我不知道德国人要施展多大的雄心抱负,但是我知道对于英国人来说,生活的滋味是对家的思念。某一日,无论相距多么遥远,他们的目光会再次转向北方小岛,那时那刻,一切就会好起来。)"But what of his wife? Where will she find excitement? By what pursuit will she repay herself for all that she has left behind her at her mother's fireside? She will love her husband. Yes; that at least! If there be not that, there will be a hell, indeed. Then she will nurse her children, and talk of her—home. When the time shall come that her promised return thither is within a year or two of its accomplishment, her thoughts will all be fixed on that coming pleasure, as are the thoughts of a young girl on her first ball for the fortnight before that event comes off."(但是他的妻子可以做什么呢？她应该去哪里找寻生活的热情呢？依靠什么样的寄托才能弥补她损失在娘家的一切呢？她可以去爱她的丈夫。是的，这是最起码的！如果不是这样，她简直就是在地狱。她也可以照料孩子，闲叙"家"事。再过一两年，允诺她归家的日子将近，她就会日思夜想那即将到来的欢乐，心情就像年轻姑娘等待两周后头一回参加的舞会一样迫不及待。)作者对身居海外的英国男人翘望家乡"小"岛的细节描写，与德国人的生活态度形成反差，在这里，我们感受不到英国男人敛取财富、称霸天下的雄心"大"志，却被他们思乡怀亲的儿女柔情深深触动，而英国女人对"娘家"的强烈思念让我们愈发体会到寄居异国他乡的孤寂之味，乡愁是他们心中隐隐的痛，归家成了他们最美好的愿望。"And people told her—the few neighbours around her—how happy, how fortunate she was to get home thus early in her life. They had been out some ten—some twenty years, and still the day of their return was distant."(人们告诉她——她周围的几个邻居说——她这么年轻就可以还乡，真是好福气。他们离家在外差不多十年、二十年，归家依然遥遥无期。)"And then their preparations for the journey went on with much flurrying and hot haste....this packing of baby-linen was delightful, and for a month or so the days went by with happy wings."(紧接着他们手忙脚乱地为旅行做各种准备。……整理小孩的衣物成了乐事，时间插上了幸福的翅膀，一个月左右的日子飞逝而去。)这对英国夫妇满心欢喜准备归家，这一打算承载着流浪在外人沉甸甸的夙愿，作者用邻居们的羡慕反衬了他们起程前的幸福，烦琐的旅行准备抵挡不住他们出发前的热情，他们对时间的错觉形象地表现了他们归心似箭的心情。

《归家》片段选译及赏析(下)

2012年,英国维多利亚时代最多产的伟大小说家 Anthony Trollope(安东尼·特罗洛普,1815～1882)逝世130周年。他的纪念碑安放在威斯敏斯特教堂(Westminster Abbey)诗人角(Poets' Corner),受世人瞻仰。除了他对英国文学发展做出的巨大贡献外,至今遍布在英国街角的红色信箱(red pillar box)也是他的社会贡献之一。

归家途中,除去婴儿,一行八人,八头骡子,其中四名西班牙或印第安裔向导徒步行走。"...the clouds soon gathered and poured forth their collected waters as though it had not rained for months among those mountains. Not that it came in big drops, or with the violence which wind can give it, beating hither and thither, breaking branches from the trees, and rising up again as it pattered against the ground. There was no violence in the rain. It fell softly in a long, continuous, noiseless stream, sinking into everything that it touched, converting the deep rich earth on all sides into mud. Not a word was said by any of them as it came on. The Indian covered the baby with her blanket, closer than she was covered before, and the guide who walked by Mrs. Arkwright's side drew her cloak around her knees. But such efforts were in vain."(很快乌云密布,聚集的雨水倾倒下来,好似山地这一带数月没下过雨。其实雨点不大,没有夹杂在狂风里四下胡乱抽打一气,也没有折断树枝,待敲落地面后飞溅。雨下得一点儿也不猛烈。它轻柔地落下,悄无声息地汇成源源不断的长流,渗进所到之处,把四方肥沃的地下土壤变成泥浆。下雨时,他们当中没有一个人开口说话。印第安人用毛毯裹住婴儿,裹得比先前更紧了,走在阿克赖特夫人身旁的向导拿她的披风盖住她的膝盖。但这样做是徒劳的。)绵软细密,无声无息地落在旅行者身上,潜入他们的心头,他们缄默不语,是精疲力竭,抑或是惶恐不安,这种声音上的留白值得体味,"covered the baby, closer than...before""drew her cloak around her knees",向导们"裹""盖"两个细节动作,侧面反映出旅行中雨虐风饕的恶劣天气。

"It is not that any active exertion is necessary—that there is anything which requires doing. The traveller has before him the simple task of sitting on his mule from hour to hour, and of seeing that his knees do not get themselves jammed against the trees; but at every step the beast he rides has to drag his legs out from the deep clinging mud, and the body of the rider never knows one moment of ease. Why the mules do not die on the road, I cannot say. They live through it, and do not appear to suffer. They have their own way in everything, for no exertion on the rider's part will make them walk either faster or slower than is their wont."(骑骡子的人没有必要自己劳筋苦骨干任何事。他面前简单的活儿就是一个小时挨过一个小时地坐在骡背上,不让树枝绊上自己的膝盖。但是他骑的牲口每走一步,就得从厚厚的黏糊的泥浆中拔出腿来,这样骑者的身体一刻也没有舒坦过。我真不知道这些骡子为什么没有死在路上。它们挺了过来,没见着痛苦。它们干什么都自行其是,不管骑者使出多大力气驱赶它们,它们还是依照自己的习惯,不会加快或者减慢步子。)作者用平缓略带戏谑的笔调勾画了骡子在泥泞路上迂回前行、不紧不慢的场景,生动反衬出旅人的焦急痛苦,真实表现了旅途的曲折艰辛。这两段典型描写都可以看出特罗洛普小说语言的特点:温润轻淡中流转出厚重深郁。美国著名作家纳撒尼尔·霍桑(Nathaniel Hawthorne)在1860年2月11日写给自己出版商的信中曾这样评价:"Have you ever read the novels of Anthony Trollope?... written on strength of beef and through inspiration of ale,...as if some giant had hewn a great lump out of the earth and put it under a glass case..."(你读过安东尼·特罗洛普的小说吗?……凭借牛肉的力量和啤酒的灵感的创作……仿佛是巨人砍下巨石,垫在玻璃橱柜下……)

疲倦和痛苦更让脆弱的阿克赖特夫人近乎疯狂,她泣不成声,哀吟不止,一遍遍煞有介事地跟丈夫诉说自己不祥的预感。他们曾得到独居林中妇人的好心宽慰,他们曾向不重金钱、遁世离俗的西班牙老夫妇借宿,当向导们用自制的简陋担架毫无怨言、不计报酬地把夫人抬到了渡口时,这对英国夫妇才看到了归家的曙光,他们为胜利解脱欢欣鼓舞,读者也为他们长舒一口气,没想到他们乘坐的船只在湍急的河水里遇险,读者的心又被提到嗓子眼。"Arkwright was soon to be seen some forty yards down, having been carried clear of the trees, and here he got out of the river on the farther bank. The distance to him was not above forty yards, but from the nature of the ground he could not get up towards his wife, unless he could have forced his way against the stream."(很快,阿克赖特被发现冲到那些树枝以外大约四十码的地方。在那里,他游出水面爬到了更远的河岸。虽然出事的地点离他不过四十码,但是地势的特点让他无法靠近他的妻子,除非他能够逆流游上去。)"The Indian who had had charge of the baby rose quickly to the surface, was carried once round in the eddy, with his head high above the water, and then was seen to throw himself among the broken wood. He had seen the dress of the poor woman, and made his effort to save her.... Mrs. Arkwright had sunk at once on being precipitated into the water, but the buoyancy of her clothes had brought her for a moment again to the surface. She had risen for a moment, and then had again gone down, immediately below the forked trunk of a huge tree—had gone down, alas, alas! never to rise again with life within her bosom. The poor Indian made two attempts to save her, and then came up himself, incapable of further effort."(先前负责照看婴儿的印第安人很快露出水面,又再次被卷入漩涡,头露出水面一大截,接着被看到卷进烂木丛中了。他看见那个可怜女人的衣裙了,奋力去救助她。……阿克赖特夫人刚落水就立即沉下去了,但是开始她还靠柔软的衣裙托着在水里浮了一阵。她露出水面一会儿,又沉了下去,直接掉进大树的树杈下,一直沉了下去,哎呀,哎呀!她再没有活着浮起来。可怜的印第安人两次试图救起她,因为无济于事,他随后独自上了岸。)"It was then that the German, the owner of the canoes, who had fought his way with great efforts across the violence of the waters, and indeed up against the stream for some few yards, made his effort to save the life of that poor frail creature. He had watched the spot at which she had gone down, and even while struggling across the river, had seen how the Indian had followed her and had failed. It was now his turn. His life was in his hand, and he was prepared to throw it away in that attempt. Having succeeded in placing himself a little above the large tree, he turned his face towards the bottom of the river, and dived down among the branches. And he also, after that, was never again seen with the life-blood flowing round his heart."(就在这时,那位德国人,船只的主人,在急流中奋勇前行,竟逆水而上游了几码,努力去营救那个可怜而脆弱的生命。他留

意了她沉水的地点，甚至他挣扎着游过河水时，还看见印第安人是如何跟上她，却没有救起她。现在轮到他了。他竭尽全力，准备舍己救人。他成功地游到那棵大树偏上的位置，接着面朝河底，俯冲进树枝丛中。那以后，他生命的血液在心脏里再也没有流动。）小说故事情节可谓一波三折，营救落水的阿克赖特夫人这一段，更是将故事推向高潮，惊心动魄，作者生动塑造了有血有肉、饱满充盈的人物形象，"A singular looking man was he, with a huge shaggy beard, and shaggy uncombed hair, but with bright blue eyes, which gave to his face a remarkable look of sweetness."（他长相奇特，蓄着大把浓密粗乱的胡须，顶着蓬松杂乱的头发，但一双炯炯有神的蓝眼睛让他的面容看上去格外亲切。）就在丈夫阿克赖特和印第安人向导都束手无策时，正是这位德国船长勇敢地跳水救人，献出了自己宝贵的生命，他尽管相貌丑异，但他美好的形象却永远定格在人们心中。幸存的丈夫哀痛逾恒，安葬完妻子后又折回了中美洲的圣若泽城，"The widowed husband could not face his darling's mother with such a tale upon his tongue as that."（丧偶的丈夫无法面对爱人的母亲，亲口诉说这样一个故事呀。）然而，讲故事人特罗洛普却已经绘声绘色地向读者讲完了这样一个震撼人心、壮烈悲凄的归家故事。

《好好先生》片段选译及赏析

新西兰著名女作家凯瑟琳·曼斯菲尔德(Kathleen Mansfield, 1888～1923)在小说集《幸福》(*Bliss*)之《好好先生》("The Man Without a Temperament")里刻画了一位好脾气的丈夫形象,他对病重休养中的妻子体贴入微的关怀照料让人不禁想起爱尔兰诗人叶芝的优美诗句:"To love you, in an old high way of love.(爱你,用古老高尚的方式。)"

The iron cage clanged open. Light dragging steps sounded across the hall, coming towards him. A hand, like a leaf, fell on his shoulder. A soft voice said: "Let's go and sit over there — where we can see the drive. The trees are so lovely." And he moved forward with the hand still on his shoulder, and the light, dragging steps beside his. He pulled out a chair and she sank into it, slowly, leaning her head against the back, her arms falling along the sides.

电梯的铁栅门"哐当"一声拉开了。轻细拖沓的脚步声穿过大厅,朝他的方向传来。一只手,像一片树叶,落在他的肩上,一个柔弱的声音说:"我们走吧,去那儿坐着。那里可以看见车道。那些树木真迷人。"他向前走去,那只手仍然扶在他的肩上,轻细拖沓的脚步声又在他身边响起。他拉出一张椅子,她瘫坐下去,缓缓地,头靠在椅背,双臂搭在椅把上。

作者用第三人称叙述角度让妻子"犹抱琵琶半遮面"出场了。电梯的铁栅门幕布式地拉开,一双脚、一只手、一个声音,寥寥几笔勾画出妻子的弱不禁风、病入膏肓的状态,丈夫的肩膀始终是妻子生命的依靠。

They sat there for a long while. The sky flamed, paled; the two white beds were like two ships...

The sky is the colour of jade. There are a great many stars; an enormous white moon hangs over the garden. Far away lightning flutters—flutters like a wing—flutters like a broken bird that tries to fly and sinks again and again struggles.

He gets very cold sitting there, staring at the balcony rail. Finally he comes inside. The moon — the room is painted white with moonlight. The light trembles in the mirrors; the two beds seem to float.

他们久久地坐在那里。天空烧得通红，然后烧成灰白；两张白色的床恰似两只船……

冷翡翠色的天空里，繁星万点，一轮硕大苍白的月悬在花园上空。远处的闪电忽明忽暗，——扑哧扑哧像一只翅膀——像折翅的鸟儿挣扎着飞起来，跌下去，飞起又跌落。

他坐在那儿，凝视着阳台栏杆，感觉冷极了。他终于进了屋。那轮月——月色把房间染成霜白。亮光在一面面镜子中颤动；两张床恍如飘浮起来。

丈夫牺牲了自己的事业，甘心陪妻子到陌生的异国他乡疗养。妻子有心脏问题，夫妇已经分床而睡。“灰白的天”“折翼的鸟”“苍白的月”“游离的床”，这些意象表现了有名无实的冷淡夫妻生活，叫人感到窒息。这样死寂的婚姻状态可以用美国当代诗人保罗·胡佛(Paul Hoover)的诗句来感叹：“I have two coffins but only one wife, who loves me like a neighbor.(我有两副棺材，却只有一个跟我相敬如宾的妻子。)”原文中颜色词 paled(灰白色)、the color of jade(冷翡翠色)、white(苍白)、painted white (霜白)，只有翻译细致妥帖了，才能够深刻再现原作品的艺术魅力。令人动颜的是，这位好脾气先生依然坚守在妻子身旁，不放弃这份沉重的家庭责任。文中不断描写一个细节：“He turned the ring, turned the signet ring on his little finger.(他转动着戒指，转动着小指上所戴的那枚图章戒。)”婚戒象征相爱一生的誓言和相守一世的承诺，丈夫不断转动它的细小动作，不断表达信守诺言的决心。

“To love you, in an old high way of love.(爱你，用古老高尚的方式。)”丈夫为妻子取披肩、穿斗篷，几乎每时每刻陪伴在她身边。妻子感动得向丈夫深情表白："You see — you're everything. You're bread and wine, Robert, bread and wine.(你瞧，你是一切，是面包和酒，罗伯特，面包和酒。)"古老高尚的爱，是人间四月柔情的天光，是牺牲奉献、体贴付出，是不求一点回报，是没有丝毫计较，心中默默甘愿分担另一个生命的苦与痛，甘做另一个生命的"面包和酒"。

Arrived in their room he went swiftly over to the washstand, shook the bottle, poured her out a dose and brought it across.

"Sit down. Drink it. And don't talk." And he stood over her while she obeyed. Then he took the glass, rinsed it and put it back in its case. "Would you like a cushion?"

"No, don't move. Stay where you are." He switches on the light, lifts the net. "Where is the little beggar? Have you spotted him?"

"Yes, there, over by the corner. Oh, I do feel such a fiend to have dragged you out of bed. Do you mind dreadfully?"

"No, of course not." For a moment he hovers in his blue and white pyjamas. Then, "got him," he said.

"Oh, good. Was he a juicy one?"

"Beastly." He went over to the washstand and dipped his fingers in water. "Are you all right now? Shall I switch off the light?"

He bends down. He kisses her. He tucks her in, he smoothes the pillow.

他一回屋，就立刻走到脸盆架旁，摇了摇瓶子，为她倒出一份药并且端过去。

"坐下来，喝了它吧。别说话。"他站在她身旁，她照办了。接着他拿走水杯，涮了涮，放回架子上，"想要个靠垫吗？"

"不，不要动。躺在原地。"他拧开灯，掀起蚊帐。"那只吸血鬼在哪里？你找到它了吗？"

"是的，在那里，就在角落里。哎，我真可恶，把你叫下床。你不怪我吧？"

"怎么会呢？"他用他那件蓝白相间的睡衣扑腾了好一阵子。然后说，"拍死它了。"

"哇，太好了，它吸饱肚子了吧？"

“血滴滴的，”他走到脸盆架旁，把手浸泡在水中。“你现在感觉好些吗？要不要熄灯？”

他弯下身去，吻了吻她，替她盖好被子，抚平枕头。

好好先生用古老高尚的方式关爱妻子。作者选取丈夫为妻子端药水，半夜起身为妻子驱蚊的点滴小事将丈夫的无私大爱表现得淋漓尽致。古老高尚的爱，像颗颗珍珠在女作家曼斯菲尔德这篇佳作里熠熠闪烁，愿君多采撷，此情最笃切。

女人如猫——《雨中的猫》片段选译及赏析

美国 20 世纪著名小说家欧内斯特·米勒尔·海明威(Ernest Miller Hemingway,1899～1961)的短篇小说"*Cat in the Rain*"(《雨中的猫》)最早发表在他 1925 年的小说集 *Our Times*(《我们的时代》)里。张爱玲曾说:女人如猫,对大多数的女人,"爱"的意思就是"被爱"。小说通过讲述漂泊异乡的美国女人寻猫、乞猫和得猫的故事,反映了一战后女人渴望回归温馨美好的家庭生活,渴望得到男人尊重和呵护的主题。

There were only two Americans stopping at the hotel. They did not know any of the people they passed on the stairs on their way to and from their room. Their room was on the second floor facing the sea. It also faced the public garden and the war monument. There were big palms and green benches in the public garden. In the good weather there was always an artist with his easel. Artists liked the way the palms grew and the bright colors of the hotels facing the gardens and the sea. Italians came from a long way off to look up at the war monument. It was made of bronze and glistened in the rain. It was raining. The rain dripped from the palm trees. Water stood in pools on the gravel paths. The sea broke in a long line in the rain and slipped back down the beach to come up and break again in a long line in the rain. The motor cars were gone from the square by the war monument. Across the square in the doorway of the cafe a waiter stood looking out at the empty square.

The American wife stood at the window looking out. Outside right under their window a cat was crouched under one of the dripping green tables. The cat was trying to make herself so compact that she would not be dripped on. "I'm going down and get that kitty," the American wife said.

"I'll do it," her husband offered from the bed.

"No, I'll get it. The poor kitty out trying to keep dry under a table."

The husband went on reading, lying propped up with the two pillows at the foot of the bed.

The wife went downstairs and the hotel owner stood up and bowed to her as she passed the office....The wife liked him. She liked the deadly serious way he received any complaints. She liked his dignity. She liked the way he wanted to serve her. She liked the way he felt about being a hotel-keeper. She liked his old, heavy face and big hands.

As the American girl passed the office, the padrone bowed from his desk. Something felt very small and tight inside the girl. The padrone made her feel very small and at the same time really important. She had a momentary feeling of being of supreme importance. She went on up the stairs. She opened the door of the room. George was on the bed, reading.

His wife was looking out of the window. It was quite dark now and still raining in the palm trees.

"Anyway, I want a cat," she said, "I want a cat. I want a cat now. If I can't have long hair or any fun I can have a cat."

George was not listening. He was reading his book. His wife looked out of the window where the light had come on in the square.

Someone knocked at the door.

"Avanti," George said. He looked up from his book.

In the doorway stood the maid. She held a big tortoise-shell cat pressed tight against her and swung down against her body.

"Excuse me," she said, "the padrone asked me to bring this for the Signora."

在这家旅馆里,只有两个美国人停留。他们进出自己的房间,在楼梯遇见的人,一个人也不认识。他们的房间在二楼,面朝大海,也可以看见公园和战争纪念碑。在公园里有高大的棕榈树和绿色的长凳。天气好时,总是有位背着画架的艺术家。艺术家喜欢棕榈树生长的样子和公园对面旅馆的明亮颜色。意大利人走很远的路来瞻仰战争纪念碑。铜铸成的纪念碑在雨中熠熠闪光。天下着雨。雨水从棕榈树上滑落。鹅卵石的路上留下一摊积水。大海在雨中翻起一线长长的水浪，涌上沙滩后退去又翻滚而来，在雨中再次掀起长长一线。纪念碑旁的广场上汽车飞驰而过。一位服务生站立在广场对面的咖啡馆门口，向空荡荡的广场张望。

美国太太站在窗前朝外看。就在窗外，一只小猫蜷缩在一张滴着雨水的绿色桌子下。小猫拼命缩紧身子，以免被雨淋湿。“我要下楼，抱回那只小猫咪。”美国妻子说。

“我去。”她丈夫躺在床上说。

“不，我去。屋外可怜的小猫想在桌子下躲雨呢。”

她丈夫用两个枕头撑在床头，继续躺着看书。

美国太太走下楼，当她经过经理办公室时，旅馆老板起身向她鞠躬。……美国太太喜欢他。她喜欢他那种任劳任怨、一本正经的模样。她喜欢他的气派。她喜欢他那乐于为她效劳的姿态。她喜欢他做旅馆老板的神气。她喜欢他那张成熟稳重的脸和一双大手。

美国女孩走过办公室时，旅馆老板从办公桌后面向她点头哈腰，女孩内心感到这点小事给人家添麻烦了。老板让她觉得小事虽小，但也是件挺要紧的事。她一时感到受宠若惊。她走上楼梯，打开门，乔治还在床上看书。

他的妻子望着窗外。现在天色已晚。雨水仍打落在棕榈树上。

“不管怎样，我要一只猫。”她说，“我要一只猫。现在我要一只猫。如果我不能留长头发或什么好玩的，我能有只猫也好。”

乔治没有听，他在看书。他的妻子望着窗外。广场上的灯亮起来。

有人敲门。

“进来，”乔治说，他放下书本，抬起头来。

门口站着女侍者。她贴身紧抱着一只毛色棕、黑、黄相间的大花猫。猫扭动着从她怀里跳下来。

“打搅了，”她说，“老板让我把这只猫送给夫人。”

赏析

海明威对人们历经战争沧桑洗礼的描写，让人不禁联想起苏轼的词《念奴娇·赤壁怀古》：惊涛拍岸，卷起千堆雪。江山如画，一时多少豪杰。第一次世界大战后美国人热衷异国探险，意大利人缅怀战争英雄，历史有如广场上的汽车飞驰过往，人们却如同咖啡馆门前的服务生面对空荡荡的未来一脸茫然。战后分崩离析的社会，许多问题纷至沓来，新旧事物交织碰撞，道德价值观交替对峙，"迷惘一代"(The Lost Generation)是海明威时代独特的历史文化现象。

《雨中的猫》的丈夫形象正是当时迷惘的美国青年的代表，残酷的战争毁灭了他的理想，他宁愿在书本里寻找慰藉。他心灰意冷，丧失了对妻子体贴入微、关爱备至的能力。一战后美国社会趋于保守。年轻女性认为妇女应回归家庭，专心地扮好妻子和母亲这一传统角色。美国太太执意要亲自抱回在雨中漂泊的小猫咪，这是战后女性渴望回归温暖家庭生活的强烈表达。小猫孤立无助，被人冷落的处境使她产生了一种心灵深处的共鸣，它激发了妻子同病相怜的情感。

面对妻子的小小愿望，美国丈夫表现出冷漠麻木的态度，太太强烈地想要寻猫，他在看书；太太执着地寻猫未果，他在看书；太太苦苦地哀求养只猫，他还在看书。在逃避现实、消极迷惘的丈夫那里，妻子得不到关爱，"我要一只猫"的反复诉求正是女性对家庭关怀的大声疾呼。美国太太对意大利旅馆老板成熟特质的一连串 5 个 like，正是她渴望男性对女性尊重和体贴的一种心理映射。女人如猫，她的撒娇只是想得到男人的疼爱和关心，她需要一个男人的时候，她才会发出独有的咕噜声。女人如猫，她不是任性矫情，也不是贪图享乐，只是想获得被爱的尊严。

海明威简约艺术的风格使小说的结尾呈现出维纳斯断臂的美感，美国妻子是否接受了那只大花猫，美国丈夫是否内心触动幡然醒悟，美国妻子和意大利旅馆老板之间是否还有故事，这样开放式的构图使得小说耐人寻味，留给读者无限想象的空间。

写给我的亲亲宝贝

我们也许永远不会知道，当我们还是个什么都不懂的小婴儿时，母亲就已经在用各种方式与我们交流了。她想象我们长大后的样子，对我们的未来充满各种憧憬，担心我们有一天会离开，又期盼我们适时归来。其实，从我们出生的第一天起，这样的母爱便开始流淌。它贯穿母亲的生命，陪伴我们走过人生的高潮和低谷。无论如何，母亲的怀抱永远对我们敞开，那双关切的眼睛也从未离开。

Before You Can Pick Your Own Nose

Dear Son,

I'm writing to you when you are at the tender age of just 37 days old in order to take the time to reflect on who you are and to be grateful for it.

You see, your dad and I realize that at this very moment in time, you are 100% dependent on us. We knew of this great responsibility once we found out we were pregnant with you.

You need us to provide you food, shelter, warmth and all your basic needs to help you grow. You haven't been potty[①] trained yet, so your diapers are our responsibility. You rely on us for everything, but you cry and sleep and poop on your own. You even rely on us to pick your nose, which we still haven't figured out how to do.

And one day, it has occurred to me, you won't need us for anything at all.

I have read so many mommy articles lately about the hardship of motherhood, with the attendant[②] rah- rah[③] over how many sacrifices moms make. And while I absolutely agree that motherhood has its challenges, I want

① potty /ˈpɒtɪ/ *n.* (小孩用的)便盆；尿壶

② attendant /əˈtendənt/ *adj.* 伴随的；随之而来的

③ rah-rah /ˈrɑːˈrɑː/ *n.* 欢呼声，叫好声，喝彩声

to also appreciate the beautiful things about motherhood, because there truly are so many things that only you and I experience together. Your growth so far has made me realize so much about myself and about your evolution from our baby to one day, a self-sufficient young man.

At some point in time, the things that can drive a new mom crazy will fade. So, for now, I will stop and find the beauty and joy in the smallest things you do.

You cry and wail at the top of your lungs[①]. I choose to be grateful that you are 100% healthy. Your lungs are functioning and until you can communicate with words. Crying is the only way to let us know that you are displeased with something. And son, we hear you loud and clear. When you were born, you let out a cry that struck a chord[②] in the hearts of both your father and me. And even though you cry mysteriously from time to time, your pitch and tone will forever be recorded in my memory.

My hope is that as you grow up, your cries are reserved for happy moments instead of tragic ones. I can't even imagine yet how gut-wrenching[③] it will feel for me when you start experiencing pain that elicits[④] tears. And since you have no spoken words yet, I am cherishing these days before you can say the word "no," but look forward to when you can tell me about your highest highs and lowest lows. So for now, I am reminded by your cries that you need something from me.

And son, I have a request for you since your mom is a health care provider: please keep your lungs free of nicotine.

You let me smother you with kisses. Little do you know it, but we give you about 1,000 kisses a day. More or less. As I had posted on my *Facebook* this week about how you just smiled at your dad and I a few mornings ago, my friend Adam said it best. To paraphrase him, there's a circle of life that happens when a child smiles at their parents. You'll enjoy us for the next 8 to 10

---

① at the top of one's lungs 声嘶力竭地;用尽量大的声音

② strike a chord 引起共鸣,触动心弦

③ gut-wrenching *adj*. 带来精神痛苦的

④ elicit /ɪˈlɪsɪt/ *vt*. 引起,引出

years, then not be as enthused to see us for another 8 to 10 years, and then you'll be back to being happy to see us with a vengeance[①].

I realize that the days of 1,000 kisses will fade from coming from your parents and be replaced by a lover one day. May you choose wisely. Very, very wisely my dear son.

You are comforted most in my arms. As I have chosen to exclusively breastfeed you, you and I share a lot of intimate time together. Easily we share 8 to 10 times a day where it is just you and I, literally connected. Yes, there have been sleepless nights, but I know those days are limited. In the coming months and years, you'll grow heavier to where I won't physically be able to hold you in my arms and lay you on my lap. So I am choosing to cherish this finite time with you.

As you grow up, you'll be comforted by other people, no doubt. Outside of your parents, you'll be comforted by friends, family and romantic partners (again choose wisely). My hope is that you always know that you can always find comfort in me.

You piss and poop a dozen times a day. All I can say to this is that you are a healthy boy! There will come a day soon when I'll stop inspecting all your orifices[②] and feeling like a champion for each day that you haven't had a diaper rash[③]. As a little boy, you'll be more obsessed with poop, farts and gas throughout the years and I'll be less interested in them I am sure. As for now, I am obsessed as making sure you burp[④] after feeds and go through enough wet and dirty diapers so that we know you are hydrated and gaining weight I am choosing to be grateful that through diapers, we can ensure you are thriving.

We hold hands every day. You have the tightest little grip for such a small baby. I am grateful that you have reflexes and you are building up your small motor skills.

---

① with a vengeance 极度地，彻底地

② orifice /ˈɒrɪfɪs/ *n.* (尤指身体上的)孔，口

③ diaper rash [医]尿布疹

④ burp /bɜː(r)p/ *vi.* 打嗝

Your hands will allow you to express so many things. You'll use your hands to write. I wish you to use your written words as kind and well-thought-out as your spoken words.

You'll use your hands for play. We hope you use your hands to nurture others as well. You'll use your hands to also comfort others, as we have often comforted you. There'll be those years where you will drop my hand as soon as you see your friends very soon. I am holding on to your hand as much as I can, for now.

It's my hope that as a new mom, we have moments of gratitude in the midst of figuring this whole thing out. I am not saying that these past 37 days have been a breeze but I will say without a doubt, you have made my life richer and have given me a sense to prioritize what's important in life and avoid the minutiae①. With you in my life, to be away from you for just a minute, must be worth it. That being said, there really aren't that many compelling reasons for me to put forth the effort. As much as I can joke about motherhood, I love it so much. However, when I am away from you, I just make sure it's worth it. Thank you for teaching me to streamline my life and focus on what matters the most.

What I am most grateful for is that you arrived outside of my womb safe and sound. I know that other friends of ours are having difficulty conceiving their baby, or are also having complicated pregnancies. I know that it is easy to focus on how hard motherhood is but I hope to be mindful that even on the toughest days, when your lungs are functioning VERY WELL, I'll remember that you have come into our lives. And that you will one day, not rely on us for anything, but choose to anyway.

With my love,
Mom

---

① minutiae /maɪˈnjuːʃiiː/ *n*. [复]细枝末节；琐事

心爱的儿子：

你是个小宝宝，出生才37天。现在我写信给你，是想花点时间仔细想想你是谁，并表达我对此的感激。

瞧，我和你爸爸意识到，此时此刻的你百分之百地依赖我们。在我们发现怀上你的那一刻，我们就知道自己要担负着这一重任。

你需要我们为你提供食、住、暖等所有基本生活需求来帮助你成长。你还没学会自己上厕所，所以我们要担当起为你换尿片的责任。你除了会自己哭闹、睡觉和拉便便，其他一切都依靠我们。你甚至需要我们为你掏鼻孔，这一点我们目前还是手足无措。

我突然想到，有一天你将完全不需要我们为你做任何事。

最近我读了许多讲述妈妈育儿艰辛的文章，这些文章都赞颂妈妈们做出了多少牺牲。我完全赞同做母亲要接受种种考验的说法，但是我也想感激做母亲带来的许多美好，因为的确有太多的事情是只有你我二人一起经历的。截至目前，你的成长让我对自己有了许多的认识，也让我更多地意识到你是如何从我们的小宝宝一步步成长，直到某一天长成一个自立的青年的。

某时某刻，那些让新妈妈抓狂的事情会逐渐消失。因此，现在我会停下来，去发现你细微的一举一动所带来的美好和欢乐。

你撕心裂肺地大哭，我选择为你百分百的健康而心存感激。你的肺功能正常，在你学会用语言交流之前，哭是你告诉我们你对某些事不满的唯一方式。儿子，你的哭声我们听得一清二楚。你出生时的第一声啼哭让我和你父亲的心弦为之颤动。就算你时不时莫名其妙地哭闹，但你哭闹的腔调将永远铭刻在我的记忆中。

我希望，随着你渐渐长大，你的眼泪都留给欢快的时刻，而不是痛苦的时刻。我甚至无法想象，如果你开始经历让你流泪的痛苦，那会让我多么心痛。你还不会说话，所以我会珍惜你还不会开口说“不”的日子，但我期盼你能开口告诉我你情绪的最高潮与最低谷的那一天。而现在，你的一声声啼哭在提醒我，你需要我为你做点什么。

儿子，妈妈是一位医疗工作者，因此我对你有一个要求：请让你的肺脏远离尼古丁的侵蚀。

你让我对你亲不够。你不知道，我们每天都会亲吻你大约一千次，或多或少。本周我在自己的Facebook上贴出了几天前你冲我和爸爸微笑的照片。对此我的朋友亚当说得太好了。他的大意是,孩子对父母微笑时,生活的循环便开始了。在接下来的十年八年,你会开心地和我们在一起;再有十年八年,你会不那么乐意看到我们,然后你又会回到见到我们极度开心的状态。

我知道父母每天亲吻你一千次的日子会一去不返,某天取而代之的是你爱人的亲吻。但愿你在选爱人时做出明智的选择。千万千万要选对人,我亲爱的儿子。

我的臂弯能给你带来最大的安慰。由于我选择纯母乳喂养,因此我们共度了许多亲密的时光,一天当中,我们轻易就有八到十次独处的机会,只有你我两人,真正地母子相连。的确,我有过许多不眠之夜,但是我知道那样的日子是有限的。在接下来的岁月里,你会变得越来越重,重到我体力不支,无法再用双臂抱你,无法再把你放到我的腿上。所以,我选择珍惜和你亲密相处的这些有限时光。

随着你渐渐长大,毫无疑问,你会得到他人的安慰。除了父母,你会得到亲朋好友和伴侣的安慰(再说一次,要明智选择)。我希望你始终明白,你永远可以在我这里找到安慰。

你一天要尿尿、拉便便十几次,对此我只能说你是个健康的男孩儿!有一天我将不再检查你的小屁股,不再在你没有尿布疹的每个日子都像拿了冠军一样开心——那一天很快就会到来。作为一个小男孩,在以后的几年里,你拉的便便、放的臭屁和打的嗝会越来越多,而我敢肯定我对它们的兴趣会越来越少。现在,我满脑子想的都是确保喂奶后你能打嗝,并把该尿湿拉脏的尿布全都尿湿拉脏——这样我们就知道你不缺水分,体重在增加。通过这些尿布,我们能确保你在茁壮成长,对此我选择心存感激。

我们每天都会牵手。对你这么小的婴儿来说,你的小手攥得可真紧。这让我感到欣慰,因为你有条件反射,你在锻炼自己小小的肌肉运动技能。

你将可以用你的双手表达很多东西。你会用自己的双手写作。我希望你写下的东西充满善意和深思熟虑,希望你口中说出的话也是如此。

你会用自己的双手去玩耍。我们希望你也用自己的双手去扶持他人。你还会用你的双手去安慰别人,就像我们经常安慰你一样。在未来的某些年里,你一看到你的朋友们就会甩开我的手,那样的日子很快就会到来。所以此时此刻,我正尽可能多地牵牵你的手。

作为新妈妈,我希望我们在摸索如何解决这一切问题的过程中时常怀有感激之情。我并不是说过去的这 37 天很轻松,但是我要确定无疑地说,你让我的生活更加丰富，让我明白了要把生活中重要的事情放在首位，忽略那些细枝末节。有你在我生命中，离开你的每一分钟都必须值得我那么做。话虽如此，但真的没有多少理由说服我付出那样的努力。虽然我可以调侃母亲这个身份，但我同样如此热爱这个身份。然而，当我不在你身边时，我会确保所做的事情是值得的。谢谢你教会我如何安排自己的生活，教会我把精力放在最重要的事情上。

我最感激的是你从我的肚子里平平安安地生了出来。我知道有些朋友很难怀上宝宝，或是还有着曲折艰辛的怀孕过程。我知道人们很容易把关注点放在做母亲的艰难上，但是我希望自己记着一件事：即使在最辛苦的日子里——那些你号啕大哭的日子里——我也会牢记你来到了我们的生命里。我会牢记，有一天你将不再依赖我们做任何事，但仍会选择依恋我们。

爱你的妈妈

离家五百里——歌曲《五百里》翻译及赏析

简约的吉他伴奏撩拨你的心弦，微颤的和声吟唱打动你的灵魂，蕴藏在英文经典歌曲“500 Miles”字里行间的情愫魅力会带给你心灵上的冲击和震撼。据说它是被翻唱次数最多的和声民谣，其中以乐队 The Brothers Four、Peter, Paul & Mary (PP&M)、Highwaymen、The Innocence Mission 演唱的版本流传最广，日本著名影星和歌手松隆子也曾演绎过日文版的“500 Miles”。获得 2014 年第 86 届奥斯卡最佳音响效果、最佳音效剪辑奖提名的影片 *Inside Llewyn Davis*（《醉乡民谣》）里还特别收录了这首民谣。影片中民谣歌手 Llewyn Davis（勒维恩 · 戴维斯）游走各处酒吧，靠卖唱为生，昏黄灯光摇曳中，面对他的听众，他有一句经典的台词："You've probably heard that one before. If it's not new and it never gets old, it is a folk song.（或许你以前听过这样的歌，它并不新鲜，但永不衰老，它就是民谣。）”“500 Miles”，一首游子心头浅吟低唱的离歌，正是一首艺术生命力常青的民谣。

500 Miles

By Hedy West

If you miss the train I'm on, you will know that I am gone.
You can hear the whistle blow a hundred miles.

A hundred miles, a hundred miles, a hundred miles, a hundred miles,
You can hear the whistle blow a hundred miles.
Lord, I'm one; Lord, I'm two.
Lord, I'm three; Lord, I'm four.
Lord, I'm five hundred miles away from home.

Away from home, away from home,

Away from home, away from home,
Lord, I'm five hundred miles away from home,
Not a shirt on my back, not a penny to my name.

Lord, I can't go back home this a-way,
This a-way, this a-way, this a-way, this a-way.
Lord, I can't go back home this a-way.

If you miss the train I'm on, you will know that I am gone.
You can hear the whistle blow a hundred miles.

五百里

你若没赶上我的火车,就知道我已经踏上征程。
百里之外,你可以听到汽笛鸣响。

一百里,一百里,一百里,一百里,
百里之外,你可以听到汽笛鸣响。
天啊,一百里,二百里。
天啊,三百里,四百里。
天啊,我已经离家五百里。

告别故乡,漂泊流浪;
远走他乡,颠沛流离,
天啊,我已离家五百里,
衣不蔽体,身无分文。

主啊,我一定要衣锦还乡,
只有这样,只有这样啊。
主啊,我一定要荣归故里。

你若没赶上我的火车，就知道我已经踏上征程。

百里之外，你可以听到汽笛鸣响。

赏析

歌词运用数词上的反复淋漓尽致表现了主人公离开家乡焦灼矛盾的心态：离乡情更切，不敢道别。在残酷艰难的生存现实面前，穷困潦倒的主人公不得不选择背井离乡，远走天涯去成就一番事业，甚至不等与亲友话别，便义无反顾匆匆踏上行程。火车载着主人公驶离家乡，一百里、二百里、三百里、四百里、五百里，渐远的是路途，煎熬的是乡愁，主人公默默数念着与家一点点拉开的距离，心与家却一点点靠得更近了，远方亲友的安危冷暖让他牵肠挂肚、心怀惦念；征程漫漫，自己的前途未卜，他祈祷主的佑护，对天发誓一定要衣锦荣归、泽被乡里。

歌词首尾回环反复，感情层层递进。开头段主人公寄情呜呜拉响的汽笛，好似他内心的呜咽抽泣、十分无奈，他唯愿百里之外的亲友能够听到，并且原谅他的不辞而别。结尾段主人公许下衣锦还乡的铮铮誓言，其实多少洇润着悲壮与苍凉的色彩。这样的誓言看似给人以希望，实则富荣穷辱、聚散生死、对比强烈。誓言若无法兑现，主人公的归家便遥遥无期，这时更有离愁别恨涌上心头，百感杂陈、千愁万思，何时才能回家乡？那一声声汽笛，化作阔别故土的号角，回荡上空，响彻云霄。

五百里路能有多远？恰是一颗游子心与家的距离，亦近亦远。

黑与白的奇妙物语——《我摸到了一条鲸鱼》片段选译

加里·施密特(Gary D. Schmidt, 1957～),美国儿童文学、青少年文学作家,密歇根州凯尔文学院(Calvin College)英语系教授,著有十多本小说。2005年,其作品《我摸到了一条鲸鱼》(*Lizzie Bright and the Buckminster Boy*)成为首部同时荣获纽伯瑞儿童文学银奖(Newbery Honor)及普林茨青少年文学银奖(Printz Honor);2008年,《星期三的战争》(*The Wednesday Wars*)再度摘得纽伯瑞儿童文学银奖。

《我摸到了一条鲸鱼》的故事发生在1912年,14岁的少年特纳·巴克敏斯特(Turner Buckminster)随父亲巴克敏斯特牧师(Reverend Buckminster)和母亲从波士顿搬到了缅因州的菲普斯堡镇(Phippsburg),起初不适应这里陌生的环境和当地的生活,也没有什么玩伴。后来,特纳结识了黑人小女孩莉齐·布莱特·格里芬(Lizzie Bright Griffin)并和她成为好朋友。以狡猾的资本家斯通克罗珀先生(Mr. Stonecrop)为代表的白人为除掉黑人,谋取私利,无所不用其极地将他们从世世代代生活的马拉加岛(Malaga Island)驱逐了出去,从而发展旅游业,特纳则试图帮助岛上的黑人……

下文节选自小说第五章,讲述了特纳和莉齐俩人一次在海边一起玩耍时,莉齐受了伤,特纳驾驶着小船送莉齐回家,在途中邂逅鲸鱼的故事。

And that was when he first heard the water ripping① near him.

The moon had roused herself fully out of the sea and was tossing② her silver bedclothes③ all around. Turner was sure that in that light he should have been able to make out④ any rocks. But he couldn't see anything breaking the surface. He listened, not moving, and heard the ripping again, but behind him this

---

① rip /rɪp/ *vi*. 撕裂;划破

② toss /tɒs/ *vt*. 到处扔;把……抛来抛去

③ bedclothes /ˈbedkləʊðz/ *n*. [复]床上用品(指床单、枕头、毯子、被子等)

④ make out (勉强地)看出,辨认出

time, and closer to shore, and ahead of him—one after another. In the moonlight he saw a silver spray[①] burst up into the air, a shower of diamond dust[②]. Then another, and another almost beside the boat, so that he could feel the spray of it against his face, and the dory[③] rocked to the rhythm of the new swells[④] as a great Presence[⑤] broke the surface of the sea and Turner knew, or felt, the vastness of the whales.

Now he almost did panic. One could come right up beneath them and turn the dory over as easily as a pine chip[⑥], and he would be floating in the sea, holding on to the upturned dory, holding on to Lizzie, who he was sure could not hold on by herself. That is, he would be holding on to her if he could find her after they capsized[⑦].

But though the dory rocked back and forth with the swell of them, the whales never came so close that the boat might capsize. Turner heard them ripping the surface all around him, and felt the diamond spray sprinkle down on him in the moonlight like a benediction[⑧]. He knew he was in the middle of something much larger than himself, and not just larger in size. It was like being in the middle of a swirling universe that could swamp[⑨] him in a moment but had no desire to. He might put out his hand into the maelstrom[⑩] and become a part of it.

But he didn't put his hand out yet, because as he watched, a whale five times as long as the dory surfaced, and rode quietly alongside him in the smooth swells. Turner could not breathe. The whale flipped[⑪] its tail up a bit and began

---

① spray /spreɪ/ *n*. 浪花;水花

② diamond dust (= ice crystal) [气]冰晶(体)

③ dory /ˈdɔːri/ *n*. 平底小渔船

④ swell /swel/ *n*. 海面的起伏,浪涌

⑤ presence /ˈprezns/ *n*. (看不见但能感觉其存在的)精灵,鬼怪

⑥ chip /tʃɪp/ *n*. (木、石、金属等的)碎屑,碎片

⑦ capsize /kæpˈsaɪz/ *vi*. (船等)倾覆,翻

⑧ benediction /ˌbenɪˈdɪkʃn/ *n*. (基督教的)祝福,赐福祷告

⑨ swamp /swɒmp/ *vt*. 淹没;浸没

⑩ maelstrom /ˈmeɪlstrɒm/ *n*. 大漩涡

⑪ flip /flɪp/ *vt*. 快速翻动,迅速翻动

to roll from side to side, a great gargantuan[①] roll like the roll of the globe, side to side, until it could slap the swells with the length of its flippers[②], gleaming silver-white in the moonlight. Turner held on to the sides of the dory and rolled side to side with it with this great vastness that had swum past the mountains and valleys of the sea. Together they rocked, and Turner wished that the rocking would never stop, that there would always be this moonlit moment.

But slowly the whale did stop rocking, and the seas calmed, and the rhythm of the swells took hold again. Quietly, more afraid than not, Turner slipped the oars[③] into the water, and with gentle strokes[④], keeping the oars beneath the surface all the time, he eased[⑤] the dory forward, hoping that the whale would wait on the surface.

It did. And so Turner reached the whale's eye, and they looked at each other. They looked at each other a long time—two souls rolling on the sea under the silvery moon, peering[⑥] into each other's eyes. Turner wished with a desire greater than anything he had ever desired that he might understand what it was in the eye of the whale that shivered his soul.

He stretched his hand out across the side of the dory and reached over as far as he could without tipping[⑦] the boat. But the whale kept a space of dark water between them, and they did not touch. Then slowly the whale sank, the water closing quietly along its black and white back.

And the whales were gone.

"Lizzie," whispered Turner.

There was no answer. He reached back and shook her leg, then her shoulder. Finally, he scooped[⑧] up water and splashed it into her face—since

---

① gargantuan /gɑːˈgæntʃuən/ *adj*. 巨大的，庞大的

② flipper /ˈflɪpə(r)/ *n*. (鲸、海豹、海龟等的)鳍(状)肢，前肢，鳍足

③ oar /ɔː(r)/ *n*. 桨，橹

④ stroke /strəʊk/ *n*. (划船的)(一次)划桨动作

⑤ ease /iːz/ *vt*. 小心缓慢地推动(或移动)，使缓缓移动

⑥ peer /pɪə(r)/ *vi*. 仔细看，费力地看，凝视

⑦ tip /tɪp/ *vt*. 使倾斜，使倾侧，使倾翻

⑧ scoop /skuːp/ *vt*. 用勺舀；用铲子铲(up)

saltwater will do for everything. "Lizzie, you've got to open your eyes."

"They're open," she said. "You splashed me."

"Lizzie, there were whales."

She didn't answer.

"Lizzie, whales."

"You touch one?"

"Tried."

She took a deep breath. "They only let you touch them if you understand what they're saying."

"What do they say?"

"You'll know when... when they let you touch them. Home yet?"

正是在这个时候,他第一次听到自己身边有划破水面的声音。

月亮已经完完全全把自己从海中唤醒了,正把自己银色的被毯撒向整个海面。特纳肯定,在这样的月光下,他本可以辨认出所有岩礁的。可他却看不到有任何东西破水而出。他一动也不动地聆听着,然后又一次听到划破水面的声音,但这一次是在他身后,而后在更靠近岸边的地方,接着又在他的前方——一次又一次划破水面的声音。在月光下,他看见一道银色的水柱向上喷涌至空中,形成一片闪闪发光的水雾。接下来又一道水柱,而后几乎从小船边上又喷涌出一道水柱,所以他都能感觉到水喷洒在自己的脸上。当一个巨大的东西冲破海面而出,小渔船随着新的浪涌的节奏来回摇晃时,特纳意识到了——或者可以说是感受到了——鲸鱼的庞大。

这下他差点儿就真慌了。鲸鱼可能刚好从他们的小渔船底下游上来,轻而易举掀翻他们的小船,就如同掀翻一块松木那样。他会漂浮在大海上,紧紧抓住被掀翻的小船,抓住莉齐,他肯定莉齐没法自己抓住小船。也就是说,如果他能在船翻后找到莉齐,他就会一直抓着她。

不过,虽然小船随着鲸鱼游动引起的浪涌来回摇晃,但鲸鱼却从未靠近小船到让小船可能会翻的地步。特纳听见它们在自己的四面八方划破水面,感觉到亮晶晶的水雾在月光下洒到自己身上,就像教堂祈福时牧师洒圣水一样。他知道他正处在比自己大很多的某个东西中间,不仅仅是块头比自己大。这种感觉就像身处一个旋动的宇宙当中，这个宇宙在瞬间就可以将他吞没，但却不想这么做。他可以将手伸进大漩涡中，成为其中的一部分。

但他还没有把手伸出去，因为在他观察时，一条身长有小渔船五倍的鲸鱼露出了水面，悄无声息地在平缓的海浪中跟着他游着。特纳无法呼吸了。那条鲸鱼快速向上翻转了一下自己的尾鳍，然后便开始在水上左右翻转，那翻转规模不小，就像地球的转动似的。它来回翻转着，直到它能用自己长长的双鳍拍打海浪——它的双鳍在月光下银光闪闪。特纳抓住小船的两侧船舷，随着小船和这个已经游过群山和海谷的庞然大物一起来回翻滚。他们一起摇晃着，特纳希望他们可以一直这样摇下去，希望永远都会有现在这般月光照耀的时刻。

但慢慢地，这条鲸鱼确实不再摇晃了，海面平静了下来，又一次只剩下海浪涌动的节奏。特纳十分害怕，他轻轻地把双桨滑入水中，然后轻轻地划着，让双桨一直处在海面之下。他小心翼翼地向前划动着小船，希望那条鲸鱼会在海面上等自己。

那条鲸鱼果然在海面上等着他。于是，特纳望见了鲸鱼的眼睛，他们互相看着彼此。他们彼此对视了很久——两个灵魂在银色月光照耀下的大海上摇晃着，还凝望着彼此的双眼。那条鲸鱼眼中透出的东西震颤了特纳的灵魂，他极度希望自己可以理解那是什么，这种渴望比以往任何时候都更为强烈。

他把手探出小船的船舷，在不把船弄翻的情况下尽可能地向外伸手。但鲸鱼与他之间一直相隔着一片黑茫茫的海水，他们没有触摸到彼此。然后，鲸鱼缓缓地沉了下去，海水沿着它那黑白相间的背脊静静地闭合了。

这群鲸鱼离开了。

“莉齐。”特纳小声说。

没有回应。他把手伸到后面摇了摇她的腿，然后又摇了摇她的肩。最后，他舀了点水撒在她的脸上，因为咸咸的海水用处大着呢。“莉齐，你得睁开眼睛。”

“已经睁开了，”她说，“你用水泼我了。”

“莉齐，刚刚鲸鱼来了。”

她没有回答。

“莉齐，成群的鲸鱼。”

“你摸到了一条？”

“试着去摸来着。”

她深深地吸了一口气。“只有当你明白它们在说什么的时候，它们才会让你摸到它们。”

“它们说的是什么呢？”

“你会明白的，当……当它们让你摸到它们的时候。我们已经到家了吗？”

时光圈里旅行的勇敢少年——《怪奇孤儿院》片段选译

兰萨姆·里格斯(Ransom Riggs, 1979～),美国作家、电影制作人,出生于佛罗里达州,是美国悬疑惊悚作家中熠熠生辉的新星。兰萨姆最著名的小说便是《怪奇孤儿院》(*Miss Peregrine's Home for Peculiar Children*),该书于2011年出版,雄踞美国亚马逊网站销售榜冠军半年之久,被《纽约时报》评为2011年度十大重磅好书之一。2014年,兰萨姆出版了该系列小说第二部《怪奇孤儿院:空城》(*Hollow City*),随后又于2015年出版了第三部《怪奇孤儿院:灵魂博物馆》(*Library of Souls*)。2016年,美国著名导演蒂姆·伯顿(Tim Burton)将其拍成了电影。

《怪奇孤儿院》的主人公是一个名叫雅各布(Jacob)的小男孩。他的爷爷离奇死亡,只留下几句听起来荒诞不羁的遗言。为了找出真相,雅各布远赴威尔士,踏上了惊心动魄的时光穿越之旅。

下文节选自本书第五章,主要讲述了雅各布发现爷爷当年生活过的孤儿院后睹物思人的故事。

By the time I reached the children's home, what had begun as a drizzle was a full-on downpour①. I stood wringing② water from my shirt and shaking out my hair, and when I was as dry as I was going to get—which was not very—I began to search. For what, I wasn't sure. A box of letters? My grandfather's name scribbled③ on a wall? It all seemed so unlikely.

I roved④ around peeling up mats of old newspaper and looking under chairs and tables. I imagined uncovering some horrible scene, but all I found were rooms that had become more outside than inside, character stripped away by moisture and wind and layers of dirt. The ground floor was hopeless. I went

① downpour /ˈdaʊnpɔː(r)/ *n.* 倾盆大雨
② wring /rɪŋ/ *vt.* 拧;拧出
③ scribble /ˈskrɪbl/ *vt.* 匆匆地写;乱涂乱画
④ rove /rəʊv/ *vi.* 流浪;漫游

back to the upstairs.

The steps protested my weight with a symphony of shudders① and creaks, but they held, and what I discovered upstairs was like a time capsule②. Arranged along a hallway striped with peeling wallpaper, the rooms were in surprisingly good shape. Though one or two had been invaded by mold③ where a broken window had let in the rain, the rest were packed with things that seemed only a layer or two of dust away from new: a shirt tossed casually over the back of a chair, loose change skimming④ a nightstand⑤. It was easy to believe that everything was just as the children had left it, as if time had stopped the night they died.

I went from room to room, examining their contents like an archaeologist. There were wooden toys moldering⑥ in a box; crayons⑦ on a windowsill, their colors dulled by the light of ten thousand afternoons. In a modest⑧ library, the creep of moisture had bowed the shelves into crooked smiles. I ran my finger along the balding spines⑨, as if considering pulling one out to read. There were classics like *Peter Pan* and *The Secret Garden*, histories written by authors forgotten by history, textbooks of Latin and Greek. In the corner were corralled⑩ a few old desks. This had been their classroom, I realized, and Miss Peregrine, their teacher.

I tried to open a pair of heavy doors, twisting the handle, but they were swelled shut—so I took a running start and rammed⑪ them with my shoulder.

---

① shudder /ˈʃʌdə(r)/ *n*. 打颤，战栗

② time capsule：时代文物秘藏器（装入具有时代特征的对象后埋入地下，以供后世发掘研究）

③ mold /ˈməʊld/ *n*. 霉；霉菌

④ skim /skɪm/ *vt*. 在……表面覆上一层东西

⑤ nightstand *n*. 床头柜

⑥ molder /ˈməʊldə(r)/ *vi*. 腐烂；朽坏

⑦ crayon /ˈkreɪən/ *n*. 颜色粉笔（或蜡笔、炭笔）

⑧ modest /ˈmɒdɪst/ *adj*.（房屋等）不太大的，不算昂贵的，普通的

⑨ spine /spaɪn/ *n*. 书脊

⑩ corral /kəːˈrɑːl/ *vt*. 把……集合在一起

⑪ ram /ræm/ *vt*. 猛撞，撞击

They flew open with a rasping[1] shriek and I fell face-first into the next room. As I picked myself up and looked around, I realized that it could only have belonged to Miss Peregrine. It was like a room in Sleeping Beauty's castle. I pictured the last time she'd been here, scrambling[2] out from under the sheets in the middle of the night to the whine[3] of an air-raid[4] siren[5], rounding up[6] the children, all groggy[7] and grasping for coats on their way downstairs.

"Were you scared?" I wondered. "Did you hear the planes coming?"

I began to feel unusual. I imagined I was being watched; that the children were still here, inside the walls. I could feel them peering at me through cracks and knotholes[8].

I drifted into the next room. Weak light shone through a window. Petals of wallpaper drooped[9] toward a couple of small beds, still clad[10] in dusty sheets. I knew, somehow, that this had been my grandfather's room.

"Why did you send me here? What was it you needed me to see?"

Then I noticed something beneath one of the beds and knelt down to look. It was an old suitcase.

"Was this yours? Is it what you carried onto the train the last time you saw your mother and father, as your first life was slipping away?"

I pulled it out. It opened easily—but except for a family of dead beetles, it was empty.

I felt empty, too, and strangely heavy, like the planet was spinning too fast, heating up gravity, pulling me toward the floor. Suddenly exhausted, I sat

---

① rasp /rɑːsp/ *vi*. 发出刺耳声
② scramble /ˈskræmbl/ *vi*. 仓促行动
③ whine /waɪn/ *n*. 哀叫声;呜咽声
④ air-raid: 空袭的;防空袭的
⑤ siren /ˈsaɪərən/ *n*. 汽笛;警报器
⑥ round up: 集拢(分散的人或物)
⑦ groggy /ˈgrɒgɪ *adj*. 摇摇晃晃的;昏昏沉沉的
⑧ knothole *n*. (木板等的)节孔
⑨ droop /druːp/ *vi*. 低垂,下垂
⑩ clad /klæd/ *adj*. 穿着……的

on the bed— *his bed*, *maybe* —and for reasons I can't quite explain, I stretched out on those sheets and stared at the ceiling.

"What did you think about, lying here at night? Did you have nightmares, too?"

I began to cry.

"When your parents died, did you know it? Could you feel them go?"

I cried harder. I didn't want to, but I couldn't stop myself.

I couldn't stop myself, so I thought about all the bad things. I thought about how my great-grandparents had starved to death. I thought about how the children who lived in this house had been burned up and blown apart because a pilot who didn't care pushed a button. I thought about how my grandfather's family had been taken from him, and how because of that my dad grew up feeling like he didn't have a dad, and now I had nightmares and was sitting alone in a falling-down house and crying hot, stupid tears all over my shirt. All because of a seventy-year-old hurt that had somehow been passed down to me like some poisonous heirloom①, and monsters I couldn't fight because they were all dead. At least my grandfather had been able to join the army and go fight them. What could I do?

等我到达孤儿院时，起初的毛毛细雨已经变成了瓢泼大雨。我站在那儿把衬衫里的水拧干，然后抖了抖头发，等到身上快干，但还不是很干的时候，我开始搜寻。寻找什么？我不确定。一盒子信？还是胡乱写在墙上的爷爷的名字？这一切看似都不大可能。

我四处转悠，翻翻旧报纸堆，看看桌椅下面。我想象会发现某个可怕的场景，但结果发现的全都是一个个更像屋外而不是屋里的房间，墙上的字迹已经在湿气、风和厚厚的尘土的作用下变模糊了。一楼是没有希望发现什么了，于是我又回到了楼上。

颤颤巍巍的楼梯台阶发出嘎吱嘎吱的响声，仿佛在演奏一首交响曲，向我的体

① heirloom /ˈeəluːm/ *n*. 祖传遗物；传家宝

重提出抗议，但它们还是撑住了，而且我发现楼上就像是一个时间胶囊。在走廊的墙上是一片片脱落的墙纸，沿着走廊有一排房间，出人意料的是，它们都保存得很好。尽管有一两个房间因为窗户坏了进了雨而长了霉，但剩下的房间则都塞满了东西（因为只落了一两层灰，所以看起来没那么旧）：一件衬衫随意地搭在椅背上，还有一些零钱散落在床头柜上。这一切很容易让人相信，所有的东西都还是孩子们留下它们时的样子，就好像时间停在了他们死去的那个夜晚。

我从一个房间走到另一个房间，像个考古学家似的检查着屋内的物品。盒子里的那些木制玩具已经腐烂，窗台上的彩色粉笔被无数个午后的阳光晒得褪了颜色。在一间不大的图书室里，湿气侵入书架，使其弯曲变形，看起来就像歪着嘴笑似的。我的手指滑过光秃秃的书脊，仿佛想要抽出一本书来读似的。书架上有《彼得·潘》《秘密花园》这类经典文学作品，有被历史遗忘的佚名作者撰写的历史故事，还有拉丁语和希腊语的课本。房间的角落堆放着几张旧书桌。我意识到，这是他们曾经的教室，而佩里格林女士曾是他们的老师。

我扭了扭门把手，试着打开那两扇厚重的门，但是门因为发胀紧闭而推不开。于是，我开始快速起跑用肩膀去撞。门被撞开了，发出尖锐刺耳的声音，而我则脸朝下摔进了隔壁房间。等我起身站好，环顾四周时，我才意识到，这间房只可能属于佩里格林女士。因为它就像是睡美人城堡里的一间屋子。我想象她最后一次睡在这里，半夜里听到空袭警报的呜呜声后迅速从被子里爬出来，把孩子们召集起来——一个个摇摇晃晃，边往楼下走边试图抓件衣服穿上。

“你们当时害怕吗？”我想知道。“你们听到飞机轰鸣而来了吗？”

我开始感到不自在。我有种幻觉，觉得有人在看着我，觉得那些孩子还在这里，就在这一面面墙里。我能感觉到他们从墙缝和木孔里窥视着我。

不知不觉中我走进了下一个房间，微弱的阳光从一扇窗户照进来。墙纸像一片片凋萎的花瓣，垂落在两张小床上。床上还铺着落满灰尘的床单。不知怎么地，我知道这个房间就是我爷爷的。

“您为什么让我来这里？您希望我看到什么呢？”

这时，我注意到其中一张床下有东西，于是跪下来去看，发现是一只旧的手提箱。

“这是您的手提箱吗？是您向第一段生活告别，最后一次见父母的时候带上火车的那只吗？”

我拽出手提箱。它很容易就打开了，但是除了一群甲壳虫的尸体外，箱子里空荡荡的。

我感觉心里也空荡荡的，却沉重得不可思议，就像是这个星球旋转得太快加剧了地心引力，把我拉向地面一样。忽然之间，我感到精疲力竭，一下子坐在床上——可能就是爷爷的床——说不上是因为什么，我就四仰八叉地躺在了那些床单上望着天花板发呆。

“您晚上躺在这里都想过些什么呢？您也做过噩梦吗？”

我哭了起来。

“您父母去世的时候您知道吗？您能感觉到他们的离去吗？”

我哭得更厉害了，我不想哭，可是我无法自已。

我无法控制自己，于是所有不好的事情一下子涌上心头。我想起我的曾祖父是如何饿死的，我想起生活在这幢房子里的孩子们是如何在飞行员冷漠地按下按钮后被炸掉烧死的。我想起我爷爷的家人是如何从他身边被夺走的，正因为如此，我爸爸在成长过程中才会觉得缺少父爱，而我现在才会噩梦不断，独自坐在一幢快要坍塌的房屋里痛哭流涕，任由愚蠢的泪水打湿我的衬衫。所有这一切都是因为70 年前的那个伤痛(编注：指 1940 年 9 月 3 日孤儿院被德军飞机轰炸)——它就像是某种有毒的传家宝一样不知怎么就传给了我——以及那群已经死去而无法让我反击的恶魔。至少我爷爷当时还能够参军去反击他们。我能做什么呢？

爱情篇

同是天涯沦落人，挚爱缱绻入画帧——《一帧画页》片段选译及赏析

2月14日，冰冷的月份，情人的日子，你会为心爱的人送上什么样暖意的礼物呢？是一大束娇艳欲滴的红玫瑰呢？还是一大块香醇丝滑的巧克力呢？然而，短篇小说《一帧画页》（“FEUILLE D'ALBUM”）的男主人公伊恩小心翼翼、笨手笨脚地向心仪已久的姑娘捧上了一颗褐壳鸡蛋，并且还满面羞红地吐露爱意：“打搅了，小姐，您掉了这个。”（“Excuse me, Mademoiselle, you dropped this.”），极富戏剧性地上演了小说的最后一幕。新西兰女作家凯瑟琳·曼斯菲尔德（Kathering Mansfield）用娴熟精练的笔法向读者描述了一个淳朴的初恋故事，勾画了一幅纯真淡雅的爱情素描。

伊恩·弗兰奇（Ian French）是女作家凯瑟琳·曼斯菲尔德的作品集 *Bliss*《幸福》中刻画的众多小人物中的一个，一位在巴黎勤奋打拼、坚持追求的单身画家，一朵摇曳在繁华大都市的乡野雏菊。他长相俊秀、才华横溢，身边不乏仰慕者和追求者，无论是给予他慈母般关爱的女性，还是外表妖娆、甜言蜜语的女性，还有巴黎灯红酒绿下奢华的浪漫约会，都没有叩开他情感的心扉，他将它们统统拒之门外，他将自己紧紧锁在斗室内，“...he kept his studio as neat as a pin. Everything was arranged to form a pattern, a little ‘still life’ as it were — the saucepans with their lids on the wall behind the gas stove, the bowl of eggs, milk jug and teapot on the shelf, the books and the lamp with the crinkly paper shade on the table. An Indian curtain that had a fringe of red leopards marching round it covered his bed by day, and on the wall beside the bed on a level with your eyes when you were lying down there was a small neatly printed notice: GET UP AT

ONCE."(……他把自己的画室拾掇得干净整洁。每件东西都摆放得井井有条，如同一小幅"静物画"——带盖儿的煮锅挂在煤气炉后面的墙壁上，盛鸡蛋的碗、牛奶罐和茶壶搁在架子上，书籍和皱巴巴的纸灯罩的灯具摆在书桌上。一袭印度风格的窗帘，镶有一圈红色豹子阔步前行的图案，成了他铺在床上的日用床单。你若躺在那里，床边墙壁上，眼睛平视的地方，贴了一张小纸片，用印刷体工整地写了警句："立刻起床。")"Every day was much the same. While the light was good he slaved at his painting, then cooked his meals and tidied up the place. And in the evenings he went off to the café, or sat at home reading or making out the most complicated list of expenses headed: 'What I ought to be able to do it on,' and ending with a sworn statement... 'I swear not to exceed this amount for next month. Signed, Ian French.'"(日复一日，几乎一成不变，当光线好时，他奋笔作画，然后煮饭、收拾房间。晚上他去咖啡馆，或坐在家中阅读，或列出最为复杂的开销清单，标题是："月度开销限额"，并以一句誓言结尾："我发誓下个月花销不超过这个数。伊恩·弗兰奇")

通过这些细节描写，一个经济生活虽清贫拮据、精神生活却丰富充实的青年画家形象跃然纸上。阴冷简陋、凄凉孤苦的居住环境里，他没有自嗟自叹、自暴自弃、自甘堕落；他也没有自轻自贱、曲意承欢，依附女性生存；他洁身自好、自律勤俭、自强不息，在自我小天地里，怡然自得。

"It had been raining — the first real spring rain of the year had fallen — a bright spangle hung on everything, and the air smelled of buds and moist earth... The trees were peppered with new green."(雨不停地下——今年迎来了第一场真正的春雨——万物熠熠闪光，空气里弥散着花苞嫩芽的香气和湿润泥土的气息。…… 一棵棵树木缀上了点点新绿。)此时此刻，青年画家伊恩一颗爱心也正在悄然发芽。一位和他年龄相仿的穷人姑娘让他内心萌动，春意漾漾。她就住在他对面的破旧房子里，"...two wings of windows opened and a girl came out on to the tiny balcony carrying a pot of daffodils. She was a strangely thin girl in a dark pinafore, with a pink handkerchief tied over her hair. Her sleeves were rolled up almost to her shoulders and her slender arms shone against the dark stuff."(……两扇长窗打开，一个女孩子走出来，手捧一盆水仙花，走到小阳台上。她出奇地瘦，系着深色围裙，头发上扎了条粉红色方巾，衣袖几乎卷到肩头，纤细的

胳膊，在深色衣衫的衬托下，白花花地耀眼。）“His heart fell out of the side window of his studio, and down to the balcony of the house opposite — buried itself in the pot of daffodils under the half-opened buds and spears of green...”（他的心儿跌出画室的侧窗，落到对屋的阳台上——埋在种着水仙花的花盆里，埋在半开的花蕾和娇绿的嫩茎下……）

穷画家爱上了这个清瘦质朴的女孩儿。哪怕她要靠整天干活来维持生计，哪怕她难露笑颜、自卑到没有任何朋友，哪怕她和卧病在床的母亲相依为命，他决意把男人的温情和力量献给这个生活更加困顿窘迫、更需要他人体贴呵护的少女；他决意与她并肩分享未来人生的酸甜苦辣、喜怒哀乐，他甚至一厢情愿地开始憧憬贫苦夫妻柴米油盐、磕磕碰碰的幸福生活：“...they quarrelled terribly at times, he and she. She had a way of stamping her foot and twisting her hands in her pinafore...furious. And she very rarely laughed. Only when she told him about an absurd little kitten she once had who used to roar and pretend to be a lion when it was given meat to eat. Things like that made her laugh... But as a rule they sat together very quietly; he, just as he was sitting now, and she with her hands folded in her lap and her feet tucked under, talking in low tones, or silent and tired after the day's work. Of course, she never asked him about his pictures, and of course he made the most wonderful drawings of her which she hated, because he made her so thin and so dark...”（……他和她，有时候会大吵一场。她嗔怒地摆出跺脚、双手绞着围裙的样子。她过去养了一只傻乎乎的小猫咪，喂它肉吃时，它会狮子般吼叫。只有在对他说起这件事时，她才会露出难得的笑容。通常他们安安静静地坐在一块儿。他，就像现在这样坐着；而她呢，双手交叉在膝上，双脚蜷缩在身下，他们俩或低声交谈，或缄默不语，一天的辛劳，让他们疲乏。当然，她从不问起他画的那些画；当然，他以她为模特儿画了许多极棒的素描，她却不喜欢，因为他把她画得那样瘦、那样黑……）

画家伊恩产生了迫切结识女孩的强烈愿望，所以在她出来买东西的晚上，他尾随她并借机表白。“There was a lovely pink light over everything. He saw it glowing in the river, and the people walking towards him had pink faces and pink hands.”（温馨的粉红色灯光笼罩了一切，他看见河水泛出粉红色的波光，朝他走过来的人们的脸和手都是粉红色的。）

粉色之夜见证了纯真浪漫的爱情，暖暖的粉色正是画家内心浓浓爱意的写照。"She suddenly turned into the dairy and he saw her through the window buying an egg. She picked it out of the basket with such care — a brown one, a beautifully shaped one, the one he would have chosen."（她突然拐进乳品店，他隔着橱窗看见她买了一只鸡蛋。她从筐里精挑细选了它——一只形状完美的褐壳蛋，换了他，他也会选中这样一只。）于是出现了伊恩捧送鸡蛋求爱的一幕，这颗圆圆的鸡蛋寄托了他对圆满爱情的渴望，他才会如此郑重其事地请求她：接受它，不轻易地掉落摔碎它。《一帧画页》这个唯美隽永的短篇故事，不愧是女作家凯瑟琳·曼斯菲尔德爱情主题长卷里值得永远珍藏的一页。

天地自是有情痴，此爱绵绵无绝期——《爱痴》片段选译及赏析

美国现代小说家杰西·斯图尔特（Jesse Stuart，1906～1984）的短篇小说《爱痴》（“Love”）描述了一个发生在动物身上生死相随、不离不弃的爱情故事。动物之间高尚坚贞的爱情让自诩是万物之灵、文明开化的人类为之动容，为之汗颜，尤其是在世风日渐浮躁、弃子抛妻时有发生的拜金社会里，这样的故事更弥足珍贵，值得传唱。

故事发生在一个晴暖干燥的春天，玉米长势喜人，但父亲深为奶牛、土松鼠等动物啃噬玉米苗所困，于是带上牧羊犬鲍勃，决定和“我”在玉米地四周扎起篱笆。不料“我们”却碰见一条大黑蛇。“It's a big bull blacksnake,” said my father. “Kill him, Bob! Kill him, Bob!”（“是条粗壮的黑蛇。”父亲命令说，“鲍勃，咬死它！鲍勃，咬死它！）“Let's don't kill the snake,” I said. “A blacksnake is a harmless snake. It kills poison snakes. It kills the copperhead. It catches more mice from the fields than a cat.” I could see the snake didn't want to fight the dog. The snake wanted to get away. Bob wouldn't let it. I wondered why it was crawling toward a heap of black loamy earth at the bench of the hill. I wondered why it had come from the chestnut oak sprouts and the matted green briars on the cliff. I looked as the snake lifted its pretty head in response to one of Bob's jumps. “It's not a bull blacksnake,” I said. “It's a she-snake. Look at the white on her throat.”（“我们不要伤害这条蛇，”我说，“黑蛇是无害的，它吞吃铜斑蛇之类的毒蛇，比猫捕捉到更多的田鼠。”我看得出黑蛇无心与牧羊犬交战，它想游走开。鲍勃不愿放过它。我好奇黑蛇为什么要游向平坦山坡肥沃的黑色土壤里，我猜想它从山崖的栗栎嫩枝和绿色石楠树丛爬下的原因。当黑蛇优雅地抬头回应鲍勃的挑衅时，我注意到了它。“它不是条公蛇。”我说出声，“她是条母蛇，快看她脖子上的白色。”）“A snake is an enemy to me,” my father snapped. “I hate a snake. Kill it, Bob. Go in there and get that snake and quit playing with it!”（“蛇是人类的天敌。”父亲厉声呵斥，“我厌恶蛇，咬死它，鲍勃！去那儿，咬死它，不

要贪玩了。”)

Bob grabbed the white patch on her throat. He cracked her long body like an ox whip in the wind.... The blood spurted from her fine-curved throat. Something hit against my legs like pellets....I looked to see what had struck my legs. It was snake eggs....She was going to the sand heap to lay her eggs, where the sun is the setting-hen that warms them and hatches them.... We counted thirty-seven eggs. I picked an egg up and held it in my hand. Only a minute ago there was life in it....“Well, Bob, I guess you see now why this snake couldn’t fight.” I said.(鲍勃一口咬住她喉部的白斑。他撕咬她,她修长的身体像风中甩动的牛鞭……鲜血从她迷人曲线的脖颈里喷涌出来。有些弹丸似的东西甩打在我腿上,……我看清了甩掷在我腿上的东西。它们是蛇蛋。……她本打算去沙堆里下蛋,那儿的暖日会像母鸡孵蛋般将它们孵化出来。……我们数了数,共有37颗蛇蛋。我挑出一颗,把它放在自己手中。就在一分钟之前,一个生命还孕育其中。……“看,鲍勃,你现在知道这只母蛇无心恋战的原因了吧!”我说。)

The sun was going down over the chestnut ridge. A lark was singing. It was late for a lark to sing. The red evening clouds floated above the pine trees on our pasture hill. My father stood beside the path. His black hair was moved by the wind. His face was red in the blue wind of day. His eyes looked toward the sinking sun.(太阳缓缓沉落到棕褐色山岭后。天色已晚,云雀仍在嘤唱。殷红的落霞飘浮在牧场山头、松树林间,父亲站在小路旁,任风儿吹动他的黑发,凛冽寒风中,他满脸通红,遥望西下的斜阳。)I thought about the agony women know of giving birth. I thought about how they will fight to save their children. Then I thought of the snake.(我想到女人生孩子时的痛苦,我想到她们竭力保住自己孩子时的挣扎,接着我就想到了那条母蛇。)

“红霞绕翠松,落日泛余晖,悲歌以当泣,远望以当归”,云雀啼啭哀鸣似乎是在为消逝的无辜生命悲伤哭泣,母蛇为了产下爱情结晶使自己置身险境,母性光辉闪现的至爱至柔感动了父亲。父亲凝望天边夕阳的举动表现了他对放犬惨杀黑蛇母子生命行为的愧疚之心,表达了他祈盼冀望母子归升安息的忏悔之情。

次日,天朗气清,惠风和畅,父亲和我扛上锄头准备下地大干一场,没想到遭遇另一条大黑蛇。It was moving like a huge black rope winds around a windlass.

“Steady,” I say to my father. “Here is the bull blacksnake.” He took one step up beside me and stood. His eyes grew wide apart.(它爬行扭动着，像一根粗大的缠绕在绞盘上的黑色绳索。“稳住了，”我交代父亲说，“这儿有条黑蛇。”父亲向前迈了一步，到我身边站定，睁大了眼睛。) “You have seen the bull blacksnake now.” I said. “Take a good look at him! He is lying beside his dead mate. He has come to her. He, perhaps, was on her trail yesterday.”(“您这次看到的才是条公蛇。”我解释说，“仔细看啦，他躺在死掉的伴侣旁。他为着她而来。他，或许，昨天寻到了她的踪迹。”)...He had come in the night, under the roof of stars, as the moon shed rays of light on the quivering clouds of green. He had found his lover dead. He was coiled beside her, and she was dead. The bull blacksnake lifted his head and followed us as we walked around the dead snake. He would have fought us to his death. He would have fought Bob to his death. “Take a stick,” said my father, “and throw him over the hill so Bob won’t find him....” I took a stick and threw him over the bank into the dewy sprouts on the cliff.(……他循着夜色而来，苍穹之间，繁星点点，明月相照，碧云漾漾。他发现爱侣已逝。他蜷依在她身旁，她却毫无生气。我们绕过死母蛇时，公蛇昂起头，尾随我们，他要找我们拼命，他会寻鲍勃决一死战。“用根树棍，”父亲吩咐道，“把它扔到山那边去，这样鲍勃就不会找到它了……”我拿来了树棍，让它缠在上面，把它扔过土堆，放它进山崖上露水晶莹的嫩枝丛里。)

过去，在父亲的眼里，蛇是冷血的妖孽、邪恶的化身，它们咬伤人、毁庄稼。他曾对黑蛇深恶痛疾，曾不听“我”的劝阻，迫不及待地放犬置母蛇于死地；此刻，父亲面对伺机复仇、以身殉情的公蛇却只有放生、帮助它脱离险境的怜惜。公蛇偎依在已离去伴侣身旁的至情至真、忠贞不渝强烈地震撼了父亲，实可谓，“天地自是有情痴，此爱绵绵无绝期。”

爱情的“信”使——《爱情的信使》片段选译及赏析

美国现代短篇小说之父欧·亨利(O. Henry,1862～1910)一生创作出大量脍炙人口的著名短篇小说,例如《麦琪的礼物》(“The Gift of Magi”)、《最后一片藤叶》(“The Last Leaf”)、《爱的牺牲》(“A Service of Love”)等等,这些小说以独到新颖的故事情节设计,独具匠心的故事结局安排,真实细腻的语言刻画和描写让中外读者啧啧称奇、拍案叫绝。他独树一帜的叙事风格堪比“剥洋葱”:读者希望得到他小说的灵魂,充满好奇地去一层层剥开小说情节,层层剥落间,不知不觉中为作品里小人物的命途多舛而泪眼盈盈,然而剥到最后,在小说结尾,却发现了洋葱本无心、一切皆虚有的真相。那一刹,电光闪现,读者或感叹真挚纯洁的友谊,或赞叹善良仁慈的人性,或喟叹变幻莫测的爱情,泪水微笑交织,悲情喜悦掺杂,小说的艺术魅力和人文价值彰显到极致。当爱情出现信任危机时,一对恋人该何去何从,他们的爱情又能否焕发新生,欧·亨利的短篇小说佳作《爱情的信使》(“By Courier”) 运用同样颇具巧思的叙事风格娓娓讲述了一段爱情风波。

It was neither the season nor the hour when the Park had frequenters; and it is likely that the young lady, who was seated on one of the benches at the side of the walk, had merely obeyed a sudden impulse to sit for a while and enjoy a foretaste of coming Spring.(在这样的季节,这样的时刻,公园人迹罕至;一位年轻姑娘,可能是一时心血来潮,在人行道旁长凳上坐了会儿,呼吸着春回大地时的气息。)She rested there, pensive and still. A certain melancholy that touched her countenance must have been of recent birth, for it had not yet altered the fine and youthful contours of her cheek, nor subdued the arch though resolute curve of her lips.(她静静地靠在那里,若有所思。她忧郁的神色,一定是刚刚流露出的,因为她靓丽青春的脸蛋还没有扭曲,她坚毅的双唇曲线也没有变形。)A tall young man came striding through the park along the path near which she sat. Behind him tagged a boy carrying a suit-case. At sight of the young lady, the man's face changed to red and back to pale again. He watched her countenance as he drew nearer, with hope and anxiety mingled on his own.(一位高个儿年轻小伙子沿着姑娘停歇的小路大步流星地穿过公园,紧随他身后的是一个提行李箱的小男孩。一见到那位年轻姑娘,小伙子苍白的脸色先是变通红,随即又变煞白。他向姑娘靠近了,怀揣期盼与忐忑地观察她的面色。) Some fifty yards further on he suddenly stopped and sat on a bench at one side. The boy dropped the suit-case and stared at him with wondering, shrewd eyes. The young man took out his handkerchief and wiped his brow. It was a good handkerchief, a good brow, and the young man was good to look at.(他又向前走了大约 50 码,突然止步,在一旁的长凳上坐下。小男孩放下行李箱,用一双好奇机灵的眼睛注视着他。年轻小伙子拿出手帕擦拭了下自己的额头。手帕很漂亮,年轻人额头饱满,长相耐看。)年轻姑娘心事重重,怅然若失;年轻男人踌躇不前,欲言又止。作者通过一对俊男靓女各自神态举止幽微细致的描写表现了他们内心的挣扎和彷徨。读者的好奇心油然而生,他们彼此认识吗?他们之间有什么感情纠葛吗?他们会一直僵持下去吗?这样的疑团和悬念让读者迫不及待地要剥开洋葱的层层外皮,与小说中的人物同悲共喜。

"I want you to take a message to that young lady on that bench.... Tell her that, since she has commanded me neither to speak nor to write to her, I take this means of making one last appeal to her sense of justice, for the sake of what has been..." The young man dropped a half-dollar into the boy's hand. The boy looked at him for a moment with bright, canny eyes out of a dirty, intelligent face, and then set off at a run. He approached the lady on the bench a little doubtfully, but unembarrassed. He touched the brim of the old plaid bicycle cap perched on the back of his head. The lady looked at him coolly, without prejudice or favour.("我想让你给那边凳子上的年轻小姐带个口信。……告诉她,既然她要求我不能和她讲话,也不许给她写信,我只能用这种办法对事实的真相做最后的诉求……"年轻小伙子把半美元放在小男孩手里。小男孩脏兮兮的脸却一脸灵性,他用明亮机敏的眼睛看了看小伙子,转身就跑掉了。小男孩走近坐在凳子上的年轻姑娘,有点迟疑但不忸怩。他摸了摸后脑勺上那顶旧的花呢格子单车帽的帽檐。姑娘冷静地望着他,不偏不倚。)正是这样一个可爱聪明、对恋爱还懵懵懂懂的小男孩为成年男女的情事充当起了"信使",而且还是用一口美国南部方言在他们之间来回牵线搭桥,这无疑为小说凝重的氛围增添了喜剧

的元素。“Lady,” he said, “dat gent on de oder bench sent yer a song and dance by me. If yer don't know de guy, and he's tryin' to do de Johnny act, say de word, and I'll call a cop in t'ree minutes. If yer does know him, and he's on de square, w'y I'll spiel yer de bunch of hot air he sent yer.” The young lady betrayed a faint interest.(“小姐,”他说,“对面凳子上的先生让我给您唱首曲,跳支舞。如果您不认识那家伙,他企图耍流氓,只要您吱声,我三分钟就把警察叫来。如果您真的认识他,他是老实人,那我就把他想说的话告诉您。”年轻姑娘流露出一丝兴趣。)...She fixed her eye on a statue standing disconsolate in the dishevelled park, and spoke into the transmitter: “...absolute loyalty and truth are the ones paramount....Tell him I saw him and Miss Ashburton beneath the pink oleander. The tableau was pretty, but the pose and juxtaposition were too eloquent and evident to require explanation. I left the conservatory, and, at the same time, the rose and my ideal. You may carry that song and dance to your impresario.” (……她凝望孤零零矗立在凌乱公园里的雕像,对传话的小男孩说:“……忠诚坚贞和正直老实才是最最重要的。……你告诉他,我看见他和阿什伯顿小姐在夹竹桃下,场景十分动人,他们交叠在一起的姿势再明显不过,用不着解释了。我离开了温室,也告别了我的玫瑰和我的理想。你可以把这幕歌舞带回给你的导演了。”)

The young man gave a low whistle and his eyes flashed with a sudden thought. His hand flew to the inside pocket of his coat, and drew out a handful of letters. Selecting one, he handed it to the boy, following it with a silver dollar from his vest-pocket. “Give that letter to the lady,” he said, “and ask her to read it. Tell her that it should explain the situation. Tell her that, if she had mingled a little trust with her conception of the ideal, much heartache might have been avoided. Tell her that the loyalty she prizes so much has never wavered. Tell her I am waiting for an answer.”(年轻小伙子轻声吹了记口哨,突然想起什么,眼睛一亮。他的手飞快地伸进上衣的内兜里,掏出一把信。他挑出一封递给小男孩,并且从内衣口袋里摸出一块银币给他。“把这封信送给那位小姐,”他说,“让她读读,这封信会解释当时的情形。你跟她讲,如果她的理想能够融入一点点‘信任’的话,就不至于那么心痛了。你告诉她,她所珍视的忠诚从未动摇过,我在等她的回音。”)年轻女孩半信半疑地打开那封信读起来。这是阿什伯顿小姐

的父亲写给那位年轻小伙子的一封感谢信，感谢在他女儿突发心脏病、即将倒下去的时候，阿诺德医生及时扶住她并提供了好意的救助。那一瞬间，一切猜忌委屈烟消云散，一切误会隔阂化为乌有。"De gent wants an answer," said the messenger. "Wot's de word?" ("那位先生想要您回话，"小信使问道，"回什么话呢？")The lady's eyes suddenly flashed on him, bright, smiling and wet. "Tell that guy on the other bench," she said, with a happy, tremulous laugh, "that his girl wants him."(女孩突然眼睛发亮地看着小男孩，双眼濡湿，漾起笑意。"告诉对面凳子上的那个家伙，"她用幸福颤抖的声音笑着说，"就说他的女孩要他过来。")

爱情的信使让一对有情人破镜重圆，但是相爱的人，更重要的是彼此信任。

《情殇玫瑰园》片段选译及赏析

David Herbert Lawrence（大卫·赫伯特·劳伦斯，1885～1930）是20世纪最伟大的英国小说家之一，他的作品以自然美学为棱镜，折射出大自然独有的光芒和人性的红黑颜色。光影流转，曲终人散，他的短篇小说《情殇玫瑰园》（"The Shadow in the Rose Garden"）上演的爱情婚姻悲剧，是灵和肉相互分离，无法统一的时候，压抑在胸口那道永远不能抹去的隐隐伤痛。

A rather small young man sat by the window of a pretty seaside cottage trying to persuade himself that he was reading the newspaper. It was about half-past eight in the morning. Outside, the glory roses hung in the morning sunshine like little bowls of fire tipped up. The young man looked at the table, then at the clock, then at his own big silver watch. An expression of stiff endurance came on to his face. Then he rose and reflected on the oil-paintings that hung on the walls of the room, giving careful but hostile attention to *The Stag at Bay*. He tried the lid of the piano, and found it locked. He caught sight of his own face in a little mirror, pulled his brown moustache, and an alert interest sprang into his eyes. He was not ill-favoured. He twisted his moustache. His figure was rather small, but alert and vigorous. As he turned from the mirror a look of self-commiseration mingled with his appreciation of his own physiognomy.

In a state of self-suppression, he went through into the garden. His jacket, however, did not look dejected. It was new, and had a smart and self-confident air, sitting upon a confident body. He contemplated the Tree of Heaven that flourished by the lawn, then sauntered on to the next plant. There was more promise in a crooked apple tree covered with brown-red fruit. Glancing round, he broke off an apple and, with his back to the house, took a clean, sharp bite. To his surprise the fruit was sweet. He took another. Then again he turned to survey the bedroom windows overlooking the garden. He started, seeing a woman's figure; but it was only his wife. She was gazing across to the sea, apparently ignorant of him.

For a moment or two he looked at her, watching her. She was a good-looking woman, who seemed older than he, rather pale, but healthy, her face yearning. Her rich auburn hair was heaped in folds on her forehead. She looked apart from him and his world, gazing away to the sea. It irked her husband that she should continue abstracted and in ignorance of him; he pulled poppy fruits and threw them at the window. She started, glanced at him with a wild smile, and looked away again. Then almost immediately she left the window. He went indoors to meet her. She had a fine carriage, very proud, and wore a dress of soft white muslin.

漂亮的海边别墅里，一位身材矮小的年轻人坐在窗边。他努力说服自己读报。早上八点半光景。窗外，晨曦中低垂的火红玫瑰如同一碗碗摇曳燃烧的小小火焰。年轻人看看桌子，又瞅瞅时钟，再瞧瞧自己的那块大银表，脸上流露出僵硬强忍的神情。接着他起身，环视屋内四周墙壁挂着的油画，对那幅《海湾雄鹿》图仔细端详，心中怨恨油生。他想掀开钢琴盖，发现它锁上了。从小镜子里，他瞥见自己的脸。捋捋棕色的小胡子，他突然眼睛一亮：他并非其貌不扬。他捻了捻自己的胡须。虽然他个头矮小，但是机灵敏捷，精力充沛。他转身离开镜子时，自叹自怜的表情里夹杂着对自我容貌的自我陶醉。

郁闷沮丧中，他走进花园。不过，他身上穿着的夹克倒是很精神，崭新而笔挺，他显得精明自信。他呆望草坪旁生长的椿树出神，随后闲步走到另一棵树前。一棵弯曲的苹果树上结满了褐红色的果子，颇为诱人。他环顾四周后，摘下一个苹果，背对着别墅，干脆利落地咬上一口，意外的是果子很甜，他又摘了一个，然后回头看向朝花园敞开的卧室窗户。他发现了一个女人的身影，不过，那只能是他的妻子。她眺望着大海，显然没有留意他。

有那么一会儿，他注视她，观察她。她长相耐看，却比他显老，面色苍白，但是健康，脸上挂着期盼和渴望。她赤褐色的浓密头发卷曲地堆积在她的额前。她凝望大海，看上去和他，和他的世界毫不相干。她对他熟视无睹，这让身为丈夫的他苦恼。他扯下几粒深红色果子，向窗内扔去。她这才瞟他一眼，苦笑一声，又将视线移开了。随即她离开窗边。他进屋去见她。她仪态端庄，神情高贵，穿一件柔软的白色棉布衣。

小说开头的不协调、不和谐和不匀称预示了故事残缺之美、悲情之美。"rather small"与"pretty"，"the glory roses"与"fire tipped up"，是视觉上美与丑的强烈反差；男主人公生活富足，外表光鲜，却无法掩饰他一个矿工在性格修养上的缺陷，两者亦形成对比。七宗罪里，骄傲（pride）如男主人公之自我迷恋，饕餮（gluttony）如男主人公之偷吃苹果，嫉妒、愤怒（envy，wrath）则成为困扰男主人公的心魔，小说对这些细节的刻画，揭示了这桩不幸婚姻貌合神离、情感冷淡的真正根源。

Slowly she went down one path, lingering, like one who has gone back into the past. Suddenly she was touching some heavy crimson roses that were soft as velvet, touching them thoughtfully, without knowing, as a mother sometimes fondles the hand of her child. She leaned slightly forward to catch the scent. Then she wandered on in abstraction. Sometimes a flame-coloured, scentless rose would hold her arrested. She stood gazing at it as if she could not understand it. Again the same softness of intimacy came over her, as she stood before a tumbling heap of pink petals. Then she wondered over the white rose, that was greenish, like ice, in the centre. So, slowly, like a white, pathetic butterfly, she drifted down the path, coming at last to a tiny terrace all full of roses. They seemed to fill the place, a sunny, gay throng. She was shy of them; they were so many and so bright. They seemed to be conversing and laughing. She felt herself in a strange crowd. It exhilarated her, carried her out of herself. She flushed with excitement. The air was pure scent.

Hastily, she went to a little seat among the white roses, and sat down. Her scarlet sunshade made a hard blot of colour. She sat quite still, feeling her own existence lapse. She was no more than a rose, a rose that could not quite come into blossom, but remained tense. A little fly dropped on her knee, on her white dress. She watched it, as if it had fallen on a rose. She was not herself.

她缓慢地走过小路，徘徊着，一个人追寻着过去。突然，她触摸到一些深红色玫瑰，丝绒般柔软，她若有所思地抚摸着它们，不知不觉，仿佛母亲时不时抚摸婴儿的小手。她微微探出身子去捕捉香味，然后精神恍惚地继续前行。有时一朵火红的、没有香味的玫瑰花会吸引她的注意。她伫立着，凝视它，似乎对它充满疑惑。当她站在层层叠叠、颤颤巍巍的粉色花瓣面前时，心中又会涌起亲密的柔情。她还惊讶地发现白色玫瑰，花心如冰，泛出淡淡的绿色。就这样，好似一只结着愁怨的白色蝴蝶，她轻挪着步子沿小路来到一个开满玫瑰花的小阳台。那儿似乎填满了玫瑰花，团团簇簇，灿烂欢快。在它们中间，她感到羞涩，它们是如此繁多，如此亮丽，它们似乎在畅谈，在大笑，她觉得自己身处一群陌生人当中，这让她激动不已，神魂颠倒。她兴奋得脸颊泛红。空气中弥漫着纯纯的花香。

很快，她在白玫瑰花丛中找到小椅子坐下。她鲜红的太阳伞显得格外耀眼。她静静地坐着，忘记了自己的存在。她自己不过也是一朵玫瑰，一朵含苞紧闭的玫瑰。一只小苍蝇飞落到她的膝盖上，停落在她白色的裙子上。她看着它，似乎它落在一朵玫瑰上。她不再是她自己。

女主人公独自一人在玫瑰园里散步，追寻流逝的时光与往昔的爱情。作家Lawrence借助女主人公的触觉、视觉、嗅觉和听觉，描写自然景物的声、色、形，物与我相互交融后所激发出来的一种艺术境界，感人至深。在与大自然交流中，女主人公的情绪瞬息变化，时而恍惚，时而疑惑，时而激动，时而忧郁。她昔日的恋人是教区长的儿子，一位谈吐文雅、举止高贵的绅士，和她一样受过良好教育。他们本来会是幸福的一对，他却奔赴了非洲战场。她不渴望他们的爱恋像火红玫瑰一样轰轰烈烈；她只希望他们的初恋犹如粉色玫瑰般浪漫温馨；她期盼她的爱情好似白玫瑰的纯洁。然而，淡绿色的白玫瑰花心、飞落在白裙子上的苍蝇、含苞紧闭的玫瑰暗示了女主人纯爱理想与残酷现实的冲突。她以为她的初恋已死在战场上，只好委身不爱的人，只得在没有灵魂的婚姻中隐忍挣扎直至婚姻破裂，小说结尾让人唏嘘、叹息。

爱情的宏大与具象——歌曲《九百万辆自行车》翻译及赏析

1985年出生于格鲁吉亚的凯特·玛露(Katie Melua)从小梦想从政或成为史学家,却不曾想偶然间踏入了音乐这条人生轨迹。2003年底,凯特被音乐制作人挖掘,以新星的姿态步入歌坛。2005年9月,凯特发行了她的第二张专辑 *Piece by Piece*。该专辑第一周进入英国流行音乐排行榜就荣登榜首,其中的一曲"Nine Million Bicycles"以其轻慢舒缓的曲调节奏、悠扬清丽的笛声配乐以及凯特清澈自然又不失温暖的独特嗓音而大获成功,仿佛一阵清新自然的春风吹过欧洲各国的流行音乐排行榜。

★There are nine million bicycles in Beijing	★北京有九百万辆自行车
That's a fact	这是个事实
It's a thing we can't deny	是我们不可否认的事
Like the fact that I will love you till I die★	正如永生永世我都爱你一样真实★
We are twelve billion light years from the edge	我们离宇宙尽头有120亿光年
That's a guess	那只是猜测
No one can ever say it's true	没有人知道它是否确实
But I know that I will always be with you	但是我知道我会永远和你在一起
I'm warmed by the fire of your love everyday	你爱的火焰日日温暖着我
So don't call me a liar	别说我撒谎
Just believe everything that I say	相信我倾诉的字字句句
There are six billion people in the world	这个世界上生活着60亿人
More or less	大概也就这个数目
And it makes me feel quite small	这让我觉得自己犹如沧海一粟
But you're the one I love the most of all	而芸芸众生之中你才是我爱的全部
We're high on the wire	高速互联网让我们尽兴冲浪
With the world in our sight	世界尽收眼底
And I'll never tire	而我从不厌倦
Of the love that you give me every night	每个夜晚你给我的爱的信息
(Refrain ★)	(重复 ★)

And there are nine million bicycles in Beijing　北京城里有九百万辆自行车
And you know that I will love you till I die　你要知道我爱你永生永世

赏析

在"Nine Million Bicycles"中，凯特率真从容地吟唱出了对爱情的忠贞不渝和执着追求。在古今中外咏叹爱情的诗或歌中，借物借景抒发感情的词句不胜枚举，这首歌的歌词也是如此，而且这首歌词中的海誓山盟还饱含着浓浓的现代气息——从北京的自行车到对宇宙的终极探索，从地球的人口问题到网络技术的飞速发展，歌词营造的意象及其创作手法让人耳目一新。

这首歌的歌词运用了多种修辞手法。其一是明喻(simile)。歌词把北京自行车的惊人数量和主人公满腔的痴情爱意放在一起，以具体比喻抽象，新奇而传神。北宋词人秦观一句"无边丝雨细如愁"就曾用无边无际的雨来比喻无影无形的愁，两者可谓有异曲同工之妙。其二是隐喻(metaphor)。"the fire of your love"便是用"of 短语"构成的隐喻，以"火焰"比喻"爱情"，生活中类似的隐喻表达有很多，如：the light of learning(智慧之光)、the warm sunshine of praise(温暖如阳的赞美)等。其三是对比(contrast)。浩瀚广袤的宇宙亦有尽头，可歌者的爱情誓言却超越了时空界限；人口数量的庞大让个人感到自身的渺小，却淹没不了歌者对爱情的专一——无限与有限、大与小、多与少形成鲜明对比。歌词中的数字极具冲击力，但即使这些惊人的数字营造的意象仍然无法企及歌者的爱意。在数字的使用上，这首歌广受好评的同时，也引发了不小的争论。有人说北京没有九百万辆自行车，只有七百多万辆。物理学家西蒙·辛格甚至在英国《卫报》(*The Guardian*)上"声讨"词作者和凯特严重缺乏科学常识，120 亿光年应该改为 137 亿光年，而称这一数字为"This is a guess."也是对当今天文学研究成果的侮蔑。Katie 后来应西蒙·辛格的要求修改了部分歌词并重新录音，并表示为自己缺乏相关常识而感到羞愧，尽管她认为物理学家的"新词"很难与曲调配合。虽然在"数字精确度"这个问题上饱受争议，但我们得承认，音乐并非科学，这些数字虽不精确，却并未妨碍其对创作者心中所想的传神表达。

这首融合着爵士乐风和流行元素的慢版抒情小调，在从容平和中透露着一种执着的信念和优雅的自在。它讲述的故事与北京有着若有若无的关联，而大众喜欢这首歌曲的原因正像凯特自己所表达的那样："I like this song because it is a simple juxtaposition of a trivial idea against an important idea."

恋爱需要正能量

You Should Fall in Love with Someone Who Inspires You

By Stephanie Althoff

There's one trait that I continuously find myself coming back to when it comes to dating: inspiration. There's one thing I need from you—one thing I really, truly value: I need you to inspire me.

Inspiration is in its simplest form, really. I want you to inspire me to be a better person. To push myself—in my career, in my education, in my beliefs, culture, and values. I want you to inspire me to try things I always said I wouldn't. To read books I never thought I'd like, to go to a place I never wanted to visit, to eat a food I always swore off. I want you to inspire me to be better, every day. Because although self-motivation is important, sometimes our steam just runs out. Sometimes we need a person running alongside us, telling us we can keep going, that we can cross that finish line.

And I want to inspire you, too. I want to be able to push you, to stretch your limits and make you step outside of your comfort zone. Because inspiration is like a weed when you have the right amount. It grows wildly and quickly, and spreads throughout the surface. When it works, when it really works, we feed off of each other. We make each other better. We consistently try new things and pursue higher heights. That's inspirational.

Inspiration makes us better. Inspiration makes us want to do something. It moves our emotions, our intellect, our behavior. And is that not what every relationship needs? We need to be influenced to feel happiness and love, influenced to deeply care for someone other than ourselves, influenced to better ourselves while we better those around us. Quite frankly, that sounds pretty healthy to me.

So that's all I want. And it encompasses so very, very, much, that one little word. Inspiration. 11 letters, 4 syllables, and a different meaning for every person walking this earth. But there's someone out there—maybe you've already found them or maybe you're still looking—but there's someone walking around with a bottle of inspiration ready to swirl and mix with your own. To create that perfect recipe that leaves us with a sweet taste in our mouth and a warm feeling in our heart.

Fill your jar. Screw that lid on tight. And unleash that beauty when you're good and ready.

Be inspired. Inspire others. Our world could use a bit more of that.

约会时，我发现自己会不断审视一种品质——拥有正能量。我需要从你那里获得一件东西，一件我真正看重的东西：你的激励。

传递正能量，再简单不过。我希望你激励我成为更好的人：无论在事业、教育，还是信仰、文化和价值观上，都不断推动自己向前。我希望你鼓励我去尝试我总说不想尝试的各种事情：去阅读我从不认为自己愿意涉猎的书籍，去造访那些我未曾想去的地方，去品尝我总是忌讳的食物。我希望受到你的激励，让自己变得一天比一天好，因为尽管自我激励很重要，但我们有时也会精疲力竭。有时，我们需要一个人在身边陪跑，为我们助威加油，鼓励我们坚持跑过终点线。

我也希望激励你，我希望能推动你向前，让你挑战自己的极限，走出舒适区。因为当你拥有了足够的正能量，它就会像野草，急切而迅速地生长，冒出地面，四处蔓延。当正能量真正释放的那一刻，我们相互给予，让彼此变得更好。我们不断尝试新的事物，攀登新的高度。这是多么令人振奋！

正能量让我们日臻完美，让我们干劲十足。它拨动我们的情感，激发我们的智力，调整我们的行为。这难道不正是每一段恋情所需要的吗？我们需要受到感染，去感受幸福和爱情，深爱某人胜过爱自己，完善自我并让周边的人更好。坦率地说，我认为这才是积极健康的恋爱。

我想要的就是这个——正能量——字眼简单，蕴藉隽永。三个字，一个词，每个人有每个人的理解。但某人就在那里，你或许已经找到，抑或还在寻觅，但某人正四处徜徉，携带一瓶正能量，准备和你的正能量搅拌交融，调和出完美的口味，让我们唇齿留香，情暖心涧。

注满你的瓶罐，拧紧瓶盖吧！当满满的正能量准备就绪，再倾倒出那份美丽。

接受正能量，释放正能量，我们的世界需要更多正能量。

爷爷的情人节卡片

Grandpa's Valentine

By Harriet

I was the only family member living close by, so I received the initial call from the nursing home. Grandpa was failing rapidly. I should come. There was nothing to do but hold his hand. "I love you, Grandpa. Thank you for always being there for me." And silently, I released him.

Memories... memories... six days a week, the farmer in the old blue shirt and bib overalls caring for those Hereford cattle he loved so much... on hot summer days lifting bales of hay from the wagon, plowing the soil, planting the corn and beans and harvesting them in the fall... always working from dawn to dusk. Survival demanded the work, work, work.

But on Sundays, after the morning chores were done, he put on his gray suit and hat. Grandma wore her wine-colored dress and the ivory beads, and they went to church. There was little other social life. Grandpa and Grandma were quiet, peaceful, unemotional people who every day did what they had to do. He was my grandpa — he had been for 35 years.

The nurse apologized for having to ask me so soon to please remove Grandpa's things from the room. It would not take long. There wasn't much. Then I found it in the top drawer of his nightstand. It looked like a very old handmade valentine. What must have been red paper at one time was a streaked faded pink. A piece of white paper had been glued to the center of the heart. On it, penned in Grandma's handwriting, were these words:

TO LEE FROM HARRIET

With All My Love,

Februrary 14, 1895

Are you alive? Real? Or are you the most beautiful dream that I have had in years? Are you an angel — or a figment of my imagination? Someone I fabricated to fill the void? To soothe the pain? Where did you find the time to listen? How could you understand?

You made me laugh when my heart was crying. You took me dancing when I couldn't take a step. You helped me set new goals when I was dying. You showed me dew drops and I had diamonds. You brought me wild flowers and I had orchids. You sang to me and angelic choirs burst forth in song. You held my hand and my whole being loved you. You gave me a ring and I belonged to you. I belonged to you and I have experienced all.

Tears streamed down my cheeks as I read the words. I pictured the old couple I had always known. It's difficult to imagine your grandparents in any other role than that. What I read was so beautiful and sacred. Grandpa had kept it all those years. Now it is framed on my dresser, a treasured part of family history.

我是唯一住处临近爷爷的家庭成员，所以我第一个接到养老院的电话。爷爷行将离世，我应该前去探望。我所能做到的只是握住他的手。“我爱您，爷爷。谢谢您为我所做的一切，”我默默地松开手。

回想起过去的日子，往事历历在目…… 一周六天，爷爷这位农夫，身着蓝色旧衬衣和带围兜的工装裤，照顾着他心爱的赫里福德牛 …… 盛夏酷暑，他从货车上扛下大捆干草，耕田犁地，种植玉米和豆子，在秋天收获 …… 他起早贪黑，为养家糊口操劳不息。

但每逢周日干完上午的活儿后，他便穿好灰色西服，戴上帽子，奶奶则穿着深红色礼服，戴上象牙珠链，同去教堂。他们几乎没有其他社交生活。爷爷和奶奶恬静淡泊、安分守己、任劳任怨。他就是我的爷爷，伴了我三十五年。

不得不让我这么快拿走爷爷留在房间的遗物，护理员感到抱歉。不过我并没

花太多工夫，因为东西并不多。我在他床头柜顶层抽屉里发现了它——一张看上去年代久远的手工情人节卡片。卡片先前的红色已褪成粉色条纹。心形卡片的中央贴着一张白纸，上面是奶奶的笔迹，写着：

李：

你是活生生的真实吗？抑或是我多年最美的梦？你是天使吗？抑或是我为了填补空虚、缓解痛苦而幻想的人？你是如何挤出时间来倾听我诉说的？你又如何能懂得我呢？

当我内心哭泣时，你逗我开怀大笑；当我不能移步时，你带我翩翩起舞；当我深感绝望时，你帮我树立新的目标。你带我看露珠，那是我眼中的宝钻；你为我采撷野花，那是我心中的幽兰；你对我吟唱，那是天使的歌声。你握住我的手，我全身心爱你；你为我戴上戒指，我属于你。我跟随你经历了人间的甘苦。一心一意爱你！

读着这些文字，泪水顺着我的脸颊流下。我想象着我所认识的老两口。很难想象你的爷爷奶奶还扮演着其他角色。我所读到的是那么优美圣洁，爷爷这些年一直保存着它。现在我将卡片装框。摆放在梳妆台上，作为家史的一份珍藏。

哈里特
1895 年 2 月 14 日

女性篇

爱的遗憾——《懊悔》片段选译及赏析

凯特·肖邦(Kate Chopin, 1851～1904),美国著名女作家,作品文字细腻动人,充满画面的质感,尤其对女性丰富微妙的内心世界刻画得入木三分,往往让读者如临其境,如见其人,如闻其声,如睹其心。从 1869 年到 1902 年间,她陆续在 *Harper's Young People*, *Vogue*, *Century*, *Atlantic Monthly* 等杂志上发表短篇小说,其中不少成为世界名作,为世人传读。短篇小说《懊悔》("Regret")发表于 1895 年 5 月 *Century* 杂志上,女主人公奥蕾莉(Aurélie)年轻时拒绝了她的追求者,年过半百,孑然一身,对此她从来就不曾感到懊悔;然而她受邻居之托,照看了几天邻居家的孩子,在孩子们离开之后,她竟然失声痛哭,这才明白什么是母爱和幸福,心中留下深深遗憾。

Mamzelle Aurélie possessed a good strong figure, ruddy cheeks, hair that was changing from brown to gray, and a determined eye. She wore a man's hat about the farm, and an old blue army overcoat when it was cold, and sometimes top-boots.

Mamzelle Aurélie had never thought of marrying. She had never been in love. At the age of twenty she had received a proposal, which she had promptly declined, and at the age of fifty she had not yet lived to regret it.

So she was quite alone in the world, except for her dog Ponto, and the negroes who lived in her cabins and worked her crops, and the fowls, a few cows, a couple of mules, her gun (with which she shot chicken-hawks), and her religion.

芒热尔・奥蕾莉身材壮硕，面色红润，头发从棕色变成灰白，眼睛坚定有神。她头戴顶男式帽在农场里走动，天气冷时还披上件蓝色的旧军大衣，有时脚穿一双长筒靴。

芒热尔・奥蕾莉从未想过结婚，从未陷入爱河。二十岁时，有人向她求婚，她当场就拒绝了。年过五十，她也从未懊悔过。

在这个世界上，她没有一个亲人，陪伴她的只有这只叫"胖头"的狗，住在她的小木屋里、为她种庄稼的黑人，一群鸡鸭，几头母牛，一对骡子，还有她的猎枪，用来猎杀那些抓小鸡的老鹰，和她的信仰。

小说女主人公奥蕾莉(Aurélie)是一个小农场主，有着男性化的外表和独立坚强的个性，作者用字词"alone"而不是"lonely"写出她形单影只，内心却不寂寞；她就像古希腊神话里的女猎手阿塔兰特(Atalanta)，向月亮女神阿耳特弥斯(Artemis)许下守护贞洁、决意不嫁的誓言。然而一天早晨，邻居家四个孩子被托付给奥蕾莉，这让未曾结婚，毫无育儿经验的她手足无措、手忙脚乱。孩子们的到来打破了奥蕾莉平静的生活。

She left them crowded into the narrow strip of shade on the porch of the long, low house; the white sunlight was beating in on the white old boards; some chickens were scratching in the grass at the foot of the steps, and one had boldly mounted, and was stepping heavily, solemnly, and aimlessly across the gallery. There was a pleasant odor of pinks in the air, and the sound of negroes' laughter was coming across the flowering cotton-field.

Ti Nomme's sticky fingers compelled her to unearth white aprons that she had not worn for years, and she had to accustom herself to his moist kisses — the expressions of an affectionate and exuberant nature. She got down her sewing-basket, which she seldom used, from the top shelf of the armoire, and placed it within the ready and easy reach which torn slips and buttonless waists demanded. It took her some days to become accustomed to the laughing, the crying, the chattering that echoed through the house and around it all day long. And it was not the first or the second night that she could sleep comfortably with little Élodie's hot, plump body pressed close against her, and the little one's warm breath beating her cheek like the fanning of a bird's wing.

她留下了他们，他们挤在低矮长屋狭窄过道的凉荫下，白炽的阳光射进来照在白色的旧木板上。一些小鸡正在台阶下的草地里觅食，有只胆大地跳上台阶，迈着沉稳的步子，大模大样、漫无目的地穿过走廊。空气里弥散着石竹花的香气，从开花的棉花地里传来黑人们的笑声。

提·诺米黏糊糊的手指迫使她翻出多年未穿的白色围裙，她还不得不习惯他湿漉漉的吻——他那热烈奔放的情感表达方式。她从大衣柜顶层的架子上取下她很少用的针线筐，放在触手可及的地方，随时缝补撕破的衬衫和掉了扣子的背心。过了好几天，她才习惯房前屋后整日的欢声笑语、哭闹嘈杂。小伊洛蒂热乎乎、胖嘟嘟的身子紧贴着她时，她才睡得踏实，像这样不是头一两个晚上了，他酣睡时一张一翕地呼吸，好似鸟儿扑扇翅膀，呼出的热气直扑她的面颊。

作者用生活细节的描写传神刻画出女主人公奥蕾莉身上发生的不可思议的变化。与孩子们的朝夕相处触碰到她心底最柔软的地方，孩子们的激情使她骨子里母性的情愫萌发了。她从冷漠如冰的小农场主摇身成为温情似水的家庭主妇，从拒绝被爱到倾心去爱，这种变化是多么神奇而美妙啊！

The excitement was all over, and they were gone. How still it was when they were gone! Mamzelle Aurélie stood upon the gallery, looking and listening. She could no longer see the cart; the red sunset and the blue-gray twilight had together flung a purple mist across the fields and road that hid it from her view. She could no longer hear the wheezing and creaking of its wheels. But she could still faintly hear the shrill, glad voices of the children.

She turned into the house. There was much work awaiting her, for the children had left a sad disorder behind them; but she did not at once set about the task of righting it. Mamzelle Aurélie seated herself beside the table. She gave one slow glance through the room, into which the evening shadows were creeping and deepening around her solitary figure. She let her head fall down upon her bended arm, and began to cry. Oh, but she cried! Not softly, as women often do. She cried like a man, with sobs that seemed to tear her very soul. She did not notice Ponto licking her hand.

他们一阵子兴奋后离开了。他们离开后是多么静寂,芒热尔·奥蕾莉站在走廊上,眺望着,聆听着。她再也看不到那辆骡子车了,绯红的日落和灰蓝的暮光交织出紫色的雾气,笼罩了田地和道路,挡住了她的视线;她再也听不到车轱辘发出的呼哧嘎吱声了,但是她还能隐约听到车上孩子们欢乐的尖叫声。

她转身回屋,那儿还有一大堆活儿等着她,孩子们把屋子弄得一团糟,但是她没有立即收拾。芒热尔·奥蕾莉瘫坐在桌旁,她缓缓地环视了房间,暮色悄悄爬进来,加深了她孤独的影子。她突然将头枕在臂弯里,痛哭起来。噢,她哭了,不是女人常有的轻柔的嘤泣,而如男人般抽噎,撕心裂肺,连她的狗"胖头"舔她的手,她都没有发觉。

一切又恢复平静的房间,夜色笼罩,只剩下奥蕾莉独自啜泣,小说结尾让读者在感性层次上产生对比强烈的视觉和听觉冲击,女主人公对孩子们依依不舍的爱恋之情使人物形象饱满充盈,这样富有戏剧化的故事情节揭示了颇有分量的主题:母性是与生俱来、圣洁无私的,母爱让女人温柔完整;女人不会因为缺失爱的伴侣而懊悔,却会因为不能给予母爱而遗憾。

走出非洲,相思成愁——《走出非洲》片段选译及赏析

在美丽神奇的丹麦,有两位让丹麦人引以为豪的讲故事高手。他们一位是为孩子们讲童话故事的安徒生,另一位是为女人们讲情感故事的凯伦·布里克森(Karen Blixen,1885～1962)。女作家布里克森在她的代表作自传体小说《走出非洲》(*Out of Africa*)里用诗化的语言吟唱出对非洲大自然的深情向往和对女性自由精神的执着追求。在非洲,布里克森度过了一生中最宝贵的青葱岁月。作为欧洲移民,她用饱含痴情的笔触表达了她对这块原始热土绮丽自然风光的深深眷恋。小说如散文般的抒情叙述,舒缓优游的笔调,温婉细腻的语言,描写出非洲独有的地貌特征、气候条件和植被动物,读后让人身临其境、爱不释手。

I had a farm in Africa, at the foot of the Ngong Hills. The Equator runs across these highlands, a hundred miles to the North, and the farm lay at an altitude of over six thousand feet. In the daytime you felt that you had got high up, near to the sun, but the early mornings and evenings were limpid and restful, and the nights were cold.

The geographical position, and the height of the land combined to create a landscape that had not its like in all the world. There was no fat on it and no luxuriance anywhere; it was Africa distilled up through six thousand feet, like the strong and refined essence of a continent. The colours were dry and burnt, like the colours in pottery. The trees had a light delicate foliage, the structure of which was different from that of the trees in Europe; it did not grow in bows or cupolas, but in horizontal layers, and the formation gave to the tall solitary trees a likeness to the palms, or a heroic and romantic air like full-rigged ships with their sails clewed up, and to the edge of a wood a strange appearance as if the whole wood were faintly vibrating. Upon the grass of the great plains the crooked bare old thorn trees were scattered, and the grass was spiced like thyme and bog myrtle; in some places the scent was so strong, that it smarted in the nostrils. All the flowers that you found on the plains, or upon the creepers and liana in the native forest, were diminutive like flowers of the downs — only just in the beginning of the long rains a number of big, massive heavy-scented lilies sprang out on the plains. The views were immensely wide. Everything that you saw made for greatness and freedom, and unequalled nobility.

The early morning air of the African highlands is of such a tangible coldness and freshness that time after time the same fancy there comes back to you: you are not on earth but in dark deep waters, going ahead along the bottom of the sea. It is not even certain that you are moving at all, the flows of chilliness against your face may be the deep sea currents, and your car, like some sluggish electric fish, may be sitting steadily upon the bottom of the Sea, staring in front of her with the glaring eyes of her lamps, and letting the submarine life pass by her. The stars are so large because they are no real stars but reflections, shimmering upon the surface of the water. Alongside your path on the sea bottom, live things, darker than their surroundings, keep on appearing, jumping up and sweeping into the long grass, as crabs and beach fleas will make their way into the sand. The light gets clearer, and, about sunrise, the sea bottom lifts itself towards the surface, a new created island.

在非洲，我有一座农场，坐落在恩贡山脉脚下。它位于海拔六千多英尺[①]的高原，向北绵延百里，赤道横穿而过。白天，你登高望远，似乎太阳也触手可及；拂晓或傍晚却来得清，来得静；到了夜间还有些许寒意。

这片高原的地理位置与海拔高度使它形成了世界上独一无二的美景，处处不染尘俗之气，举手投足皆显淳朴。非洲大陆在经过海拔六千英里[②]的沉淀筛滤，到这里，就像高度浓缩的精华。大地色彩干焦，和陶器上的着色一样，有如烧制般考究。树上的叶子稀疏纤细，生长的形状与欧洲的截然不同。它们没有弓状或圆形的树冠，而是朝水平方向层层伸展开来。这样的树形结构让一株株参天独木酷似

① 1英尺=0.3048米

② 1英里=1.609344千米

手掌，又像是整装待发、扬帆起航的船舰，洋溢着英雄主义气概，散发出浪漫主义气息；这也为树林周边蒙上了诡异的面纱，似乎整座森林都在微微颤动。旷野草地上，散落生长着光秃的荆棘树，年代已远，枝条虬曲；青草散发出百里香和香桃木的芳香；有些地方香气浓烈得熏鼻。在草原上找得到的花儿，或是长在当地森林里藤蔓植物上的花儿，就像丘陵地带的花儿，娇小玲珑。只有当漫长雨季开始时，草原上才会冒出成片芬芳馥郁的硕大百合。这里视野无比开阔，放眼望去，宏大宽广、无拘无束的景象，拥有无与伦比的高贵气质。

黎明时分，非洲高原的空气，似乎触摸得到的凉爽清新，让你一次又一次产生幻觉：不是在陆地上，仿佛置身昏暗的深海海底行走。你甚至不确信自己是在行走，一阵阵拂面凉风好似一股股涌动的深海水流推动你前行。你的汽车，像是行动迟缓的电鱼，可以稳稳停靠在海底，汽车车灯用发光的眼睛注视前方，让海底生物得以从她身边游过。一颗颗星星那么大，它们不是天空里的星星，而是水面上闪烁摇曳的倒影。海底里与你同行的生物，体色深过周围环境，如同螃蟹、沙蚤寻路钻进沙堆里，它们不断出现、蹦跳着，涌进深草丛中。光线越来越强，太阳喷薄欲出，海底抬升至水面，一座崭新的岛屿孕育而生。

小说结尾，农场经营失败、陷入破产，女作家布里克森离开了所热爱的非洲大陆，却始终走不出对非洲世界的日夜思念。她如怨如慕，如泣如诉，缠绵悱恻，柔肠百转，任由一腔思绪情愁肆意倾泻于笔端。

If I know a song of Africa, — I thought, — of the Giraffe, and the African new moon lying on her back, of the ploughs in the fields, and the sweaty faces of the coffee-pickers, does Africa know a song of me? Would the air over the plain quiver with a colour that I had had on, or the children invent a game in which my name was, or the full moon throw a shadow over the gravel of the drive that was like me, or would the eagles of Ngong look out for me?

如果我所熟悉的非洲之歌，在我听来，是一首吟唱长颈鹿和天边新月停歇在非洲大陆脊背上的歌，是一首颂唱农夫在田间犁作，汗流满面采摘咖啡的歌，那么非洲是否记得一支和我有关的歌？非洲高原的天穹会为我往昔衣装的色彩而震颤吗？孩子们发明的游戏里是否提及我的名字？圆月可否在鹅卵石的车道上投下形似我的身影？恩贡山的雄鹰会翘首以盼我的到来吗？

非洲在女作家布里克森生命里留下了刻骨铭心、不可磨灭的印痕。在非洲，布里克森历经种种生活磨难，非洲却让她洗尽铅华、拾回自我、学会坚韧，非洲带给她巨大的精神财富。在与非洲丰富的自然人文世界交流中，布里克森对自己与瑞典男爵失败的婚姻进行了深刻反思，当地的风俗观念唤起了布里克森对女性价值与尊严的重新认识。那里有她钟爱的森林原野、珍稀动物，有她敬佩的索马里妇女，那里有她喂养的雌瞪羚璐璐，有她医治的土著居民。在非洲广袤自由的世界里，女作家布里克森寻回了女性失落的自我，实现了女性生命的意义，她的灵魂已经融入非洲辽阔壮美的大自然，与那里的天地万物合而为一。

于无声处听惊雷——《空白页》片段选译及赏析

短篇小说《空白页》(“The Blank Page”)选自《最后的故事》(*The Last Tale*),小说故事结构之精妙,故事主题之深远,令人叹为观止。女作家凯伦·布里克森极尽艺术创作之能事,秉承《一千零一夜》里山鲁佐德讲故事的叙述风格,推崇的是古老神秘的说书技艺,让说故事的人娓娓讲述了一个个传奇故事,有修道院创设的历史,修女种植亚麻的故事,由此引出亚麻籽的神话故事和亚麻布的宫廷传统,最后讲到一张纯白的亚麻布的故事戛然而止,让小说艺术表现力达到登峰造极的境界。这些故事隐晦微妙地表现了修道院修女凄苦孤寂的生活,封建婚姻枷锁对宫廷妇女身心的压制束缚,女性的声音为当时社会的男权统治所淹没,所以人性解放的故事主题愈显突出有力、掷地有声、振聋发聩。作家留白的写作智慧让读者心领神会,让作品耐人寻味。

小说的开头部分,运用魔幻诡异的表现手法,让说故事人披纱蒙面神秘登场,一位讲了两百年故事的老婆婆,蠕动着牙齿脱落的干瘪嘴巴,向众人炫耀自己说故事的本领,她提及的所谓“无声胜有声”的留白技艺,正是作家借老婆婆的口增强故事叙述张力,吸引读者兴趣的高明手法。

By the ancient city gate sat an old coffee-brown, black-veiled woman who made her living by telling stories. She said: “You want a tale, sweet lady and gentleman? Indeed I have told many tales, one more than a thousand...It was my mother’s mother, the black-eyed dancer, ... who in the end — wrinkled like a winter apple and crouching beneath the mercy of the veil — took upon herself to teach me the art of story-telling. Her own mother’s mother had taught it to her, and both were better storytellers than I am. But that, by now, is of no consequence, since to the people they and I have become one, and I am most highly honoured because I have told stories for two hundred years.”

“With my grandmother,” she said, “I went through a hard school. ‘Be loyal to the story,' the old hag would say to me. 'Be eternally and unswervingly loyal to the story...Where the story-teller is loyal, eternally and unswervingly loyal to the story, there, in the end, silence will speak. Where the story has been betrayed, silence is but emptiness...'" "Who then," she continues, "tells a finer tale than any of us? Silence does. And where does one read a deeper tale than upon the most perfectly printed page of the most precious book? Upon the blank page. When a royal and gallant pen, in the moment of its highest inspiration, has written down its tale with the rarest ink of all — where, then, may one read a still deeper, sweeter, merrier and more cruel tale than that? Upon the blank page."

古老的城墙下倚坐着一位咖啡色皮肤,头戴黑色面纱的年老女人,她靠讲故事来谋生。她叫卖着:"你想听故事吗,亲爱的女士、先生?我可说过很多故事,有一千零一个故事……我的母亲的母亲曾是位黑眼睛的舞女,最后当她满脸的皱纹像冬天的蔫苹果,她不得不掩藏在面纱之后时,她开始教会我说故事的艺术。她母亲的母亲教会了她,她们都比我更会说故事。但是到现在,在我的听众心里,我就成了她们。我是最受欢迎的讲故事人,我已经讲了两百年的故事。"

"跟着祖母,"她回忆着,"我接受过严格训练,'忠实于故事,'老婆子向我传授道,'要永远不偏不倚真实地讲述故事,只有说故事人忠实于故事,始终不渝真实地讲出真相,讲到最后,沉默的人群里才会爆发喝彩声;如果故事讲得虚假,沉默的人群则继续保持沉默。'""那么有谁能比我们任何人讲出更好的故事呢?"她顿了顿,接着说:"是沉没的声音。那么在哪里才能读到比印刷在最精美的书页上更动听的故事呢?只有在空白页上。用高贵精致的钢笔在最富有灵感的时刻,用最珍贵的墨水写下的故事,那么又是在哪里才能读到比这更深刻、更甜蜜、更欢快和更悲惨的故事呢?还是在空白页上。"

于是老婆婆平静舒缓地讲述了几个小故事,故事中有故事,环环相扣,层层交织,其中修女们种植、采摘和加工亚麻的描写借助夸张的渲染,形象的比喻,颇为细致生动。

The long field below the convent is plowed with gentle-eyed, milk-white bullocks, and the seed is skillfully sown out by labour-hardened virginal hands with mold under the nails. At the time when the flax field flowers, the whole valley becomes air-blue... During this month the villagers many miles round raise their eyes to the flax field and ask one another: "Has the convent been lifted into heaven? Or have our good little sisters succeeded in pulling down heaven to them?"

Later in due course the flax is pulled, scatched and hackled; thereafter the delicate thread is spun, and the linen woven, and at the very end the fabric is laid out on the grass to bleach, and is watered time after time, until one may believe that snow has fallen round the convent walls.... The linen, baled high on the backs of small gray donkeys and sent out through the convent gate, downwards and ever downwards to the towns, is as flower-white, smooth and dainty as was my own little foot when fourteen years old, I had washed it in the brook to go to a dance in the village.

修道院下面，眼神温顺，乳白色的小牛犁着长长的田地，修女们用圣洁的双手手持农具熟练地播撒下亚麻种子。当亚麻地开花时，整个山谷一片天蓝色，在那个月里，数百英里[①]开外的村民抬头望见亚麻地，会相互打听："是修道院抬升上了天堂，还是我们善良的小修女姊妹将天堂搬到了人间？"

在接下来的工序里，亚麻被采摘下来，打散压轧，然后被抽出细柔的亚麻线，纺织出亚麻布，最后被铺放在草地上漂白，用水反复浸润，直到修道院的院墙周围铺满像下了雪似的片片白色。加工好的亚麻布高高捆绑在小灰驴的背上，被送出修道院，往下，再往下被送到各处小镇，它们就像14岁时的我去乡村跳舞前在小溪里冲刷过的小脚丫一样，花瓣般白嫩，柔滑细腻。

修女们用勤劳的汗水编织出圣洁雪白的亚麻布，原来是被用作检验少女婚前是否贞洁的工具，公主大婚时留有"女儿红"的每一小块亚麻布还会在修道院的长

① 1英里=1.609344千米

廊里展示，无异于标榜女性“美德”的一块块贞节牌坊。小说高潮，最出彩的部分正是在空白页上。

But in the midst of the long row there hangs a canvas which differs from the others. The frame of it is as fine and as heavy as any, and as proudly as any carries the golden plate with the royal crown. But on this one plate no name is inscribed, and the linen within the frame is snow-white from corner to corner, a blank page.

在这一长排正中间却悬挂着一块与众不同的亚麻布，它同样有精美厚重的画框，和供放皇冠的金色托盘的画框一样，傲然挂立，但是它的托盘没刻上名字，画框里的亚麻布，竟然整块雪白雪白的，是一幅空白页。

讲故事的老妇人，也就是作者布里克森自己对这位公主新娘的亚麻布还是洁白的原因只字不提，她把一切想象留给听众，但是小说结尾，皇族王妃和修道院修女同在那片空白的亚麻布前肃然沉思，让小说故事主题升华到一个新高度，女作家为被束缚与被侮辱的女性的自由和尊严喊出了最强音，使读者于无声处听惊雷，惊心动魄。

栀子花的魔力

Spell of the Gardenia

By Cynthia

In my hometown, in summertime, gardenia is in full blossom, blooming under fences, on hills, in gardens, in courtyards as well as in balconies. Gardenias, as white as snow, splash everywhere, pure white, in bosses① of ivory and in large bulks. The tiny flowers gleam② on the dark green foliage and stems and grass. Its sweet fragrance spreads into the surrounding air, being free from every taint③, ending its unique scent to people's lips, purifying the crowded city air. Very often, in such scene, I am indulged myself④ and intoxicated⑤ with a special feeling.

In earlier mornings, country girls are on streets and lanes, selling gardenias. The flowers are in the girls' exquisite⑥ blankets, white and thick, tiny and fragile⑦, with a few petite⑧ green leaves decoration. Its special fragrance draws a big gathering. Very soon, the crowds disperse⑨, with gardenias in their hands, and smile on their faces. Then, the gardenias' scent is roaming in the city's air and the whole summer. I seldom buy gardenia because I cannot tolerate its withering in glass.

---

① boss /bɒs/ *n*. 凸起的装饰，浮雕

② gleam /gliːm/ *v*. 闪烁，发出微光

③ taint /teɪnt/ *n*. 污染，腐烂

④ indulge oneself (with sth.) 让自己沉溺于……

⑤ intoxicated /ɪnˈtɒksɪkeɪtɪd/ *adj*. 喝醉的，极度兴奋的

⑥ exquisite /ˈekskwɪzɪt/ *adj*. 精致的，优美的，高雅的

⑦ fragile /ˈfrædʒaɪl/ *adj*. 脆的，娇嫩的

⑧ petite /pəˈtiːt/ *adj*. 小的，细的

⑨ disperse /dɪsˈpəːs/ *v*. 散开，疏散

It is said that gardenia alludes to[①] feminine charm. So the flower is always beautiful in my eyes. It gives me magic and joy as I touch the soft and smooth petals. In evenings, I like to come to a garden in moonlight. Usually, the air is cozily[②] cool with vaporous[③] warmth, and the stillness is unbroken. At such moment, gardenias, the eyes of this land, open their hearts to meet the moonbeam[④], like the sparking stars on the blue sky, seemingly each flower is murmuring to each star. In the concealed stillness, I can hear their whispering. For me, the gardenias' scent is the special word sending to their stars; it is the reason why the delightful stars glitter so brightly in summer time. The white flowers, twinkling stars, moonlit, gentle summer breeze together create a poetic dream. In such dream, I deeply sense the mood of charm and tenderness, the mood of cleanness and calmness, the greatness of nature; in such a dream, all troubles are away from me, all earthly tie is cut off; in such a dream, I have gained warm kindness and caress[⑤].

I have learned from a book that gardenia embodies a coy[⑥] "I love you secretly". Is that really so? If yes, I can better understand why the flower is so quiet, so lonely and why every time, I have sympathy on it. Who can take away its loneliness and melancholy[⑦], a star in the sky? I ask myself and go to deep thinking. Suddenly a gust of gentle breeze comes to break my pondering and brings me the fragrance of gardenia, My heart is seized with an unexpected sense and totally moved. Thousands of words are crowded in my mind and tears in eyes. Staring at the white flowers while taking a deep breath of the fragrant air, I know probably gardenias are longing for quietness too, because it is the very moment for themselves, the very moment they can talk to their own stars,

---

① allude to 暗指,影射

② cozily /ˈkəuzɪlɪ/ *adv*. 舒服地,安逸地

③ vaporous /ˈveɪpərəs/ *adj*. 似蒸汽的

④ moonbeam 月光

⑤ caress /kəˈres/ *n*. 爱抚,珍爱

⑥ coy /kɒɪ/ *adj*. 腼腆的,怕羞的

⑦ melancholy /ˈmelənkəlɪ/ *n*. 忧郁,抑郁

the very moment they are in their own dream. So, I whisper tenderly gardenias and leave the garden silently...

在我家乡,夏季里栀子花开得非常繁茂,开在篱笆下,山坡上,花园里,庭院内和阳台上。洁白如雪的栀子花四处绽放,好似洁白的象牙雕成的球,团团簇拥。这些小花在深绿色的叶子,茎干和草地上熠熠闪光,怡人的芳香弥漫在空中,没有丝毫异味,独特的芳香沁人心脾,净化了拥挤的城市的空气。在这样的环境里,我经常沉浸陶醉在一种特别的感觉里。

一大早,乡村女孩走上街头小巷卖栀子花。这些鲜花放在女孩们精致的毯子里,洁白厚实的花小巧柔嫩,还衬着几片细小的绿叶。它特有的香气吸引了大群人围观。很快人群散开,大家手里拿着栀子花,脸上洋溢着微笑。之后栀子花的香味弥漫着整个城市和整个夏天。我很少买栀子花,因为不忍心看它在玻璃花瓶里枯萎。

据说栀子花是女性魅力的象征,所以这种花在我眼里永远美丽。每当我触摸它柔软平滑的花瓣时总感觉有一种魔力的快感袭来。晚上,我喜欢来到月色笼罩的花园,空气往往凉爽宜人,湿润温馨,四周万籁俱寂。此刻的栀子花就像墨蓝夜空上闪烁的星星,成为这片国度的眼睛,敞开心扉去迎接月光,似乎每朵花儿都在同一颗星星喃喃细语。在深藏的静谧里,我能听到它们低语。我觉得栀子花馥郁的芳香是传递给星星的低语,这就是可爱的星星在夏天如此璀璨的原因。白色的花,闪烁的星,迷茫的月色,习习的夏风,这一切营造出诗一般的梦境。在这样的梦中,我能深感魅力与柔情、纯洁恬静的心境和自然的伟大;在这样的梦中,我远离所有的纷扰,割断一切世俗的纠葛;在这样的梦中,我收获了温情与抚慰。

从一本书上我得知栀子花包含了羞涩的"我暗恋你"之意。果真如此吗?如果真是这样,我更明白为什么这种花会如此安静孤寂,为什么每次我都会对它心生怜惜。谁能排解它的寂寞和忧愁,天上的星星吗?我追问自己,陷入深思。忽然,一阵微风吹来打断了我的思绪,为我送上栀子花香。一种突如其来的感觉攫住我的心,让我深受感动。千言万语涌上心头,眼泪在眼眶里涌动。我凝视着这些白色的花,深深呼吸一口清新的空气。我知道栀子花或许也渴望寂静,因为这一刻属于它自己,这一刻它可以和自己的星星交谈,这一刻它在自己的梦中。所以,我对栀子花轻声告别,悄悄离开了花园……

“她”的天堂——歌曲《天堂》翻译及赏析

当代流行音乐乐坛上有一支具有旺盛艺术生命力的神奇乐队。这支乐队创作出一首首荡气回肠、感心动耳的流行音乐，让全球摇滚乐迷为之倾倒。这支乐队硕果累累、战绩辉煌，迄今为止，它共获得 8 项格莱美音乐大奖。这支乐队就是酷玩乐队(Coldplay)。

2011 年 10 月 24 日 Coldplay 又推出一张新专辑 *Mylo Xyloto*，其中的一首“Paradise”曾获得当时英国单曲第一的好成绩，2012 年还被指定为李安导演的电影《少年派的奇幻漂流》(*Life of Pi*)宣传片的主题曲。

Paradise	**天　堂**
When she was just a girl,	当她只是个小女孩，
she expected the world,	她对世界充满期待。
but it flew away from her reach,	但理想却触不可及，
so she ran away in her sleep,	她唯在睡梦中躲避。
dreamed of paradise,	只要轻轻闭上眼睛，
every time she closed her eyes.	美丽天堂就在心间。
When she was just a girl,	当她只是个小女孩，
she expected the world,	她对世界充满期待。
but it flew away from her reach,	可是愿望触不可及，
and the bullets catching in her teeth.	子弹穿过她的牙齿，
Life goes on; it gets so heavy.	生活步伐不再轻盈。
The wheel breaks the butterfly,	车轮滚滚碾断蝴蝶，
every tear a waterfall.	每滴眼泪汇注成河。
In a night, a stormy night,	一个暴风骤雨之夜，

she closed her eyes.	她轻轻合上了双眼;
In a night, a stormy night,	一个暴风骤雨之夜,
away she flies, and dreams of paradise.	她飞去梦想的天堂。
So lying underneath the stormy skies,	躺在阴霾的天空下,
She'd say,	她依然坚守着信念:
"Oh, I know the sun must set to rise."	旭日必定喷薄而升。
This could be paradise.	那就是光明与天堂。

赏析

歌词中的"She"充满了隐喻色彩,"她"代表了被损害的、被欺辱的,"她"对天堂的向往、对梦想的坚守,震撼人类的灵魂,唤醒人类的良知。歌词"The wheel breaks the butterfly"引自历史典故,来源于18世纪英国诗人Alexander Pope的诗句:"Who breaks a butterfly on a wheel.(是谁用车轮碾碎了一只蝴蝶。)""她"的梦想并不是揽月摘星、不可企及,"她"的梦想只是求生的愿望,或是求知的渴望,如同鲜活美丽、纤小柔弱的蝴蝶,却被野蛮与愚昧肆意地践踏,凶暴地蹂躏,实现这样小小的梦想也步履维艰。"她"是惨遭猎杀、濒临灭绝的津巴布韦小母象,"她"的天堂在津巴布韦一望无际的大草原上,"她"的梦想就是在大草原上自由驰骋,不再为人类贪婪、觊觎自己的牙齿而忧心忡忡;"她"是为失学儿童呼吁的巴基斯坦小女孩马拉拉,"她"的天堂在窗明几净的校园里,"她"的梦想就是妇女儿童能够重返课堂,接受教育,不再饱受战乱冲突之苦。

歌曲在歌手为"她"的天堂、美好梦想的呐喊声中结束,乐队大气磅礴的音乐却久久回响在我们心间。

我若为精神的王——歌曲《王》翻译及赏析

2014年1月26日，第56届格莱美音乐大奖（the Grammy Awards）宣布《王》（“Royals”）为年度热曲（Song of the Year），它的词曲作者和演唱者是年仅17岁的新西兰天才少女洛德（Lorde），一时引发热议。编曲大气磅礴的节拍、歌手冷魅迷幻的嗓音、歌词视浮华为粪土的精神，这些大概是征服大奖评委和吸引广大歌迷的法宝。

Royals

I've never seen a diamond in the flesh;
I cut my teeth on wedding rings in the movies.
And I'm not proud of my address,
In the torn-up town, no post code envy.

★But every song's like gold teeth, Grey Goose, trippin' in the bathroom,
Blood stains, ball gowns, trashin' the hotel room.
We don't care; we're driving Cadillacs in our dreams.
But everybody's like Cristal, Maybach, diamonds on your time piece,
Jet planes, islands, tigers on a gold leash.
We don't care; we aren't caught up in your love affair.

And we'll never be royals.
It won't run in our blood;
That kind of lux just ain't for us.
We crave a different kind of buzz.
Let me be your ruler;

You can call me Queen Bee.
And baby I'll rule, I'll rule, I'll rule, I'll rule.
Let me live that fantasy.★

My friends and I — we've cracked the code.
We count our dollars on the train to the party.
And everyone who knows us knows that we're fine with this.
We didn't come for money.

We're bigger than we ever dreamed,
And I'm in love with being Queen.
Life is a game without care.
We aren't caught up in your love affair.
(Refrain★)

我若为精神的王

我从未亲眼见过佩戴的钻戒；
我只是在电影里才见过婚戒。
我不为自己的住址感到骄傲，
破烂小镇的邮编也不被嫉妒。

★但歌词里总提到金牙、美酒、在浴室里嗑药，
斗殴时的血迹、舞会的华服、酒店里喝到吐。
我们不在乎，我们在梦中驾驶凯迪拉克，
但每个人总提到名贵香槟、豪华汽车、镶钻手表、
喷气式飞机、度假小岛、圈养老虎。
我们不在乎，你(们)的风流韵事与我们无关。

我们永远不会是物质的贵族。

我们不会流淌物质贵族的血液；
那样的奢华不属于我们，
我们渴求不同的生活，
让我统治你们，
我是蜂王，
我会主宰一切，一切，一切，
就让我生活在幻想中。★

我和朋友们——坦然接受现实。
我们在去派对的火车上数着零钱，
懂我们的人都知道我们安于贫困，
我们不为金钱而活。

我们比自己的梦想强大，
我痴心成为蜂王，
人生是一场无所谓的游戏。
你(们)的风流韵事与我们无关。
(重复★)

赏析

富有质感的鼓槌声和悠扬层叠的和声，仿佛召唤着听众走进歌手幻构的原始而神秘、简朴却高贵的精神王国。这里不崇拜现代物质社会的纸醉金迷、奢腐堕落，这里没有钻戒金牙、名酒豪车、私人飞机；没有镶钻的手表、圈养的老虎；没有华丽的派对服装、狼藉的酒店房间。在这个精神王国里，挣脱物欲的羁绊束缚，每个人都是自己的王，都是自己心灵的主宰；在这个精神王国里，与贵族的炫富奢靡无关，与富豪的风流韵事无关，每个人都是自己的王，追求的是蜜蜂采蜜、终日嗡嗡的辛勤劳作，孜孜不倦地酿造甜蜜的梦想，正如英国浪漫派诗人威廉·布雷克(William Blake)所说："The busy bee has no time for sorrow(忙碌的蜜蜂无暇痛苦。)"

歌曲副歌部分运用头韵、尾韵和腹韵，使得歌词朗朗上口，"And we'll never

be royals... Let me be your ruler；You can call me Queen Bee."词句间看似相互矛盾，仔细推敲后发现蕴意深长："毋做物质贵族，宁为精神的王"，矛盾、对比、修辞撞击出来的听觉效果使歌曲充满张力，让人过耳不忘、刻骨铭心。

有趣的是，女歌手 Lorde 本名为 Ella Yelich-O'Connor，13 岁刚出道时，她为自己取了艺名 Lorde，别出心裁地在英文单词 lord（王）词尾加上了字母 e，赋予单词女性化的特质，表达了她做音乐 Queen Bee（女王）的雄心壮志。正是这个大气动听的艺名"Lorde"，伴随她不懈努力，一直拿到全球颇具影响力的格莱美大奖。歌曲《王》歌唱的梦想变为现实，女歌手 Lorde 真的成为精神盛宴 —— 格莱美音乐颁奖盛典上的"女王"，她的艺术天赋倍受瞩目，她的精神理想迷倒众生。

生 活 篇

《救救溺水鱼》片段选译及赏析

谭恩美(Amy Tan,1952～),美国华裔作家,被人誉为"是一个具有罕见才华的优秀作家,能触及人们的心灵",美国《华盛顿邮报》说她是讲故事的天才,也有评论家说她是营造氛围的高手。她的作品正是用一个个细碎的生活片段,拼贴出具有穿越时空意义的宏大主题,她的成名作小说《喜福会》(*Joy Luck Club*, 1989)生动演绎了中国移民母亲和美国女儿之间微妙的情感纠葛,其中母亲望女成凤的小故事《两类人》("Two Kinds")被收录进《现代大学英语》精读课本。下面节选自谭恩美近年来的得力之作《救救溺水鱼》(*Saving Fish from Drowning*, 2005)。她细致入微的观察力,娴熟细腻的表现力,时而幽默调侃、时而柔情脉脉的叙事风格引人入胜。《救救溺水鱼》讲述了 12 个美国人出国旅行的所见所闻,小说空间更加广阔,横跨美国、中国、缅甸等几个国家的文化,借用"救救溺水鱼"的寓意故事,表达了强势文化冲击和干预下坚守弱势文化身份的迷茫与痛苦,传达出全球化时代背景下异质文化之间应该相互尊重,共同发展的声音。

"我"分别通过朋友和自己的不同视角勾勒出中国、缅甸自然景观上的异同,空间上的变化甚至让"我"产生时间上的错觉,这样的描述再现了缅甸的神秘原始,让读者感同身受。

Crossing the border into Burma, one can spot the same pretty flowers seen from the bus window in China: yellow daisies and scarlet hibiscus, lantana growing as plentifully as weeds. Nothing had changed from one country to the next, or so it appeared to my friends.

But in fact all had suddenly become denser, wilder, devouring itself as nature does when it is neglected for a hundred years. That was the sense I had in crossing that border, as if I, like H.G. Wells in his time machine, possessed the same consciousness but had been plopped in the past... Like my friends, I, too have found the literature of yesteryear intoxicating, engorged with the perfumes and pastiches of the exotic and languid life.

On their way out, they passed a pile of shiny carp, the mouths of the fish still moving. "I thought this was a Buddhist country," Heidi said. "I thought they didn't kill animals." A few yards to the right was the bloody carnage of a dead pig. Heidi had glimpsed it and now would not look that way.

"The butchers and fishermen are usually not Buddhist," Walter said. "But even if they are, they approach their fishing with reverence. They scoop up the fish and bring them to shore. They say they are saving fish from drowning. Unfortunately..."He looked downward, like a penitent. "...the fish do not recover."

Heidi was unable to speak. Did these people actually believe they were doing a good deed? Why, they had no intention of saving anything! Look at those fish. They were gasping for oxygen, and the sellers who squatted nearby, smoking their cheroots, hardly possessed the caring demeanor of emergency doctors or hospice workers."It's horrible," she said at last. "It's worse than if they just killed them outright rather than justifying it as an act of kindness."

"No worse than what we do in other countries," Dwight said. ..."Saving people for their own good," he replied. "Invading countries, having them suffer collateral damage, as we call it. Killing them as an unfortunate consequence of helping them. You know, like Vietnam, Bosnia." "...The question is, who pays for the consequences? Saving fish from drowning. Same thing. Who's saved? Who's not?"

穿越中缅边境，汽车车窗外可以发现和在中国看到的一样美丽的花：黄色的雏菊、鲜红的芙蓉、像野草般生长蔓延的马樱丹。从一个国家到另一个国家，景色没有任何变化，至少在我的朋友们看来是这样。

但是事实上，和上百年未经开发的大自然一样，忽然之间，所有的一切变得更加浓密原始，湮没了现代的一切。这就是我穿越边境时的感受，恍若坐上赫伯特·乔治·威尔斯的时间机器，虽然拥有同样的意识，却扑通一声掉落到过去。和我的朋友们一样，我也觉得陈旧的东西叫人心醉，异域风情的香味、慵懒生活的画面让人兴奋。

出门的路上，他们经过一堆光泽灵动的鲤鱼，鱼嘴儿还一张一合。“我以为这是一个佛教国家，”海蒂说。“我以为他们不屠杀动物。”向右几步路的地方正在血淋淋地宰猪，海蒂瞥了一眼，就不愿意看下去了。

“屠夫和渔夫一般不是佛教徒。”（导游）沃尔特说。“但若是他们信佛，他们会很虔诚地捕鱼。他们捞鱼上岸，说是不让鱼被水淹死。不幸的是……，”他低头忏悔，“鱼断气了。”

海蒂说不出话来。这些人真的认为他们是在干一件好事？显然，他们并不想拯救任何生命，看看这些鱼，因为缺氧而大口喘气，这些鱼贩子却蹲坐在一旁，抽着大烟，没有表现出救护人员的丝毫关心。“太可怕了，”她终于开口说话了。“他们还不如直接杀死鱼，何必要假仁假义地说是去解救它们？”

“其实，我们美国在别的国家干的那些事儿也好不到哪去。”德怀特说。……“说是为了拯救别国人民，”他回复道，“去侵犯他们，让他们受难，名义上给予援助，结果是不幸让他们丧生，就像你们熟知的美越战争、波黑战争。”“……问题是，谁对后果负责？这和救出溺水鱼是一回事，救了谁？又害了谁？”

我们知道人会溺水，鱼却只能在水中存活，它们靠鳃呼吸水中的氧气，因为陆地干燥、鳃的粘连，鱼反倒无法在陆地上正常呼吸而窒息死亡。当地渔夫打捞鱼、兜售鱼，亵渎生命，还冠冕堂皇地偷换概念、振振有词：“救救溺水鱼。”作者借用几个美国游客的口，暗讽了强权文化对弱势文化的侵蚀。一个只能在水中生存的文化，却被强权文化以拯救的名义强行带到陆地，离开了它赖以生存的环境，痛苦挣扎，岌岌可危，奄奄一息，面临消亡。

这一行美国游客中的本尼（Bennie）为当地路边上的一位老妇人画了一张肖像画，老妇人笑面盈盈地替他扎了袋甘蓝泡菜。

What the hell. How much could it cost? He offered her a few bills, the equivalent of thirty cents, which was a fantastically huge sum for a bag of fermented turnips, but she looked insulted and firmly pushed his hand away. He finally came to understand: *Oh*, a gift. A gift! She gave a firm nod. He gave her a gift, and she was giving him a gift. Wow! He was overwhelmed. This was the true kindness of strangers. *This* was a *National Geographic* moment: two people, vastly different, separated by language and culture and a whole lot else, yet giving and giving back the best they had to offer, their own humanity, their cartoons, their pickles. He gratefully accepted the pink plastic bag with its soggy lump, this beautiful token of universal friendship. It was incredible, so warming to the heart. He would keep it forever...

天啦,这得值多少钱?他给了她几张钞票,相当于三十美分,对一袋甘蓝泡菜来说,开价很高了,可是她像是被羞辱了,断然推开了他的手。他最后才明白:"哦,一份回报的礼物。"对的,这是一份礼物。她用力点点头。他赠送她一张画像,她也回赠给他一份礼物。哇!他的心灵受到震撼。这是陌生人之间的以诚相待,这是《国家地理》杂志应该拍录下的瞬间:两个不同国度的人,语言不通,文化迥异,还有其他许多差异,但是仍然相互馈赠彼此最美好的东西,他们的博爱,他们的绘画,他们的咸菜。他感激地接过装有泡菜的粉色塑料袋,这是世界友谊的美好象征,这份礼物棒极了,情暖人心,他将永远珍藏它……

上述一段描述是多么美妙,多么和谐,多么神圣,让人不禁想用美国当代著名作家雷莫德·卡佛(Raymond Carver)的诗句来感叹:"水与另外一片水交汇的地方。那些地方像圣地一样,矗立在我的脑海中。……我可以数小时地坐在这儿望着这些河流。它们每一条都与众不同。"是啊,多元异质文化在交流融合时,因为相互欣赏、理解,才更显得彼此弥足珍贵;因为相互尊重、包容,才能共同繁荣、和合共生。

谭恩美的小说《救救溺水鱼》立意隽远,让人感悦意境之美;思睿观通,让人体味思想之美;情真意切,让人赞叹情感之美;字字珠玑,让人享受语言之美,它,是一道值得欣赏的美景。

《英格兰的乡村生活》片段选译及赏析

华盛顿·欧文(Washington Irving，1783～1859)，被世人誉为“美国短篇小说之父”“美国散文大师”，是美国文学奠基人之一。他文笔清新自然，感情细腻充沛，是美国早期浪漫主义文学的代表作家，其主要作品有《见闻札记》(*The Sketch Book*)、《旅客谈》(*Tales of a Traveler*)、《布雷斯布里奇田庄》(*Bracebridge Hall*)等。欧文一生曾三度赴欧，探寨问俗，访镇寻风，走遍英、法、德、西等国家，陆续发表了不少散文随笔、奇闻轶事，并汇集成《见闻札记》一书。此书既有散文的优美抒情，又有小说的曲折离奇，在英国一经出版，立刻引起轰动。《英格兰的乡村生活》(“Rural Life in England”)一文正是取自《见闻札记》。在这篇随笔中，作者将宁静恬淡的乡村生活与浮躁喧哗的城市生活做对比，描绘出一幅幅具有英格兰浓郁乡土气息的画面，让读者真切感受到英格兰乡村生活的独特与美好。

Those who see the Englishman only in town, are apt to form an unfavorable opinion of his social character. He is either absorbed in business, or distracted by the thousand engagements that dissipate time, thought, and feeling, in this huge metropolis. He has, therefore, too commonly, a look of hurry and abstraction. Wherever he happens to be, he is on the point of going somewhere else; at the moment he is talking on one subject, his mind is wandering to another; and while paying a friendly visit, he is calculating how he shall economize time so as to pay the other visits allotted to the morning. An immense metropolis, like London, is calculated to make men selfish and uninteresting. In their casual and transient meetings, they can but deal briefly in commonplaces. They present but the cold superfices of character—its rich and genial qualities have no time to be warmed into a flow.

It is in the country that the Englishman gives scope to his natural feelings. He breaks loose gladly from the cold formalities and negative civilities of town;

throws off his habits of shy reserve, and becomes joyous and free-hearted. He manages to collect round him all the conveniences and elegancies of polite life, and to banish its restraints. His country-seat abounds with every requisite, either for studious retirement, tasteful gratification, or rural exercise. Books, paintings, music, horses, dogs, and sporting implements of all kinds, are at hand. He puts no constraint, either upon his guests or himself, but, in the true spirit of hospitality, provides the means of enjoyment, and leaves every one to partake according to his inclination.

你若遇到仅仅身居在城里的英国人,就容易对他的社交性格产生成见。在大都市里,他要么忙于公事,要么耽于无数个耗费时间、思想、情感的约会。他因此常常行色匆匆,神情恍惚。他无论恰巧身在何处,都正准备赶赴别处;他谈论这个话题时,脑筋里寻思着又一个话题;他走亲访友时,心里盘算着如何省下时间,完成早晨安排好的其他拜访。像伦敦这样的大都市,注定让人自私无趣。人们在偶然短暂的会面中,往往只是简单地寒暄上几句。他们总表现出个性冷漠的外表,丰富多彩、和蔼可亲的情感热流根本没有余暇涌动起来。

只有在乡下,英国人才自然流露出情感。他乐于从都市冷漠的礼节和消沉的客套中挣脱出来,将拘谨保守的生活习惯抛之脑后,从而变得欢欣快乐,无忧无虑。他汲取文明生活中的各种便利和高雅,却摒弃其束缚和局限。他在乡间的住所应有尽有,或读书以怡情,怡情以自乐,或参加乡间体育运动。书籍、绘画、音乐、马、狗以及各种体育器具都唾手可得。他既不约束客人,也不拘束自己,真心实意,殷勤待客,做到让每一个人尽兴畅快。

通过上述两段细节描写,城市和乡村迥异的生活环境对英国人性格的不同影响表现得淋漓尽致。英国都市生活的快节奏和高压力雪藏了英国人的真实内心,让他们热情奔放的天性得不到释放,只有在广阔自由的英格兰乡间,英国人才重新焕发出活力,展现出人性中美好的一面。回归自然、欢快融洽的英格兰乡村生活让人无限向往。

Nothing can be more imposing than the magnificence of English park scenery. Vast lawns that extend like sheets of vivid green, with here and there clumps of gigantic trees, heaping up rich piles of foliage: the solemn pomp of groves and woodland glades, with the deer trooping in silent herds across them; the hare, bounding away to the covert; or the pheasant, suddenly bursting upon the wing; the brook, taught to wind in natural meanderings or expand into a glassy lake; the sequestered pool, reflecting the quivering trees, with the yellow leaf sleeping on its bosom, and the trout roaming fearlessly about its limpid waters; while some rustic temple or sylvan statue, grown green and dank with age, gives an air of classic sanctity to the seclusion.

It is a pleasing sight of a Sunday morning, when the bell is sending its sober melody across the quiet fields, to behold the peasantry in their best finery, with ruddy faces and modest cheerfulness, thronging tranquilly along the green lanes to church; but it is still more pleasing to see them in the evenings, gathering about their cottage doors, and appearing to exult in the humble comforts and embellishments which their own hands have spread around them.

没有什么比气势恢宏的英格兰田园风光更令人难忘了。一望无边的草坪像一块块铺展的鲜绿色地毯，其上四处丛生的参天大树，翠绿欲滴。小树林和林中空地庄严肃穆，鹿群结队默默地穿行其间；野兔蹦跳进林中深处；野鸡猛然拍打翅膀；小溪蜿蜒曲折，汇聚成一汪明净的湖水；僻静的池塘中，摇曳着树木的倒影，黄色的树叶在水面上打着盹儿，鲑鱼在清水里肆意游弋；某座乡村寺庙或神像，由于年代久远受潮而泛出绿色，为寂寥幽僻的环境增添了古雅圣洁的气氛。

礼拜日清晨，神圣的教堂钟声有节奏地在寂静田野上空响起，不绝于耳，农夫们衣着盛装，面色红润，恭谦虔诚，神清气爽，沿着一条条青葱小路，一群群安静地涌进教堂，此情此景，让人悦目赏心。每逢傍晚，农夫们聚集在村舍门口，看来是在为他们自己亲手装点的简朴舒适的生活环境陶醉不已，目睹此景，更叫人心旷神怡。

以上描写色彩鲜明，动静结合，采用了明喻(simile)、拟人(personification)、对比(contrast)、层进(climax)等多样修辞手法。在作家华盛顿·欧文的笔下，英格兰迷人的田园风景,恬静安逸不失活泼,肃穆庄重不失俏皮,森林、湖泊、村庄、野生动物、植被,无不浸润着纯真情感,孕育着淳朴道德。

英国前首相斯坦利·鲍德温爵士(Sir Stanley Baldwin)曾无限感叹:"对我来说,英格兰就是乡村,乡村才是英格兰。"在英国人看来,英格兰之魂在乡村,英格兰的乡村生活是画,是诗,是歌。美国作家华盛顿·欧文(Washington Irving)这篇作品尤其受到英国读者的喜爱。它之所以成为经久传诵的佳作,正是因为他用语言雕刻出英格兰乡村生活的特点,挖掘出英国人眼中的珍宝,道出了英国人内心深处的梦想。

心若幽兰，静如止水——歌曲《心如止水》翻译及赏析

老鹰乐队是美国乃至世界最杰出的摇滚乐队之一。虽然主唱唐·亨里(Don Henley)曾在当时的演唱会上笑称创作这首歌曲纯属偶得，他们仅仅在举办演唱会的前一个小时编排了它，但是它精致优美的曲调、蕴藉哲理的歌词却震撼影响了整整几代人。歌词"sheep without a shepherd"出自 *Bible Gateway Isaiah 13*（《以赛亚书》第13章），引用了羊羔迷途知返的圣经故事。词句"Learn to be still"充满了禅宗的味道：在纷繁复杂的大千世界里，需要在自己的心田里种上一株兰花，芳香流泽，气定神闲；"Learn to be still"，静如止水，静以养生，静而生慧。禅定静滤后，水中的泥沙才会沉淀，我们的心灵才会澄澈，我们的灵魂才能轻松上路。

心若幽兰，静如止水，短小精悍的词作表达出博大精深的智慧，这大概是老鹰乐队的"Learn to Be Still"经久传唱、百听不厌的秘方。

Learn to Be Still

It's just another day in paradise.
As you stumble to your bed,
You'd give anything to silence.
Those voices ringing in your head:
You thought you could find happiness
Just over that green hill;
You thought you would be satisfied,
But you never will —
Learn to be still.

We are like sheep without a shepherd.
We don't know how to be alone,
So we wander 'round this desert,

And wind up following the wrong gods home.
But the flock cries out for another,
And they keep answering that bell.
And one more starry-eyed Messiah
Meets a violent farewell —
Learn to be still,
Learn to be still.

Now the flowers in your garden,
They don't smell so sweet.
Maybe you've forgotten,
The heaven lying at your feet.
Learn to be still,
Learn to be still.
You just keep on runnin', keep on runnin'.

心如止水

又一个阴霾的日子，
你跌跌撞撞地躺上床，
一切纷扰归于沉寂。
这样的声音在脑海里回响：
你以为你能找到幸福，
就在青山绿意的世外桃源；
你以为你会心满意足，
但你从来不会——
心如止水。

我们像没有牧人的羊，
我们不知道如何独处，
我们在荒漠里游荡，
误入迷途。

羊群相互召唤，
不断回应铃响。
它们与救主弥赛亚
渐行渐远——
心如止水，
心如止水。

心灵花园里的百花，
不再吐露芬芳。
或许你已经遗忘，
天堂就在你脚下。
心如止水
心如止水
你只要不停奔跑，不停奔跑。

赏析

钢筋水泥浇注的城市沙漠里，绿意葱茏的人类精神家园日渐荒芜。灰白的天际，一抹夕阳如偾张的血脉，细细缕缕铺散开来，淌着血色，渐渐弥漫了半边天。绀金色的日头恍若一大块沉甸甸金色圆币，悬在天边，不堪重负，一点点坠落了。我们在繁华都市汹涌的车潮、攒动的人潮中微颤地挣扎着，踉踉跄跄地想摆脱被淹没的命运。如同迷途的羔羊，我们何去何从，我们忧心忡忡。

悠扬明快的节奏、浑厚激昂的嗓音，当老鹰乐队(Eagles)演唱的这首经典再次在我们耳畔响起，敲打我们的心房时，我们哼唱浅吟，细细品味，沉醉其中。乐队主唱唐·亨里(Don Henley)犹如慈父长兄般的谆谆教导："Learn to be still(心如止水)。"我们浮躁不安的心开始渐趋平静，丝丝暖意融入，须臾间，花蕾吐蕊、嫩苗破土，我们身体每一处细胞得到扩张放松。我们重获能量、重拾信心，在人生道路上继续努力向美好的未来奔跑。我们不禁感慨，触碰灵魂深处的经典作品，历尽岁月洗礼而弥足珍贵，它是指引人们前行的福音，是拯救世人的先知弥赛亚。

在撒哈拉游泳

The world's largest desert was once a green Eden. One day it will be again.

The Sahara, which covers nearly a third of Africa, was once a lush savanna, teeming with wildlife, fish-filled lakes, and ancient humans. "Between 10,500 and around 5,550 years ago, it was a good place to live," says Stefan Kröpelin, a geoarchaeologist at the University of Cologne in Germany, who has spent the last 30 years leading excavations in the eastern Sahara, a region that until recently has been largely unexplored.

Kröpelin and his colleague Rudolph Kuper have unearthed hundreds of geologic samples and more than 500 archaeological artifacts—everything from animal bones to cave art—at over 100 sites. From these findings, the researchers are piecing together a grand story linking climate change and cultural evolution. For five millennia, says Kröpelin, humans thrived in the Sahara, fishing, herding cattle, and making pottery and art—hallmarks of the Neolithic lifestyle that supplanted hunting and gathering. When rain started to become scarce around 5, 500 years ago, they migrated east to the Nile Valley. "It's no coincidence that this major climate shift coincides with the rise of the early Egyptian empires," Kröpelin says."Only when the Sahara became a desert again did the emergence of the early Egyptian civilization occur."

Although the Sahara has been bone-dry for most of its history, it undergoes an approximately 5,000-year humid period every 100,000 years as a result of variations in Earth's tilt and the shape of its orbit that change the way sunlight hits the planet. When that happens, it takes only a few centuries for the desert to become savanna, says Kröpelin. Global warming could make the next wet spell happen sooner than we think. "Since 1988 we have found evidence of increasing vegetation and rainfall," he says. "If we have five to six degrees of warming in the next centuries, evaporation on the oceans may turn the Sahara into a savanna, as it was 10,000 years ago."

撒哈拉,这个世界上最大的沙漠曾是绿色的伊甸园,将来的某天它会恢复原貌。

撒哈拉沙漠占据了非洲大陆将近 1/3 的面积,曾经是丰腴的热带大草原,这里野生动植物繁多,湖水充沛、渔产丰富,是众多远古人类定居之处。"距今约5 550年至1.05 万年以前,撒哈拉是一个适宜居住的地方。"德国科隆大学的地质考古学家斯蒂凡·克路佩林说。他花费了过去 30 年的时间率先开展了撒哈拉东部地区的发掘工作,迄今为止这一地区大部分还未被勘查。

克路佩林和他的同事鲁道夫·库珀在 100 多处地方挖掘出数以百计的地质标本和 500 多件考古学上的手工制品——从动物骨骼到洞穴壁画等各式各样的考古发现。从这些发现中,研究者正在拼合一部连接气候变化和文化发展的恢宏的故事。克路佩林说,人类在撒哈拉沙漠繁衍生息了 5 000 年,捕鱼、放牧、制作陶器和艺术品——这些具有新石器时代特点的生活方式取代了狩猎和采集。大约 5500 年前,雨水开始变得稀少,人们向东迁徙到了尼罗河谷。"这种巨大的气候变化和早期埃及帝国的崛起同时发生,这绝不是巧合。"克路佩林说,"只有撒哈拉地区再次成了沙漠,早期埃及文明才得以出现。"

虽然在历史上大部分时间里撒哈拉是极其干燥的,但是每 10 万年它就会经历一个大约 5 000 年的湿润期,这是由地球倾斜角度和运转轨道形状的变化改变了太阳光照射地球的方式造成的。克路佩林说,当这种变化发生时,只需要几个世纪的时间,沙漠就会变成热带大草原。全球气候变暖可能会使下一个湿润期来得比我们预想的要早。"自 1988 年以来,我们就发现了植被和降雨量增多的迹象。"他说,"在下几个世纪里,如果地球有 5 至 6 度的升温,海洋蒸发的水就可以让撒哈拉沙漠变成热带大草原,就像它 1 万年前那样。"

信箱里的便笺

The note I picked up from my mailbox at school read, "Call Margaret at 555-6167." Both the name and number were unfamiliar to me, but as a high-school automotive instructor, I got calls all the time from people who were looking for someone to fix their cars. During my lunchtime at school that day, I dialed the number.

"I'm calling for a Margaret," I said.

"Yes, this is Margaret," a voice answered.

"This is Ron Wenn. I have a message here that says to call you," I continued, all the while wondering what kind of car trouble this woman had.

"Oh, I'm glad you called. If you'll just give me a few minutes of your time, I have something to tell you that I think you'll be interested in hearing."

"All right," I answered looking at the clock. I only had a few minutes before I needed to be back in class.

"I'm a nurse at St. Luke's Presbyterian Hospital, and yesterday on my way home from work I was driving down Road 290 when my car started acting up."

"Uh huh." I said looking at the clock again.

"It was late at night, and I was alone. I was so afraid to pull over, but finally my car just quit, so I coasted to the shoulder. I sat there for a few minutes wondering what to do."

I didn't want to sound impatient, but I really needed to get back to class. "Would you like me to take a look at your car, ma'am?" I asked.

"Just let me finish," the woman answered.

I tapped my pencil on the stack of papers in front of me as Margaret continued her story. "Suddenly, two young guys, about twenty years old, pulled up behind me and got out. I didn't know what these guys were going to do. I was so scared."

"They asked me what happened, and they said that from the sound of things that they might be able to get the car running again, so I popped the hood. I sat in the car praying that these guys weren't up to no good. A few minutes later, they yelled at me to try to start the car. I couldn't believe it! It started right up! The guys slammed the hood and told me the car would be fine but that I should take it somewhere soon and get it checked out."

"And you'd like me to take a look at it and make sure everything's okay, right?" I asked.

"No, not at all, just listen," the woman went on. "I was so grateful. I thanked them over and over and offered them money, but they wouldn't take it. That's then they told me they were former students of yours."

"What?" I asked in surprise. "Students of mine? Who were they?"

"They wouldn't tell me. They just gave me your name and the school's number and made me promise to call to thank you."

I couldn't believe it. I didn't know what to say. Besides teaching my students about fixing cars, I always tried to teach them things about life—about going the extra mile, being honest and using what you know to help other people. The thing is I never really knew if the students learned any of this.

"Mr. Wenn, are you still there?" Margaret asked.

"I'm still here," I answered.

"Well, I hope you know how grateful I am," Margaret said.

"I hope you know how grateful I am to you, Margaret. Thanks for calling," I said and hung up the phone.

I walked back to class feeling inspired with the knowledge that my students had helped someone because of what I taught them in my classroom. I had just gotten the greatest reward a teacher could ever get.

我从学校信箱里取出的便笺上写着:"请给玛格丽特打电话,号码是555-6167。"这个名字和电话号码我都不熟悉,但作为中学的汽车教员,我总是接到人们找人修理汽车的电话。那天在学校吃午饭的时候,我拨通了这个电话。

"我找玛格丽特。"我说。

"是的,我是玛格丽特。"一个声音回答道。

"我是罗恩·文。有人给我留言让我给您打电话。"我继续说,心里则一直在猜测这位女士的汽车遇到了什么麻烦。

"哦,我很高兴您能打电话。如果您给我几分钟,我会告诉您一些我认为您会感兴趣的事。"

"好吧!"我一边回答一边看了看时钟。还有几分钟我就得回班里授课了。

"我是圣·卢克长老会医院的护士,昨天下班回家沿着290公路驾驶时,我的汽车出了毛病。"

"嗯,啊。"我说着又看了看时钟。

"天已经很晚了,我独自一人。我非常害怕把车停到路边。但最后车还是不动了,我把车滑行到路肩(编者注:高速公路两边比正常行车道略窄的紧急停车道),在那里坐了一会儿,不知道如何是好。"

我不想让她听出我的不耐烦,但我确实要回去上课了。"我可以检查一下您的车吗,女士?"我问道。

"请让我说完。"女士答道。

我用铅笔轻轻敲了敲放在面前的一摞考卷,玛格丽特则继续讲述她的故事:"突然,两个二十来岁的小伙子出现了,他们将车停在了我后面,下了车。我不清楚他们要干什么。我害怕极了。"

"他们询问了我的情况,并说从汽车的声音来判断,他们也许能重新启动汽车,于是我掀开了引擎盖。我坐在车里祈祷这两个小伙子别不怀好意。几分钟后,他们招呼我试着发动汽车。我真不敢相信!汽车立即启动了!小伙子们关上引擎盖,告诉我汽车没事,但应该尽快找地方做一次检修。"

"所以您想让我检查一下您的车以确保车没有问题,对吗?"我问。

"不,不是这么回事,您接着听我说,"女士继续说道,"我非常感激,向他们不停道谢,要给他们报酬但他们不接受,就是那时他们告诉我,他们是您从前教过的学生。"

"什么?"我诧异地问。"我的学生?他们叫什么名字?"

"他们不肯告诉我,只给我留下您的姓名和学校电话,并且让我承诺会打电话给您道谢。”

我无法相信所发生的一切，我不知道说什么才好。除了教会学生修车，我也总是试图教给他们生活的道理——例如比别人多努力一点，要诚实，以及用所学的知识帮助他人。我实际上从不知道学生是否会把这些牢记在心。

“文先生，您还在听吗？”玛格丽特问。

“我在听。”我回答。

“喔，我希望您知道我是多么感谢您。”玛格丽特说。

“我也非常感谢您，玛格丽特。谢谢您给我打电话。”说完，我便挂上了电话。

返回教室时，我备受鼓舞，因为知道了我的学生由于我在课堂上对他们的教育而帮助了别人。我刚刚收获了一名教师所能获得的最大回报。

诗 歌 篇

《晚安》翻译及赏析

Good Night

By Seamus Heaney

A latch lifting, an edged cave of light
Opens across the yard. Out of the low door
They stoop in to the honeyed corridor,
Then walk straight through the wall of the dark.
A puddle, cobble-stones, jambs and doorstep
Are set steady in a block of brightness
Till she strides in again beyond her shadows
And cancels everything behind her.

门闩拉开,从窑洞壁透出的灯光
照向小院。走出低矮的屋门,
他们弯身迈进甜蜜的走廊,
径直穿过黑夜的围墙。
池塘、卵石、门柱、台阶,
都被定格身后的全部一笔勾销。
在那抹光亮之下。
直到她又大步迈出自己的影子,
身后的全部一笔勾销。

赏析

爱尔兰诗人谢默斯·希尼(Seamus Heaney),1995年诺贝尔文学奖获得者,其作品被誉为"有种抒情美感和伦理深度,歌颂了日常生活中的奇迹和鲜活的往事(his works of lyrical beauty and ethical depth, which exalt everyday miracles and the living past)"。《晚安》("Good Night")描写了在静谧恬淡的夜晚背景下发生的一个不平静故事:一对恋人勇敢地做出重要决定,冲出黑色夜幕,她挣脱一切桎梏羁绊,与他相伴踏上幸福光明之路。夜之深,情之浓,标题"Good Night"《晚安》表达了诗人"有情人终成眷属"最美好的祝愿,他运用比拟(light **opens** across the yard)、移就(the **honeyed** corridor)、暗喻(the wall **of** the dark)等修辞手法营造了诗歌新奇而鲜活的意象,具有强烈的艺术感染力。

《金色之歌》翻译及赏析

Theme in Yellow

By Carl Sandburg

I spot the hills
With yellow balls in autumn.
I light the prairie cornfields
Orange and tawny gold clusters
And I am called pumpkins.

On the last of October
When dusk is fallen
Children join hands
And circle round me
Singing ghost songs
And love to the harvest moon;
I am a jack-o'-lantern
With terrible teeth
And the children know
I am fooling.

金秋时节
我用金色瓜球
点缀座座山岗。
团团簇结
我用橘黄金粉
点亮玉米田野

我就叫南瓜。

十月即逝
暮色笼上
孩童把手牵
绕我组个圈
向秋月唱鬼歌
对满月表爱意；
我是南瓜灯
獠牙面狰狞
孩童都知晓
我在吓唬人。

赏析

每年10月31日的万圣节(Halloween)前夜，是西方国家的传统节日。时值金秋十月，万物丰收之季，圆圆胖胖的金黄色南瓜更为人们所喜爱。人们将南瓜去瓤，雕刻五官，放入蜡烛，南瓜灯("jack-o'-lantern")就成为万圣节最应景的道具之一，传说人们用南瓜雕刻成鬼脸灯笼是为了在万圣节前夜吓走游魂。事实上它更是孩子们欢闹的日子：点南瓜灯，吃南瓜饼，唱节日歌，扮鬼怪，讨糖果，赏明月。十月，人们沉浸在秋收的喜悦之中，四处洋溢着欢声笑语。美国芝加哥派诗人卡尔·桑德堡(Carl Sandburg)(1878～1967)的这首《金色之歌》朴实自然，用字凝练，以拟人(personification)手法让南瓜自述它的生长地点、收获季节和节日用途，生动形象，活泼俏皮。

《雨日》翻译及赏析

亨利·沃兹沃思·朗费罗(Henry Wadsworth Longfellow, 1807～1882),美国历史上最伟大的诗人之一,深受19世纪欧美读者的欢迎。他一生写下了大量音韵优美的抒情诗,例如:《人生礼赞》("A Psalm of Life")、《夜的赞歌》("Voice of the Night")等,这些诗深受儿童和一些成年人的喜爱仰慕。人们将他的半身像安放在英国威斯敏斯特教堂的诗人角,他是第一位获此殊荣的美国作家。

The Rainy Day

By Henry Wadsworth Longfellow

The day is cold, and dark, and dreary;
It rains, and the wind is never weary;
The vine still clings to the moldering wall,
But at every gust the dead leaves fall,
And the day is dark and dreary.

My life is cold, and dark, and dreary;
It rains, and the wind is never weary;
My thoughts still cling to the moldering past,
But the hopes of youth fall thick in the blast,
And the days are dark and dreary.

Be still, sad heart! and cease repining;
Behind the clouds is the sun still shining;
Thy fate is the common fate of all,
Into each life some rain must fall,
Some days must be dark and dreary.

雨 日

天寒冷，暗淡，闷沉，
雨霏霏，狂风不停。
墙颓圮，犹绕缠藤，
骤风起，残叶飘零，
真是天暗闷沉沉。

我生活，冷晦，郁沉，
雨霏霏，狂风不停。
过往事，结愁留恨，
烈风吹散少年梦，
真是天暗闷沉沉。

平静吧，忧伤的心，
停止吧，抱怨愁绪！
阳光总在乌云后，
他人与你亦同命，
会逢日暗和雨淋。

赏析

原诗共三节，每节五行，层层叠进，一咏三叹，从开始描写萧败凋零的雨景再到隐喻颓败凄冷的人生，最后画龙点睛句“cease repining; the sun still shining”使全诗意境升华到催人奋进的高潮；写景寓情，借景寓理，用“the day”的阴冷沉闷来隐喻“my life”，用“the vine”的攀附纠缠来隐喻“my thoughts”，用“the moldering wall”的残败破损来隐喻“the moldering past”，用“the dead leaves”的零落纷坠来隐喻“the hopes of youth”，“Behind the clouds is the sun still shining”则表明困境中要坚信美好事物存在的道理，意象鲜明，寓意深刻；诗歌每节尾行和前两节首尾行重叠复沓词语“day”“dark”“dreary”，加强了咏叹的情味，突显了风雨肆虐之恶，“我”内心郁结之深；诗歌后两节结构安排新颖独到，“my”和“thy”抒情角度的变化，借助对话形式引出劝勉之词，流露的不再是个人患得患失的狭隘意识和自我哀叹的戚戚之心，而是豁达开朗和乐观向上的积极人生态度，全诗就此升华到一个新的思想高度。

它格律严正，音韵谐美，朗朗上口：抑扬格（Iambic）和抑抑扬格（Anapaest）的变换使用（如 The ˊday/ is ˊcold, /and ˊdark,/ and ˊdreary; It ˊrains, /and the ˊwind/ is ˊne/ver ˊweary）既增强了诗歌顿挫的节奏感，也与全诗先抑后扬的艺术手法相呼应；头韵/d/（The **d**ay is cold, and **d**ark, and **d**reary）好似冷雨的啪嗒声、/w/（...the **w**ind is never **w**eary）宛若凄风的呜咽声、/s/（Be **s**till, **s**ad heart! and **c**ease repining; ...the **s**un **s**till **sh**ining）和尾韵 a a b b a、a a c c a、d d b b a 的巧妙运用赋予全诗以音乐的和谐声调。

原英文诗歌“哀而不伤”的情感美与“铿锵有韵”的音乐美，让人不禁联想到中国韵律诗歌的美。东方神韵的美学讲究“理智节制情感”，用字工整对称，诗韵与内容情绪合一。试将英诗“The Rainy Day”依照宋词牌《雨霖铃》翻译如下：

雨霖铃

寒天阴郁，雨潇风瑟，未倦吹舞。缠藤断壁犹抱，枯叶落、狂风飘处。吾命偏逢晦日，亦寒惨悲苦。雨簌簌、风啸无歇，往事萦牵断肠肚。

疾风扫卷门前路，少年心、破碎飘如絮！流年翳闷何奈？毋自悔、静心平蹙。雨霁云开，应是阳光灿烂如故。莫己怨、凄雨阴天，注定人人遇。

《雪花》翻译及赏析

Snowflakes

By Henny Wadsworth Longfellow

Out of the bosom of the air,
Out of the cloud-folds of her garments shaken,
Over the woodlands brown and bare,
Over the harvest-fields forsaken,
Silent, and soft, and slow
Descends the snow.

Even as our cloudy fancies take
Suddenly shape in some divine expression,
Even as the troubled heart doth make
In the white countenance confession,
The troubled sky reveals
The grief it feels.

This is the poem of the air,
Slowly in silent syllables recorded;
This is the secret of despair,
Long in its cloudy bosom hoarded,
Now whispered and revealed
To wood and field.

飘落自天空的胸膛,
抖落自她的云裳,

在褐色光秃的林地，
和荒弃的丰田上徜徉，
静静地，柔柔地，缓缓地
雪花，飞扬！

恰如我们云似缥渺的玄想
蓦然寻到绝好的表述，
恰如心中的痛苦惆怅
凝结在苍白的脸上，
阴郁的苍天袒露
内心，感伤！

这是天空的诗篇
慢慢谱成静默的节拍；
这是失望的秘密，
长久堆积在它云层胸间，
此刻被悄声诉说给
树林、田庄！

赏析

《雪花》这首诗句法严格正统，语言简洁朴实，意境情景交融，字里行间展现出冬天雪景静穆之奇特美。虽然昏黑的天空郁积着作者内心的愁苦和哀怨，但是白色的雪花如同上天派来的使者带走他的落寞和感伤。全诗韵律齐整，既有头韵(alliteration)和尾韵(rhyme)，读来纡徐从容、委婉顿挫、朗朗上口，又巧妙运用暗喻(metaphor)、拟人(personification)和移就(transferred epithet)等修辞，生动形象，极富表现力和感染力。

《孩子们》翻译及赏析

Children

By Henny Wadsworth Longfellow

Come to me, O ye children!
For I hear you at your play,
And the questions that perplexed me
Have vanished quite away.

Ye open the eastern windows,
That look towards the sun,
Where thoughts are singing swallows
And the brooks of morning run.

In your hearts are the birds and the sunshine,
In your thoughts the brooklet's flow,
But in mine is the wind of Autumn
And the first fall of the snow.

Ah! what would the world be to us
If the children were no more?
We should dread the desert behind us
Worse than the dark before.

What the leaves are to the forest,
With light and air for food,
Ere their sweet and tender juices

Have been hardened into wood, —

That to the world are children;
Through them it feels the glow
Of a brighter and sunnier climate
Than reaches the trunks below.

Come to me, O ye children!
And whisper in my ear
What the birds and the winds are singing
In your sunny atmosphere.

For what are all our contrivings,
And the wisdom of our books,
When compared with your caresses,
And the gladness of your looks?

Ye are better than all the ballads
That ever were sung or said;
For ye are living poems,
And all the rest are dead.

来我这里,啊,孩子们!
你们的嬉闹声,
让困惑我的烦闷
冰释涣然。

是你们敞开东窗,
面朝太阳,
那里活跃的思绪,如飞燕吟唱,

晨溪潺潺。

你们心中有飞鸟、灿阳，
你们遐思里有溪水涓涓，
而我的内心却是秋风扫卷，
初雪飘荡。

啊，没有你们，
世界将会怎样？
我们将为眼前的黑暗，更为身后的荒原
忧心如焚。

如森林之树叶片片，
啜灵气而咀华光，
直到它们甘甜柔滑的浆汁凝变
硬木坚桩，——

世界有了孩子们，
才感受到树干之上
天光日照格外熠熠闪亮，
明朗晴暖。

来我这里，啊，孩子们！
在我耳旁呢喃，
你们明媚的气息，让鸟儿欢唱，
风儿荡漾。

我们所有的谋划伎俩，
我们书本的智慧思想，
在你们爱抚笑颜的映衬下，

黯淡无光。

你们胜过一切歌谣颂唱，
因为那些已枯竭消亡；
而你们谱写的诗篇，
生机盎然。

赏析

《孩子们》这首诗大量使用明喻（simile）、暗喻（metaphor）和对比（contrast）等修辞，真切流露出对孩童的喜爱和赞美。纯朴天真、活泼烂漫的孩子们如灿阳飞鸟，似晨溪绿叶，胜过一切歌谣，让愚昧虚伪、守旧固化的成人自惭形秽，英国浪漫主义诗人华兹华斯也曾一语道破："儿童乃成人之父。"无欲无忧、朝气蓬勃的孩子们才是智慧之源泉，道德之滥觞，未来之希望，带给世界以光明和温暖。中国先秦时期的哲学典籍《道德经》早有教诲："为天下溪，常德不离，复归于婴儿"，"含德之厚，比于赤子"。诗中主题句"Come to me, O ye children!"在在修辞上的反复，正是诗人朗费罗对回归童真的追寻和召唤，实际上反映了诗人自己质朴高洁的赤子之心。

汉译英

《人间词话》译本(节选)

一

词以境界为最上;有境界则自成高格,自有名句。五代、北宋之词所以独绝者在此。

1. *Jing-jie*(境界;pinyin: jìng jiè), the image world of the *ci* poetry(词; pinyin: cí) is of primary importance. The *ci* poetry, which reflects *jing-jie*, the image world, naturally presents souls of lofty worth and lines of mighty truth. That is why *ci* poetry of the Five Dynasties(五代 AD 907～960;pinyin: wǔ dài) and Northern Song periods(北宋 AD 960～1127;pinyin: běi sòng) are uniquely excellent.

赏析:在王国维看来,有境界的词才是上乘的词。境界,是从叔本华美学借鉴过来的一个概念,可以理解为情与景交融所形成、所开拓的意识空间。这种艺术文字在表现形象上,靠五官捕捉、心灵感应获得的有类似画面、音乐、建筑、雕塑等的美感;在思想内涵上,有立意的高度、深度、宽度和广度,"能写真景物、真感情"。

二

有造境,有写境,此理想与写实二派之所由分。

然二者颇难分别。因大诗人所造之境,必合乎自然,所写之境,亦必邻于理想故也。

2. *Jing-jie*, the image world, either created(造境;pinyin: zào jìng) or described(写境;pinyin: xiě jìng), hereby divides the *ci* poetry between the idealism(理想派;pinyin: lǐxiǎng pài) and the realism(写实派;pinyin: xiě shí pài). However, it is hard to tell the two because *jing-jie*, the image world, created by a great poet, is always loyal to nature, while the one described is always close to the ideal.

赏析:造境与写境,即理想与写实二派之别,好似画画,造境如浪漫派画,写境如写实派画。造境是理想派，则脱胎于自然（现实），我手写我想，我笔勾我意，寥寥几笔，就架构了一个丰富的艺术世界；写境是写实派，临摹自然（现实），表达理想抱负。理想，是源自柏拉图的一个美学概念，正如最完美的正圆，仅仅存在于我们心中，在现实世界里只有它不完美的摹本。

三

有有我之境，有无我之境。

"泪眼问花花不语，乱红飞过秋千去"，

"可堪孤馆闭春寒，杜鹃声里斜阳暮"，有我之境也。

"采菊东篱下，悠然见南山"，

"寒波澹澹起，白鸟悠悠下"，无我之境也。

有我之境，以我观物，故物皆着我之色彩。

无我之境，以物观物，故不知何者为我，何者为物。

古人为词，写有我之境者为多，然未始不能写无我之境，此在豪杰之士能自树立耳。

3. There is *jing-jie*, the image world, with the self (有我之境；pinyin：yǒu wǒ zhī jìng) and in itself (无我之境；pinyin：wú wǒ zhī jìng).

Jing-jie, the image world, with the self, is illustrated in such classical poetic lines as:

"Flowers have no response to my inquiry with tearful eyes; red petals have wings over the swing in a mess";

"How can I bear the loneliness of the inn shut in the chilly spring, and the loudness of the cuckoos crying in the setting sun".

Jing-jie, the image world, in itself, is illustrated in such classical poetic lines as:

"While picking chrysanthemums by the eastern fence, catch sight of the southern mountain at ease";

"Gently and gently, have the cold waves risen; leisurely and leisurely, are the white birds fluttering down".

In *jing-jie*, the image world with the self, an object is viewed from "my" perspective and is hereby colored with "my" feelings; in *jing-jie*, the image world in itself, an object is viewed from the perspective of other objects and hence it is hard to tell "I" from "the object".

Most *ci* poets describe *jing-jie*, the image world with the self, yet only those who are geniuses could establish *jing-jie*, the image world in itself.

赏析："有我之境"与"无我之境"可以将词分为"主观词"与"客观词"，前者融入写词人自我的主观感情色彩和意欲，以己喜或悲；后者则摆脱写词人自我的意欲，不以己喜，不以物悲，物我同化。王国维的词评受到康德、叔本华哲学、美学观点的影响。康德认为只有天才可以感悟体验到"物自体"的客观世界；叔本华认为只有从受欲望驱动的世俗羁绊中超脱，才具有客观理性的审美。因此，王国维认为很多词人能够表现"有我之境"，但从"有我之境"到"无我之境"，只有豪杰之士，即"天才"能做到。

四

无我之境，人唯于静中得之。有我之境，于由动之静时得之。故一优美，一宏壮也。

4. *Jing-jie*, the image world in itself, is attained only in tranquility, whereas *jing-jie*, the image world with the self, is attained by repose after action. Therefore, the former is beauty（优美；pinyin：yōu měi）; the latter, sublimity（宏壮；pinyin：hóng zhuàng）.

赏析：静有静的优美，是自我与外物水乳交融时保持的和谐之美，如庄子化蝶；而动有动的气势，由动转静，是自我对外物进行抗争时产生的悲壮之美，如望帝化鹃。

五

自然中之物，互相关系，互相限制。然其写之于文学及美术中也，必遗其关系限制之处。故虽写实家亦理想家也。又虽如何虚构之境，其材料必求之于自然，而其构造亦必从自然之法律。故虽理想家亦写实家也。

5. On the one hand, objects in nature are mutually related and restricted to one another; nevertheless, while described in literary and art works, they must

be free from the relations and restrictions. Thus, a realist is also an idealist. On the other hand, albeit it is a fictional world, its materials must be acquired from nature and its structure must follow the law of nature. Thus, an idealist is also a realist.

赏析：写实家写实，理想家虚构，但写实家亦是理想家，理想家亦是写实家，真境逼而神境生，理想的独特气质，往往是脱胎于现实，意念瞬间闪现而凝聚的美。

六

境非独谓景物也，喜怒哀乐，亦人心中之一境界。故能写真景物，真感情者，谓之有境界。否则谓之无境界。

6. *Jing-jie*, the image world is not made up of merely outer scenes and objects, but also of happy, angry, gloomy or merry inner mind. Therefore, poems which can depict genuine scenes and sentiments, may be said to mirror it, otherwise they fail to do so.

赏析：正如 19 世纪早期英国诗人济慈在《希腊古瓮颂》里所说，"Beauty is truth, truth beauty.（美即真，真即美。）"王国维也认为只有写真景物、真感情的词作，才能沁人心脾豁人耳目，成为大家之作。

七

"红杏枝头春意闹"，著一"闹"字而境界全出。"云破月来花弄影"，著一"弄"字而境界全出矣。

7. "The spring bustles with red apricot blossoms". With the choice of the word "bustle"（闹；pinyin：nào）, between the lines wholly emerges *jing-jie*, the image world; likewise, "the clouds tear the moon open and the flowers play with their shadows". With the choice of the word "play"（弄；pinyin：nòng）, between the lines also emerges *jing-jie*, the whole image world.

赏析：王国维欣赏词句中的"闹""弄"字，一用联觉（synaesthesia），视觉里获得听觉的感受，一用拟人（personification），植物被赋予人的动作和感情，词人将"红杏枝头""月下花影"这些本来无声、静态的画面，活灵活现地写出了有声、动态的境界。

八

境界有大小，不以是而分优劣。“细雨鱼儿出，微风燕子斜”，何遽不若“落日照大旗，马鸣风萧萧”？“宝帘闲挂小银钩”，何遽不若“雾失楼台，月迷津渡”也？

8. The excellence of a poem does not consist in whether *jing-jie*, the image world, is big or small. Isn't the poetic line "**Little** fish jump up in the drizzle; swallows fly down in the breeze" comparable with the line "The setting sun shines the **mighty** standard; the neighing horse echoes the rustling wind"? Likewise, isn't the line "On the pearled curtain loosely hang **tiny** silver hooks" comparable with the line "The pavilion dissolves in the mist; the ferry crossing gets lost in the moonlight"?

赏析：微小的境界“细雨微风”与宏大的境界“落日马鸣”形成对比，明朗的境界“宝帘银钩”与朦胧的境界“雾失月迷”形成对比，小境界与大境界，阴柔与阳刚，各有千秋，各呈其美。

九

严沧浪《诗话》谓：“盛唐诸公唯在兴趣，羚羊挂角，无迹可求。故其妙处，透彻玲珑，不可凑拍，如空中之音，相中之色，水中之影，镜中之像，言有尽而意无穷。”余谓北宋以前之词亦复如是。然沧浪所谓兴趣，阮亭所谓神韵，犹不过道其面目。不若鄙人拈出“境界”二字为探其本也。

9. Yan Canglang said in his *Canglang's Remarks on Poetry* (《沧浪诗话》; pinyin: cāng làng shī huà), "The poets in the glorious age of the Tang Dynasty (盛唐, AD 713～739; pinyin: shèng táng) attach great importance to inspiration and interest in composing poems. Their poetry is of superlative poetic art, like the antelope hanging its horns on the tree, leaving no trace on the ground. Therefore, the delicacy of those poems lies in their ethereality and spirituality, like sounds in the space, colors in the face, shadows in the water, reflections in the mirror, no more or no less. There's an end to poetic words, but not to their message". In my opinion, it is the same with the *ci* poetry before the Northern Song Dynasty. However, the concepts of "*xing-qu*" (inspired interest, 兴趣;

pinyin：xìng qù) proposed by Yan Canglang and "*shen-yun*" (charming spirit, 神韵；pinyin：shén yùn) by Wang Ruanting, which describe the surface of poetry, are not so good as my humble probe into its essence with the choice of two words："*jing-jie*" (the image world,境界；pinyin：jìng jiè).

赏析：王国维词话研究的"境界说"是对严沧浪(严羽，约 1192～1245)诗话研究的"兴趣说"和王阮亭(王士禛，1634～1711)"神韵说"的继承与发展。"兴趣说"是诗人进行创作之前的动机，"神韵说"是诗人寄予作品之外的感受，两者只是从诗人的主观悟性进行探讨，而"境界说"则探究诗之本体，反映喜、怒、哀、乐等主观心境与日、月、山、川等客观物境的交融相感。

十

太白纯以气象胜。"西风残照，汉家陵阙"，寥寥八字，遂关千古登临之口。后世唯范文正之《渔家傲》，夏英公之《喜迁莺》，差足继武，然气象已不逮矣。

10. Li Bai is a Tang poet of superb talent of *qi-xiang* (imagery,气象；pinyin：qì xiàng). His poetic line "West wind, evening glow, over mausoleums of Han", with only a few words of these eight, seals all the other lines uttered by height climbers of centuries. Only Fan Wenzheng's *ci* to the tune of "Yu Jia Ao" ("The Fisherman's Pride",《渔家傲》；pinyin：yú jiā ào) and Xia Yinggong's *ci* to the tune of "Xi Qian Ying" ("The Happily Migrant Oriole",《喜迁莺》；pinyin：xǐ qiān yīng) barely follow in footsteps of Li's, but they still have deficiency in poetic imagery.

赏析：气象是文学作品所特有的意象风貌。正如萧伯纳所说，"意之所到，风格随之"，好的文学作品要善于孕育意象，激发美感，形成独有的风格，李白诗歌所创造的雄浑壮阔的气象，后世的文人很难企及。范文正(范仲淹，989～1052)的《渔家傲·秋思》和夏英公(夏竦，985～1051)的《喜迁莺·霞散绮》的词句勉强与之比肩。

十一

张皋文谓飞卿之词"深美闳约"，余谓此四字唯冯正中足以当之。刘融斋谓飞卿"精艳绝人"，差近之耳。

11. Zhang Gaowen makes a remark that Wen Feiqing's *ci* poems are "broad and profound, delicate and succinct". From my perspective, only Feng Zhengzhong's *ci* poems better deserve the remark. Liu Rongzhai's comment that Wen Feiqing's *ci* poems are "exquisite and excellent" comes closer to the truth.

赏析：温飞卿(温庭筠,818～870)和冯正中(冯延巳,903～960)都是婉约派的代表人物,王国维认为温的词重笔精雕、浓艳细刻,而冯的词有情景交融、幽美深婉的境界。以下两首闺怨词描写的都是相思女清晨起床时的生活片段,二者不尽相同,温从人物所佩戴头饰的繁丽、化妆戴花的娇态,再到身着服饰的华贵,一一精致刻画、"精妙绝人";而冯用"欲曙""成灰""无绪""宿雾""惊飞""无情"等字眼,外界景物的灰度与人物内心的幽怨妙合、"深美闳约"。

十二

"画屏金鹧鸪",飞卿语也,其词品似之。"弦上黄莺语",端己语也,其词品亦似之。正中词品,若欲于其词句中求之,则"和泪试严妆"殆近之欤。

12. The poetic line"golden partridges painted on a screen" written by Wen Feiqing represents his style, so does the line "orioles warbling on a lute string" written by Wei Duanji. If we select from Feng Zhengzhong's *ci* poems, the poetic line "With tears, try to put on formal makeup" comes closer to his style.

赏析：温飞卿(温庭筠,818～870)的词句"画屏金鹧鸪"、韦端己(韦庄,836～910)的词句"弦上黄莺语"和冯正中(冯延巳,903～960)的词句"和泪试严妆"具象了他们三人各自的词品:温"精妙绝人"、韦"情深语秀"、冯"深美闳约"。

十三

南唐中主词"菡萏香销翠叶残,西风愁起绿波间",大有"众芳芜秽""美人迟暮"之感。乃古今独赏其"细雨梦回鸡塞远,小楼吹彻玉笙寒",故知解人正不易得。

13. Poetic lines in *ci* poems written by Emperor Zhongzhu of the Southern Tang State (南唐,AD 937～975;pinyin:nán táng):"The fragrance of the lotus fades with withering emerald leaves; the west wind wrinkles and worries the green waves" depict the images of the flowers overgrown with weeds and the

beauties aging in their twilight years. Ancient readers and contemporaries are only appreciative of another lines: "Dream back in the drizzle to the remote frontier; play the jade *sheng* (a Chinese mouth-blown free reed instrument) in the cold tower", but, alas, it is hard to find a critical reader.

赏析:词作表达了南唐中主李璟面临亡国危难之时,叹息惆怅又无可奈何之情,经冬历夏、风雨无阻、日日夜夜思念驻戍边塞将士的凯旋,残花残叶、残曲残梦。在王国维看来,李璟的词句:"菡萏香销翠叶残,西风愁起绿波间"才是有境界的上乘词句,王国维尤其欣赏这一句,是因为它"大有众芳芜秽,美人迟暮之感",认为它能将夏末初秋,池塘荷花香消凋萎的景象,瞬间与词人自己无比凄凉的内心融合在一起,惟妙惟肖地呈现在读者面前。

十四

温飞卿之词,句秀也。韦端已之词,骨秀也。李重光之词,神秀也。

14. Wen Feiqing's *ci* poems are credited with sentences; Wei Duanji's *ci* with structures; Emperor Li Chongguang's *ci* with spirits.

赏析:(唐)温庭筠《望江南·梳洗罢》:梳洗罢,独倚望江楼。过尽千帆皆不是,斜晖脉脉水悠悠。肠断白苹洲。这一首词体现了温的词"句秀","脉脉"是指默默地用眼神或行动表达情意,本来是形容主人公含情的样子,却用来修饰"斜晖",傍晚西斜的阳光。

十五

词至李后主而眼界始大,感慨遂深,遂变伶工之词而为士大夫之词。周介存置诸温、韦之下,可谓颠倒黑白矣。"自是人生长恨水长东","流水落花春去也,天上人间"!《金荃》《浣花》,能有此气象耶!

15. It is not until the period of Emperor Li Houzhu of the Southern Tang State that *ci* poems tend to broaden their horizon with deeper feelings and to be composed not by singers or actors, but by scholar-officials. Zhou Jiecun ranking Li's *ci* poems below Wen Feiqing's and Wei Duanji's can be said as confounding black and white. In terms of *qi-xiang*, imagery, are such *ci* collections as *Jin Quan*, (*The Golden Vanilla*,《金荃》; pinyin: jīn quán) and *Huan Hua*,

(*Washing Flowers*,《浣花》;pinyin: huàn huā) comparable to such poetic lines as "Man's life is beset with sorrow, as relentlessly as eastward waters ever flow", and "The youth and spring of Man has gone, like water flowing and flowers fallen, yet never to return, who stands with one foot in Hell, and the other in Heaven"?

赏析:周介存(周济,1781~1839),清代词人、词论家。

"天以百凶成就一词人",王国维认为南唐后主李煜从一国之君沦为阶下之囚,大起大落的坎坷经历使得他的词意境开阔,气象悲壮,感慨人生,嗟叹命运,流水天上,亘越时空,与浓艳温香的温庭筠词集和情致缠绵的韦庄词集所表达的狭隘的儿女私情相比,境界更加深广。歌德也曾经说过:"当我处境很好的时候,我的诗歌之火相当微弱。但在逃离迫在眉睫的灾害时,它却熊熊燃烧。优美的诗歌就像彩虹,只能描画暗淡的背景。诗人的才情喜欢咀嚼忧郁的心情。"

十六

词人者,不失其赤子之心者也。故生于深宫之中,长于妇人之手,是后主为人君所短处,亦即为词人所长处。

16. A *ci* poet is one who has not lost his childlike character. Emperor Li Houzhu of the Southern Tang State was born in the forbidden palace and brought up in the maid's hands, which contributes to his failure to become a good king, but his success of being a good poet.

赏析:王国维读过《叔本华思想随笔·论天才》,并且把叔本华的说法"childlike character"引述为:"赤子之心",这是借鉴了老子《道德经》的语句"含德之厚,比于赤子"和孟子《离娄下》的语句"大人者,不失其赤子之心者也"。叔本华认为天才都有"孩子气",他们摆脱意欲、天真单纯、饶有兴趣地去探索主客观世界。王国维认同叔本华的观点,在他看来,李后主就是个"大孩子",涉世不深、单纯天真的个性,是他成为天才词人的长处,而在尔虞我诈的权欲斗争中自然成为短处。

十七

客观之诗人,不可不多阅世,阅世愈深,则材料愈丰富,愈变化,《水浒传》《红楼梦》之作者是也。主观之诗人,不必多阅世,阅世愈浅,则性情愈真,李后主是也。

17. An objective poet must be deeply experienced in worldly affairs. The more they experience, the more rich and colorful materials they employ. The authors of *Shui Hu Zhuan* (*The Water Margin*, 《水浒传》; pinyin: shuǐ hǔ zhuàn) and *Hong Lou Meng* (*A Dream of Red Mansions*, 《红楼梦》; pinyin: hóng lóu mèng) are good cases in point. A subjective poet must be less experienced in worldly affairs. The less they experience, the more innocent they will be. Emperor Li Houzhu of the Southern Tang State is a good case in point.

赏析:"世事洞明皆学问,人情练达即文章"(《红楼梦》的对联),客观词人必须洞察世事幽微,品尝人情淡薄;"流水落花春去也,天上人间"(李煜的词句),主观词人则恰好相反,必须远离世俗污染,保持纯粹率真,这样创造出的作品才能直抵人心,表现出非凡的艺术功底。

十八

尼采谓:"一切文学,余爱以血书者。"后主之词,真所谓"以血书者"也。宋道君皇帝《燕山亭》词亦略似之。然道君不过自道身世之戚,后主则俨有释迦、基督担荷人类罪恶之意,其大小固不同矣。

18. Nietzsche said, "Of all that is written, I love only that which one writes with one's own blood". The *ci* written by Emperor Li Houzhu of the Southern Tang State is what is called "that which one writes with one's own blood", so is slightly the *ci* to the tune of "Yan Shan Ting" ("The Pavilion on the Yan Mountain", 《燕山亭》; pinyin: yān shān tíng) by Emperor Song Daojun of the Northern Song. However, the latter sobs out his own grievances of a sad life, whereas the former solemnly shoulders the burden of human sins as the Buddha and Jesus do, whose *jing-jie*, the image world, is loftier and mightier.

赏析:尼采(1844～1900):德国哲学家、思想家与诗人。王国维所说的"尼采谓……以血书者"出自尼采的《查拉图斯特拉如是说》第一部之七《读与写》。

宋道君皇帝:宋徽宗赵佶(1082～1135),笃信道教,故又尊为教主道君皇帝。

十九

冯正中词虽不失五代风格,而堂庑特大,开北宋一代风气。与中、后二主词皆在《花间》范围之外，宜《花间集》中不登其只字也。

19. Feng Zhengzhong's *ci* poems are characteristic of the Five Dynasties, yet have a wider scope and bring in a new style to the Northern Song, which, together with ones written by Emperor Li Zhongzhu and Li Houzhu of the Southern Tang State, transcend the realm of *Hua Jian* (*The Anthology of Ci Poetry in the Flowers*,《花间集》; pinyin: huā jiān jí). Therefore, not a single *ci* poem of his is collected in the Anthology.

二十

正中词，除《鹊踏枝》《菩萨蛮》十数阙最煊赫外，如《醉花间》之"高树鹊衔巢，斜月明寒草"，余谓韦苏州之"流萤度高阁"，孟襄阳之"疏雨滴梧桐"，不能过也。

20. Apart from ten most renowned *ci* poems, such as "Que Ta Zhi" ("Magpie Treading on Twigs",《鹊踏枝》; pinyin: què tà zhī), "Pu Sa Man" ("Lyrics to the Bodhisattva Melody",《菩萨蛮》; pinyin: pú sà mán) written by Feng Zhengzhong, the lines of his *ci* "Zui Hua Jian" ("Drunk in Flowers",《醉花间》; pinyin: zuì huā jiān): "In a tall tree take magpies mud to build nest; on the frosty grass shines the slanting moonlight", in my humble opinion, are not surpassed by those lines of Wei Suzhou's *shi* poem: "Fireflies flit across a high pavilion" and of Meng Xiangyang's: "Light rain drips down phoenix trees".

赏析：南唐宰相冯正中（冯延巳）的《阳春集》收录了他的代表作品《鹊踏枝》十四首，《菩萨蛮》九首。

韦应物（韦苏州）和孟浩然（孟襄阳）是唐代五言古体诗歌的高手，在寻常名词里嵌入一个传神的动词，动静结合，是古雅的五言写景的手法，"流萤度高阁"里的"度"，"疏雨滴梧桐"里的"滴"，是画龙点睛之笔。王国维认为冯延巳词句"高树鹊衔巢，斜月明寒草"里的"衔""明"用字生动，境界全出，与韦、孟二人的五言佳作有异曲同工之妙，是把词放在很高的地位来进行评价。

《幼学琼林》译本(节选)

《幼学琼林》是一部中华幼儿启蒙书籍,明末的西昌人程登吉所著,清代至民国时期修订,它是用骈体文写成,以双句(俪句、偶句)为主,对仗工整、声律铿锵,包括明清之前的历朝历代的格言警句、诗歌辞赋、成语典故,语言生动活泼、朗朗上口,内容高度凝练、丰富充实,伟人毛泽东就能熟读这本书。节选的《朋友宾主》篇里不乏金玉良言,对现代人的为人交友行事,仍然有积极的启示作用。

朋友宾主

Friends, Guests and Hosts

取善辅仁,皆资朋友;

Associate with friends adorned with virtues.

(“取善”出自《论语・述而》:“三人行,必有我师焉。择其善者而从之……”;资:依靠)

往来交际,迭为主宾。

In social intercourse, be hosts or guests in turns.

(西汉的戴圣《礼记・曲礼上》记载:“礼尚往来,往而不来,非礼也;来而不往,亦非礼也。”迭:轮流)

尔我同心,曰金兰;

You and I have one soul, called *Jin-lan*, Golden Orchis, which symbolizes close and intimate friendship.

(《易经・系辞上》记载:“二人同心,其利断金;同心之言,其臭如兰”,金兰指亲密深交的朋友。)

朋友相资，日丽泽。

Friends are mutually supported in study, called *Li-ze*, Water Mixed, which symbolizes exchange of academic ideas.

(《周易》兑卦记载："丽泽，兑；君子以朋友讲习。"丽，是并连的意思，兑为泽，两泽相连，交互滋润，其水流犹如朋友之间的学问交流。)

东家曰东主，师傅曰西宾。

As a rule, ones who sit east and face west are the hosts while the others in the opposite are the guests.

父所交游，尊为父执；

Friends who keep Father company are respected as Father's intimates.

己所共事，谓之同袍。

The ones whom I work with are called my companions.

心志相孚为莫逆，老幼相交曰忘年。

The ones who inspire trust in one another become very close friends; despite great difference in age, the old and the young become good friends.

(相孚：相互信任；莫逆：思想一致；忘年：忘年交)

刎颈交，相如与廉颇；总角好，孙策与周瑜。

Such friends as Minister Xiangru and General Lianpo had been ready to die for each other; since childhood, Warlord Sun Ce and General Zhou Yu had been getting on well together.

(总角：古代儿童把头发扎成向上的小辫，借指童年时代)

胶漆相投，陈重之与雷义；鸡黍之约，元伯之与巨卿。

Chen Zhong and Lei Yi had a deep affection for each other like peas and carrots; Yuanbo kept the two-year appointment of regaling his classmate Juqing with chicken and millets.

(《后汉书·范式传》记载：范式(字巨卿)和张劭(字元伯)是京城洛阳太学里的同学，各自返家之前定下了两年之约，两年后范式如期到张劭家拜其母亲，后来用"鸡黍之约"表示朋友之间的信义。)

与善人交，如入芝兰之室，久而不闻其香；与恶人交，如入鲍鱼之肆，久而不闻其臭。

Associate with the noble as if staying long enough at an abode of irises and orchids and getting used to the fragrance; associate with the evil as if staying long enough at a salted fish stall and getting used to the stinks.

(芝兰之室：种满芝和兰两种香草的居室，比喻贤士居住的地方；鲍鱼之肆：售卖咸鱼的集市，比喻恶人聚集的地方。)

肝胆相照，斯为腹心之友；意气不负，谓之口头之交。

Friends who treat each other with all sincerity are bosom ones; friends who turn back on each other are seeming ones.

彼此不合，谓之参商；尔我相仇，如同冰炭。

The ones go against each other, like Orion and Antares; you and I hate each other, like cat and dog.

("参星"指西官白虎七宿中的参宿，"商星"指东官苍龙七宿中的心宿，二者在星空中此出则彼没，两不相见。)

民之失德，干糇以愆；他山之石，可以攻玉。

Forsake the good for sake of bits of food; the stones from other hills may polish jade.

(干糇：干粮；衍：差错、失误，语出《诗经·小雅·伐木》)

落月屋梁，相思颜色；暮云春树，想望丰仪。

O'er the beams of a house, for friends the sinking moon sheds yearning;

twilight clouds and spring trees watch and wait for friends' graceful bearing.

（颜色：面容，杜甫《梦李白二首》有诗句：落月满屋梁，犹疑照颜色；丰仪：仪表，杜甫《春日忆李白》有诗句：渭北春天树，江东日暮云。）

王阳在位，贡禹弹冠以待荐；杜伯非罪，左儒宁死不徇君。

In the Han Dynasty, Wang Yang became an official and his friend Gong Yu wiped dust off the old official hat and waited to get promoted; in the Zhou Dynasty, Du Bo was wronged by King Xuan and his friend Zuo Ru would rather die than submit to the tyrant.

（《汉书·王吉传》记载：汉代王阳与贡禹是好友，王阳做了官，贡禹掸去帽子上的尘土，等待他推荐自己。后来用"弹冠相庆"指一人当了官，他的同伙也互相庆贺将来有官可做。多含贬义；《东周列国志》记载：周宣王滥杀杜伯，左儒力争，也被杀死。）

分首判袂，叙别之辞；拥彗扫门，迎迓之敬。

Part heads and separate sleeves to bid farewell to friends; ply a broom and sweep a room to extend welcome to visitors.

（判袂：衣袖分开，表示朋友离别；迎迓：迎接）

陆凯折梅逢驿使，聊寄江南一枝春；
王维折柳赠行人，遂唱《阳关三叠》曲。

Lu Kai snapped off a plum branch and handed it over to a courier to message faraway friends that early spring is coming; Wang Wei broke off a willow branch as a gift to see off friends who are going away before singing "A Parting Tune with a Thrice Repeated Refrain".

（萧统《昭明文选》记载：折花逢驿使，寄与陇头人，江南无所有，聊赠一枝春。）

频来无忌，乃云入幕之宾；不请自来，谓之不速之客。

Those who are free to visit are distinguished guests, while those who come uncalled are uninvited guests.

（《晋书·郗超传》记载：晋朝时期，大将军桓温图谋篡夺皇位。他在召见敌对派谢安时，让郗超躲在幕后偷听。风把幕帐吹开暴露了郗超。谢安风趣地称他为入幕之宾。）

醴酒不设，楚王戊待士之意怠；投辖于井，汉陈遵留客之心诚。

King Wu of the State of Chu neglected and failed to serve Scholar Mu Sheng sweet wine well; Chen Zun in the Han Dynasty sincerely persuaded the guests to stay by throwing their carriage's locking pin into the well.

（《汉书·楚元王传》："可以逝矣！醴酒不设，王之意怠，不去，楚人将钳我于市。"西汉楚元王每次设宴都为穆生准备甜酒，后楚王戊继位，渐渐忘了准备甜酒，鲁穆生从楚王戊不设醴酒而失礼的小事上，预感到日后危机四伏而离去，后遂用"醴酒不设"比喻待人礼貌渐衰；《汉书·游侠传·陈遵传》记载：汉代陈遵好客，每宴宾客，必关大门，并把客人的车轴上的销钉扔进井中，使客人无法离去。后用"投辖""投辖闭门"表示诚心留客。）

蔡邕倒屣以迎宾，周公握发而待士。

Cai Yong slipped on slippers hurriedly to extend welcome to guests; Zhou Gong tied up hair three times during a Bath in order to see callers.

（《三国志·魏志·王粲传》记载：蔡邕德高望重，家中往往车马盈门，高朋满座。有一天，蔡邕突然得知王粲上门求见，慌得倒拖着鞋子出来迎接，并向众宾客介绍说："王粲有异才，我不如他。"《韩诗外传》卷三《史记·鲁周公世家》记载：周公为了招揽天下的贤士，不怠慢求见的人，即使是正在洗头，也要握起头发来接待。后来则用这些典故表示礼贤下士，求才殷切，鞠躬尽瘁。）

陈蕃器重徐稚，下榻相延；孔子道遇程生，倾盖而语。

Chen Fan thought highly of Xu Zhi and arranged the seat of honor for his visit; Confucius met Cheng Sheng on the road and lowered the cover of the carriage to greet.

（《后汉书·徐稚传》记载：豫章太守陈蕃很器重隐士徐稚，专门为他准备一个坐榻；《孔子·家语·致思》记载：孔子在郯地路上遇到程子，两人停车交谈，形状如伞的车盖互相倾斜。后来用“倾盖而语”来形容朋友相遇亲切交谈，志同道合。）

伯牙绝弦失子期，更无知音之辈；管宁割席拒华歆，调非同志之人。

Yu Boya has stopped playing the guqin since he lost Zhong Ziqi, his bosom friend in the musical field; Guan Ning refused to share the sitting mat with his classmate, Hua Xin, who couldn't bend his mind to academic pursuit.

（《吕氏春秋·本味》记载：俞伯牙善于弹琴，钟子期善于听琴，伯牙琴音志在高山，或志在流水，子期都能心领神会，一听便知。子期死后，伯牙不再弹琴，认为世上再没有这样的知音了。后来用“绝弦”比喻哀悼亡友或慨叹无有知音之苦。《世说新语·德行》记载：东汉末年，管宁与华歆同席读书。一次，门外很热闹，管宁读书如故，而华歆却放下书去看热闹。管宁于是将席子割成两半，从此与华歆分开坐。后来用“割席”指朋友绝交。）

分金多与，鲍叔独知管仲之贫；绨袍垂爱，须贾深怜范叔之寒。

Bao Shu gave more money to help Guan Zhong out of poverty; Xu Jia gave Fan Ju a silk robe and tender care out of pity.

（《史记·范雎蔡泽列传》记载：战国时范雎曾受须贾陷害，惨遭毒打，几乎死去，后改名张禄，逃到秦国担任相国。须贾出使秦国，范雎破衣去见，须贾送他一件绨袍。第二日，须贾才发现范雎已经是秦国相国，于是肉袒谢罪。范雎因为须贾赠予绨袍，所以便宽恕他。后来用“绨袍垂爱”来形容不忘贫寒旧友。）

要知主宾联以情，须尽东南之美；朋友合以义，当展切偲之诚。

Cement the ties of friendship between a host and a guest only among the outstanding figures in southeast China; company with friends who are morally upright, and sincerely improve each other.

（《滕王阁序》里有句子：“宾主尽东南之美”，即宾主都是东南地区优秀人士。展切偲之诚：以诚相待，互相切磋、勉励）

附录

隽语箴言英汉翻译

何辉斌（浙江大学外国语言文化与国际交流学院教授）

1. There is enough in the world for everyone's need; there is not enough for everyone's greed. —Mohandas Gandhi
   这个世界有足够的财富满足每个人的需求；但没有足够的财富满足每个人的贪婪。——莫汉达斯·甘地
2. Anyone can count the seeds in an apple; no one can count the apples in a seed. — Anonymous
   谁都可以数清一个苹果中有多少粒种子，但谁也算不出一粒种子能结出多少个苹果。——佚名
3. Some people confuse acceptance with apathy but there's all the difference in the world. Apathy fails to distinguish what can and cannot be helped; acceptance makes the distinction. —Arthur Gordon
   有人混淆了接受现实与冷漠无情，但两者截然不同。无情者无法分辨可以改变的和不可以改变的；接受现实的人则能做出这种区分。——亚瑟·戈登
4. Man is now only more active — not more happy, nor more wise than he was 6,000 years ago. —Edgar Allan Poe
   现在的人只是更加忙碌，但并不比6000年前更加幸福或者聪明。——埃德加·爱伦·坡
5. The soul of all action is blindness. He who knows, cannot act any longer. Knowing means forgoing action and renouncing passion. —Egon Friedell
   行动的灵魂在于盲目。知道太多的人不能行动。知道意味着放弃行动，否定激情。——伊冈·弗里德尔

6. Tragedy is like a strong acid — it dissolves away all but the very gold of truth. —D. H. Lawrence

悲剧就像强酸，把一切都消融掉，只留下真理的金子。——D. H.劳伦斯

7. You cannot create experience. You must undergo it. —Albert Camus

你不可能创造出经验，必须自己经历。——阿尔贝·加缪

8. The busy bee has no time for sorrow. —William Blake

忙碌的蜜蜂没有给悲伤留下时间。——威廉·布莱克

9. The most generous vine, if not pruned, runs out into many superfluous stems and grows at last weak and fruitless; so doth the best man if he be not cut short in his desires, and pruned with afflictions. —Joseph Hall

再会结果的葡萄藤，如果不修剪，会产生许多分枝，最后变得虚弱并无法结果；最优秀的人，如果不减少欲望，穿过痛苦的炼狱，也会一事无成。——约瑟夫·霍尔

10. Difficulties strengthen the mind, as labor does the body. —Seneca

困难可以使心灵变得强大，正如劳动可以使身体变得结实。——塞内加

11. Adversity has the effect of eliciting talents which in prosperous times would have lain dormant. — Horace

逆境可以激发天才，而顺境则使之安睡。——贺拉斯

12. Adversity is the midwife of genius. —Napoleon Bonaparte

逆境是天才的助产士。——拿破仑·波拿巴

13. Calamity is the perfect glass wherein we truly see and know ourselves. —William Davenant

灾难是一面完美的镜子，使我们真实地看到并认识到自我。——威廉·戴夫南特

14. When a man seeks your advice he generally wants your praise. —Philip Chesterfield

当一个人征求你的建议时，他往往是想得到你的赞扬。——菲利普·切斯特菲尔德

15. A slave has one master; an ambitious man has many masters. —Jean La Bruyere

一个奴隶只有一个主子，一个野心家却有许多主子。——让·拉布吕耶尔

16. Ambition is bubbles on the rapid stream of life. —Edward Young

野心是生活急流上的泡沫。——爱德华·杨

17. Most of the trouble in the world is caused by people wanting to be important. —T. S. Eliot

世界上的大多数麻烦都由那些试图成为名流的人造成的。——T. S. 艾略特

18. Ambition is like love, impatient of delays and rivals. —John Denham

野心就像爱情，无法容忍拖延与情敌。——约翰·德纳姆

19. When angry, count to ten before you speak; if very angry, one hundred. —Thomas Jefferson

当你生气的时候，数十个数字再说话；非常生气的时候，数到一百再说话。——托马斯·杰弗森

20. To be angry is to revenge the faults of others upon ourselves. —Alexander Pope

愤怒是为了别人的错误对我们自己进行报复。——亚历山大·蒲柏

21. For every minute you are angry you lose sixty seconds of happiness. —Ralph Emerson

每生气一分钟，你就失去了60秒的幸福。——拉尔夫·艾默生

22. Anyone who conducts an argument by appealing to authority is not using his intelligence. — Leonardo da Vinci

引用权威进行辩论不是在使用智力。——列奥纳多·达·芬奇

23. Anger begins in folly, and ends in repentance. —Pythagoras

愤怒以愚蠢开端，以后悔收场。——毕达哥拉斯

24. An angry man opens his mouth and closes his eyes. —Cato the Elder

一个愤怒的人张开他的嘴，却闭上他的眼睛。——老加图

25. The intoxication of anger, like that of the grape, shows us to others, but hides us from ourselves. —Charles C. Colton

愤怒冲昏头脑，就像醉酒一样，使自己的内心暴露在别人的眼底下，却遮蔽了自知的视野。——查尔斯·C. 科尔顿

26. If a man cannot control his temper, how much less can he control others.

—Solomon Ibn Gabirol

如果无法控制自己的脾气，免谈管理他人。——罗门·伊本·盖比鲁勒

27. Men easily believe what they wish to believe. —Julius Caesar

人们会轻易地相信他们乐意看到的。——裘力斯·恺撒

28. In idleness there is perpetual despair. —Thomas Carlyle

无所事事是永无止境的绝望。——托马斯·卡莱尔

29. If you're doing nothing, you're doing wrong. —Lord Mountbatten

如果你什么都不做，就是在做错事。——蒙巴顿勋爵

30. A healthy body is a guest-chamber for the soul; a sick body is a prison. —Francis Bacon

健康的身体是心灵的客房；得病的身体是心灵的监狱。——弗朗西斯·培根

31. Books are the most patient of teachers. —Charles L. Eliot

书本是最有耐心的老师。——查尔斯·L. 艾略特

32. Teaching is lighting a lamp and not filling a bucket.—Frank Crane

教育是点亮一盏灯，而不是装满一桶水。——弗兰克·克雷恩

33. The real voyage of discovery consists not in seeking new landscapes but in having new eyes. —Marcel Proust

真正的发现之旅不在于探索新风景，而在于新的眼光。——马塞尔·普鲁斯特

34. The millions are awake enough for physical labor; but only one in a million is awake enough for effective intellectual exertion, only one in a hundred million to a poetic or divine life. To be awake is to be alive. ——Henry David Thoreau

就觉醒的程度而言，数以百万计的人只足以进行体力劳作；百万分之一的人足以进行智力劳动；亿分之一的人可以问鼎诗意的或者神圣的生活。觉醒才算活着。——亨利·戴维·梭罗

35. Though we travel the world to find the beautiful we must carry it within us or we find it not. —Ralph Waldo Emerson

为了寻找美景，我们环游世界，但我们必须心怀美好，才能发现它。——拉尔夫·沃尔多·爱默生

36. It is useless and futile to try to change other people. The only person I can change is myself. —William Curtiss

试图改变他人无用且无效。唯一我能够改变的人是我自己。——威廉·柯蒂斯

37. Beauty, unaccompanied by virtue, is a flower without perfume.

—French proverb

漂亮而没有美德,就好像花朵没有芬芳。——法国谚语

38. Beauty is God's handwriting. —Charles Kingsley

美是上帝的书法。——查尔斯·金斯利

39. The criterion of true beauty is that it increases upon examination; if false, that it lessens. —Fulke Greville

真正美的标准在于越看越美;虚假的美则不耐看。——福尔克格·雷维尔

40. What distinguishes the majority of men from the few is their inability to act according to their beliefs. —Henry Miller

大众与精英的不同之处在于他们无法根据自己的信念行动。——亨利·米勒

41. Nothing is so easy as to deceive one's self; for what we wish, that we readily believe. — Demosthenes

自我欺骗最为容易,因为我们乐于相信我们所期待的。——德摩斯梯尼

42. The more things change, the more they remain the same. —Alphonse Karr

越是变化,越是保持原样。——阿方斯·卡尔

43. Charity is the pure gold which makes us rich in eternal wealth. —Jean P. Camus

慈善是纯金,可以帮我们获得永恒的富足。——让·P. 加缪

44. The poor man's charity is to wish the rich man well. —Anonymous

穷人的慈善在于祝愿富人安好。——佚名

45. Everyone believes very easily whatever he fears or desires. —Jean La Fontaine

人易于相信他所惧怕的或者想要的。——让·拉封丹

46. The man who has no inner life is a slave of his surroundings, as the barometer is the obedient servant of the air. —Henry F. Amiel

没有强大的内心生活就是环境的奴隶，正如气压表是空气的顺从的奴仆一样。——亨利·F. 埃米尔

47. A wicked man who reproaches a virtuous one is like one who looks up and spits at heaven; the spittle soils not the heaven but comes back and defiles his own person. —Gautama Buddha

一个邪恶的人辱骂一个有美德的人，就像抬头往天上吐痰；他的唾沫无法玷污天空，只会落下来把自己弄得一身脏。——释迦牟尼

48. Consider how hard it is to change yourself, and what little chance you have of trying to change others. —Jacob M. Braude

想一想改变自我的难度，你就会知道试图改变他人的概率之小。——雅各伯·M. 布劳德

49. Perhaps man, having remade his environment, will turn around at last and begin to remake himself. —Will Durant

在改变了环境之后，人最后也许会转过身来改变自己。——威尔·杜兰特

50. No one can persuade another to change. Each of us guards a gate of change that can only be unlocked from the inside. We cannot open the gate of another, either by argument or by emotional appeal. —Marilyn Ferguson

没有人可以说服别人做出改变。每个人的变化之门的锁只能从内部打开。我们无法打开这扇门，不管是晓之以理还是动之以情。——玛丽莲·弗格森

51. Times of change are times of fearfulness and times of opportunity. Which they may be for you depends upon your attitude toward them. —Ernest C. Wilson

变革的时代是可怕的时代，也是充满机遇的时代。它对于你是什么，取决于你的态度。——欧内斯特·C. 威尔逊

52. Integrity includes but goes beyond honesty. Honesty is telling the truth — in other words, conforming our words to reality. Integrity is conforming reality to our words — in other words, keeping promises and fulfilling expectations. —Stephen R. Covey

正直包括诚实，但高于诚实。诚实在于说真话——就是说，让言语和现实一致。正直在于让现实符合言语——就是说，信守诺言，不让人失望。——斯蒂芬·

R. 科维

53. Contentment is natural wealth, luxury is artificial poverty. —Socrates

满足是自然的财富,奢华是人为的贫穷。——苏格拉底

54. Be more concerned with your character than your reputation, because your character is what you really are, while your reputation is merely what others think you are. —John Wooden

请关心自己的性格而不是声誉,因为性格代表着真实的你,而声誉只是别人对你的评价。——约翰·吴登

55. There is a broad distinction between character and reputation, for one may be destroyed by slander, while the other can never be harmed save by the possessor. —Josiah Holland

性格与声誉明显不同,声誉可能被诽谤夺走,而性格却能够免受伤害,除非自己不珍惜。——约西亚·霍兰德

56. Character is what God and the angels know of us; reputation is what men and women think of us. —Horace Mann

性格是上帝和天使对我们的评价;荣誉是世间凡人对我们的看法。——贺拉斯·曼

57. There are two kinds of charity, remedial and preventive. The former is often injurious in its tendency; the latter is always praiseworthy and beneficial. —Tryon Edwards

慈善有两种,弥补性质的与预防性质的。前者往往是有害的;后者总是有益,值得称赞。——特赖恩·爱德华兹

58. The best way to do good to ourselves is to do it to others; the right way to gather is to scatter. —Seneca

对自己好的最佳途径在于对他人好;积累财富的最好方法在于广泛布施。

——塞内加

59. Give work rather than alms to the poor. The former drives out indolence, the latter industry. —Tryon Edwards

给穷人以工作而不是钱财。前者可以赶走懒惰,而后者可以赶走勤奋。——特赖恩·爱德华兹

60. The mother-child relationship is paradoxical and, in a sense, tragic. It requires the most intense love on the mother's side, yet this very love must help the child grow away from the mother and become fully independent. —Erich Fromon

母亲-子女的关系充满悖论,甚至是悲剧性的。母亲这边总是有炽热的爱,但这种爱却必须帮助孩子长大,离开母亲,变得完全独立。——埃里奇·弗洛姆

61. Every child comes with the message that God is not yet discouraged of man. —Rabindranath Tagore

每一个孩子的出生都带来了这样的信息:上帝还没有对人类失去希望。——拉宾德拉纳特·泰戈尔

62. Children need love, especially when they do not deserve it. —Harold S. Hubert

小孩子需要爱,特别是在他们不配爱的时候。——哈罗德·S. 休伯特

63. Fate chooses our relatives. We choose our friends. —Jacques Bossuet

命运选择我们的亲戚。我们自己选择朋友。——雅克·波舒哀

64. Be the master of your will, and the slave of your conscience. —Yiddish saying

争取成为意志的主人,良心的奴隶。——意第绪格言

65. Blind is he who sees not his conscience; lame is he who wanders from the right way. — Saint Anthony of Padua

看不到良心的人是盲人;偏离正道的人是跛子。——帕多瓦的圣安东尼

66. I am always content with what happens; for I know that what God chooses is better than what I choose. —Epictetus

我总是对发生的事情感到满意;因为我知道神的选择比我自己的选择更好。——爱比克泰德

67. If a man is not content in the state he is in, he will not be content in the state he would be in. —Erskine Mason

如果一个人对现有的地位不满意,就算进入他渴求的状态也难以满意。——厄斯金·梅森

68. Discontent is like ink poured into water, which fills the whole fountain full

of blackness. — Owen Felltham

不高兴就像滴入水中的墨汁，可以使泉水全部变黑。——欧文·费尔萨姆

69. Contentment is the Philosopher's Stone, that turns all it touches to gold. —Benjamin Franklin

满足是哲人之石，能够将接触到的一切变成金子。——本杰明·富兰克林

70. Courage is almost a contradiction in terms. It means a strong desire to live taking the form of a readiness to die. —G. K. Chesterton

勇敢是一个自相矛盾的概念，意味着强烈的生存欲望，却采用了乐意赴死的形式。——G. K. 切斯特顿

71. Ignorance and fear of death overshadow life, while knowing and accepting death erases this shadow. —Lily Pincus

对死亡的无知和恐惧会给生活蒙上阴影，而了解和接受死亡可以消除这个阴影。——莉莉·平卡斯

72. The fear of death is indeed the pretense of wisdom, and not real wisdom, being a pretense of knowing the unknown; and no one knows whether death, which men in their fear apprehend to be the greatest evil, may not be the greatest good. —Plato

害怕死亡是假装聪明，只是强装知道未知的东西，不是真智慧；谈死色变的人视之为最大的恶，但谁又能够说那不是最大的善。——柏拉图

73. I see clearly that there are two deaths: to cease loving and being loved is unbearable. But to cease to live is of no consequence. —Voltaire

我清楚地看到了两种死亡：无法忍受停止爱与被爱，但停止生命是无足轻重的。——伏尔泰

74. Death means no more to me than what a caterpillar experiences when it sheds its old skin and emerges into the full light of a new day as a butterfly. —David Manners

死对于我来说，仅仅是毛毛虫在新的一天的阳光下蜕下旧皮肤变为蝴蝶。——大卫·玛纳斯

75. Death? Translated into the heavenly tongue, that word means life. —Henry W. Beecher

死亡？翻译成天国的语言就是生命。——亨利·W. 比彻

76. After your death you will be what you were before your birth. —Arthur Schopenhauer

死亡之后你将进入出生之前的状态。——亚瑟·叔本华

77. Nature invented death that there might be new life. —Johann W. Goethe

大自然创造了死亡，使新的生命变得可能。——约翰·W. 歌德

78. On the day of his death, a man feels he has lived but a single day. —*The Zohar*

在死亡到来的时候，人们往往觉得人生只有一天那么长。——《光明篇》

79. Death: where the changing mist of doubts will vanish at a breath, and the mountain peaks of truth will appear. —Rabindranath Tagore

死亡：多变的怀疑之迷雾在一口气间消失，坚硬的真理之山峰将出现。——拉宾德拉纳特·泰戈尔

80. A man abandons worn-out clothes and acquires new ones, so when the body is worn out a new one is acquired by the self, who lives within. —*Bhagavad-Gita*

衣服破烂了就要换新的，身体破损，内在的灵魂也将换新的身躯。——《薄伽梵歌》

81. Man's unhappiness comes of his greatness; it is because there is an Infinite in him, which, with all his cunning, he cannot quite bury under the finite. —Thomas Carlyle

人的不幸来自他的伟大；不管能力多强，他都无法将心中的"无限"掩埋于有限之下。——托马斯·卡莱尔

82. Despondency is ingratitude; hope is God's worship. —Henry W. Beecher

失落是不知感恩；希望是对上帝的崇拜。——亨利·W. 比彻

83. Melancholy is born of self-importance. —Nancy D. Potts

郁闷来自自负。——南希·D. 帕茨

84. Desire tells us, each time, "Now get thou this, and then you shall be happy."...The fact is, desire is a bottomless pit which can never fill up, or like the all-consuming fire which burns the fiercer, the more we feed it.

—Lakshmana Sarma

欲望每次都告诉我们,“得到这个,你就幸福了。”……但事实上欲望是一个永远填不满的无底洞,或者说,它就像焚烧一切的大火,越是喂之以燃料,火势必然更加凶猛。——拉什玛纳·萨尔玛

85. The deepest human urge is the desire to be important. —John Dewey

人类最深层次的追求是试图变得重要。——约翰·杜威

86. I have always thought the actions of men the best interpreters of their thoughts.—John Locke

我总是认为行动是思想的最好阐述者。——约翰·洛克

87. Time is what we want most, but what alas! we use worst.—William Penn

我们最渴求时间,天哪,却最不会使用时间。——威廉·佩恩

88. Desire grows in strength if you follow it, but dies if you turn from it and abstain...Desire is slavery; renunciation is freedom. —Hermes

紧紧追随,欲望威力大增;转身放弃,则欲望必死……欲望是奴役;放弃是自由。——赫尔墨斯

89. Fiction reveals truths that really obscures. —Jessamyn West

虚构的作品可以揭示被现实遮蔽的真理。——杰萨姆·韦斯特

90. Self-conquest is the greatest of victories. —Plato

战胜自己是最伟大的胜利。——柏拉图

91. Dreams are true while they last, and do we not live in dreams? —Alfred L. Tennyson

只要梦还在延续,它们就是真的,难道我们不是生活在梦中吗?——阿尔佛雷德·L.丁尼生

92. Man is a dream of a shadow. —Pindar

人是影子做的梦。——品达

93. Flattery is counterfeit money which, but for vanity, would have no circulation. —Francois De La Rochefoucauld

拍马屁是假币,不管怎么努力,都不可能真的流通。——弗朗索瓦·德·拉·罗什富科

94. The soul that is without suffering does not feel the need of knowing the

ultimate cause of the universe. Sickness, grief and hardships are all indispensable elements in the spiritual ascent. —Anandamayi Ma

没有痛苦的磨炼，人就感觉不到了解宇宙的终极原因。疾病、痛苦和苦难是提升精神境界的不可或缺的要素。——阿南达玛依·玛

95. Most people are quitters. This is wonderful news for those of us who decide to be successful. It means that if we stick to what we are doing, we will, in a very short time, be ahead of the multitudes.—Andrew Matthews

大部分人都是知难而退的。这对于希望取得成功的人是绝妙的消息。这就意味着，如果我们坚持不懈，不久就可以领先很多人。——安德鲁·马修

96. Find out what a person fears most and that is where he will develop next. —Carl Jung

找出一个人最害怕的是什么，那就是他以后需要发展的方面。——卡尔·荣格

97. Never disregard what your enemies say. They may be severe, they may be prejudiced, they may be determined to see only in one direction, but still in that direction they see clearly. They do not speak all the truth, but they generally speak the truth from one point of view; so far as that goes, attend to them. —Benjamin Haydon

不要把敌人说的话当作耳边风。他们的话可能过于严厉，充满偏见，只是一孔之见，但从那个视角看的确有见地。他们没有说出所有的真理，但通常来说道出了某个视角中的真理；只要是这样，认真听听。——本杰明·海顿

98. It is much safer to reconcile an enemy than to conquer him; victory may deprive him of his poison, but reconciliation, of his will. —Owen Felltham

和解比征服更安全；因为胜利可以剥夺敌人的毒汁，但和解可以祛除他的敌意。——欧文·费尔萨姆

言语行为理论视阈下的人物对话翻译

摘　要：人物对话作为文学作品的重要组成部分，是作家为了表达人物心理意图，塑造人物个性形象，引出行为动作，开展故事情节而刻意安排的。人物对话翻译的好坏直接影响到文学作品的整体翻译。言语行为理论为理解并翻译人物对话提供了很好的视角，译者通过分析言内行为、言外行为和言后行为之间的关系使人物对话翻译更加准确生动。

关键词：言语行为理论；人物对话；翻译

人物对话是塑造人物性格形象，推动故事情节发展和表现文学作品主题思想的重要手段。人物对话往往是作家为了展现人物冲突，引出人物动作而精心设计和巧妙安排的。人物对话翻译的好坏直接关系到译语读者能否对原著准确把握和理解到位。本文将从语用学角度出发，运用言语行为理论模式来分析和理解文学作品中人物对话的合理性，挖掘人物的心理状态、感情态度和思想活动，从而使人物对话翻译更能达意传神。

言语行为理论简述

1. 理论的核心内容

言语行为理论（Speech Act Theory）是语言语用研究中的一个重要理论。它最初是英国牛津大学哲学教授约翰·奥斯汀（Austin，J.L）在 20 世纪 50 年代提出的[①]。根据言语行为理论，我们说话的同时是在实施某种行为，即言语就是行为，它分为言内行为（locutionary act），言外行为（illocutionary act）和言后行为（perlocutionary act）三个层次。言内行为是说话人发出语音、音节，说出单词、短语和句子来表达字面意义的行为；言外行为是说话人话语（utterance）表达意图的行为，如传递信息、发出命令、威胁恫吓、问候致意、解雇下属、宣布开会等；言后行

① AUSTIN J L. How to Do Things with Words? [M]. Oxford: Clarendon Press, 1962.

为是说话人话语带来的后果或变化，听话人领会说话人意图并按照说话人意图行事才发生言后行为①(何兆熊，2000：93)。在这三种言语行为中，言内行为可以理解成话语的字面意思或说话人的信息意图；言外行为则是言内行为的言外之意或说话人的交际意图。Austin的言语行为理论提出后立即引出了大量哲学论述，其中美国哲学家塞尔(Searle，J.R)的影响最大。他提出了间接言语行为(indirect speech act)这一特殊的言语行为类型。一个人直接通过话语形式的字面意义来实现其交际意图，这是直接的言语行为；当"通过施行另一种言外行为来间接地实施某一种言外行为"②(Searle：1975：60)，这就是间接言语行为；Searle把说话人在间接地使用语言时所实施的两种言外行为分别称为首要言外行为(primary illocutionary act)和次要言外行为(secondary illocutionary act)。首要言外行为才体现了说话人的真正意图，而次要言外行为是说话人为了实施首要言外行为所实施的另一言外行为(何兆熊，2000：124)。例如下面的对话：

Father：Is this your pen?

Son：Alright，I'll put it in my pencil-box.

"Is this your pencil?"这一言语行为，其言内行为就是用疑问句的形式说出这三个单词，次要言外行为实施说话人向听话人询问的交际意图，首要言外行为实施说话人指令听话人收拾好钢笔的这一真实意图，听话人听从说话人要求就是言后行为。

2. 理论的交际意义

根据言语行为理论，话语可以被认作包括三个层次上的信息传递：言内行为、言外行为和言后行为。说话人不仅会选择某些语音、词汇和结构作为信息载体用话语信息来直接表达自己的交际意图，而且经常间接地传达自己的意图，他们期望听话人利用语境及各种背景知识，结合自己提供的话语意思，通过推理得出自己话语传达的真实意图③(何自然，2004：196)。言后行为的发生意味着听话人领会说话人的真实意图并按照该意图行事，对说话人做出积极反馈；如果听话人没有领会说话人真实意图，或者虽然领会了说话人意图，但不按照这一意图去行事，就是对说话人消极反馈，从而导致交际的失败(何兆熊，2000：93)。图1反映了言语行为

---

① 何兆熊.新编语用学概要[M].上海：上海外语教育出版社，2000.

② SEARLE J R. Indirect Speech Acts [A]. In Cole，P. & Morgan，J. (eds) *Syntax and Semantics*，Vol. 3：*Speech Acts*，New York：Academic Press，1975.

③ 何自然，陈新仁. 当代语用学[M]. 北京：外语教学与研究出版社，2004.

是如何参与构建整个信息传递过程的。

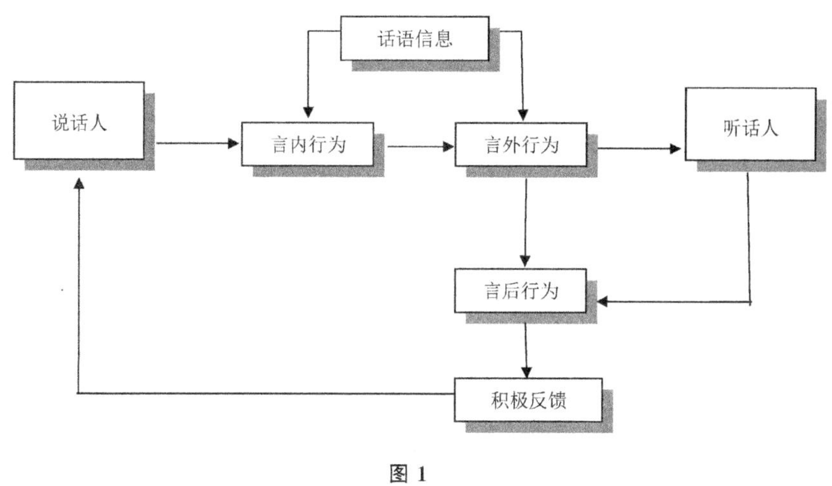

图 1

言语行为理论和人物对话翻译

人物对话是文学作品常见的表现手法。成功的作家都会为其文学作品中的人物设计出表现人物个性身份、态度观点和思想感情的语言，通过人物对话，使所塑造的一个个人物形象更为生动鲜活、栩栩如生，使故事情节更加耐人寻味、引人入胜。通过言语行为理论，我们在翻译人物对话时，会注意挖掘人物对话的交际意图和真实意图，用恰当的言内行为传达言外行为，使言后行为符合言外行为。

1. 言内行为传达言外行为

作为信息载体的言内行为采用丰富的手段和方式来实现表达交际意图和真实意图的言外行为，这些手段包括语音、词汇、句法等，所以我们在翻译人物对话时，先必须利用语境和背景知识分析出原语中说话人的交际意图和真实意图即言外行为，然后在译语中找到可以传达该言外行为的言内行为，如图 2 所示：

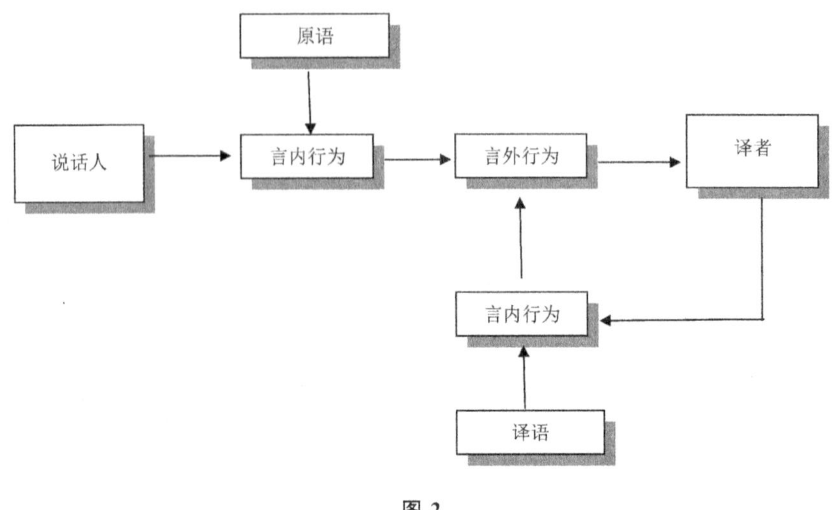

图 2

言内行为传达的言外行为，Searle 把它们分成五大类：①阐述类(representatives)：说话人必须相信自己所说话的真实性，所表达的心理状态是“相信”；②指令类(directives)：说话人试图让听话人去做某一件事情，所表达的心理状态是“希望或愿望”；③承诺类(commissives)：使听话人对某一未来的行为做出许诺，所表达的心理状态是“意欲”；④表达类（expressives)：说话人对某种客观事态表达自己的心理状态，所表达的心理状态主要有“感谢”“祝贺”“欢迎”“道歉”等；⑤宣告类(declarations)：使客观现实符合所说的话语。(何兆熊，2000：105)

根据以上分析，结合具体实例，我们来看看人物对话翻译中的得和失：

(1)语音层面

例：周萍：打他！

……

鲁大海：(挣扎)放开我，你们这一群强盗！

周萍：(向仆人们)把他拉下去。

鲁侍萍：(大哭)这真是一群强盗！(走至周萍面前)你是**萍**，——**凭**——**凭**——什么打我的儿子？(曹禺《雷雨》第二幕)

译文 1：PING：Give him what for!

…

HAI (struggling)：Let go of me，you hooligans!

PING (to the servants): Hustle him outside!

MA (breaking down): You are hooligans, too! (Going across to Zhou Ping.) You're **my—mighty** free with your fists! What right have you to hit my son? [①](王佐良,2001:174-175)

译文 2:PING: Beat him!

...

HAI (struggling): Let me go, you a band of robbers!

PING (to the servants): Pull him out!

MA (crying loudly): You are robbers, indeed! (Going up to Zhou Ping.) You are **Ping—whereby** will you strike my son?

汉字"萍"和"凭"同音,生动地表现了鲁侍萍的心理矛盾:一方面相信自己阔别三十年的儿子周萍近在眼前,想认却不敢认,即阐述类的言外之的;另一方面为面前周萍的冷酷无情感到痛心疾首,试图阻止他和鲁大海兄弟之间的手足残杀,即指令类的言外之的。译文 1 借助英语中有相同音节/mai/的两个单词"my"和"mighty"恰到好处地表现了鲁侍萍复杂言外行为的过渡。译文 2 则没有考虑鲁侍萍言内行为语音层面上的特点,改变了人物对话产生的实际效果。

(2)词汇层面

① 贾琏垂头含笑想了想,拍手道:"我如今**竟**糊涂了……"(曹雪芹《红楼梦》第72 回)

霍克斯译:Jia Lian looked down smilingly and reflected, then clapped his hands suddenly as he remembered. "**Why ,yes ,of course** . How stupid of me !..."[②](霍克斯,1973:75)

杨宪益译:Chia Lian lowered his head and was silent for some time. "I'd

---

① 曹禺著.雷雨.王佐良,巴恩斯译.Thunderstorm[M].北京:外文出版社,2001.

② 曹雪芹著.红楼梦.霍克斯(David Hawkes)译.*The Story of the Stone*[M].Penguin Group,1973.

forgotten..."[①](杨宪益,1978:102)

原文对话中,贾琏误会了王熙凤私自收下外路和尚孝敬的蜡油冻佛手,在鸳鸯和平儿的解释下,他意识到是自己忘性而胡乱地责备了他人,一个"竟"字强烈地表达了他内心的歉意。在翻译这句对话时,霍克斯通过英语语气词"why""yes"和肯定词组"of course"以及感叹句"How stupid of me!"到位地表达了贾琏认错时羞愧的心理状态。杨译则没有看到原语中语气词"竟"在贾琏表达类言外行为中的重要作用,忽略了对它的翻译。

② "**Well**—it's my **duty** to help them out of it."

"It's your **duty** to invite all the rats in the world to gnaw at your bones." (D. H. Lawrence: *Women in Love*)

译文1:"**唉**——我**该帮帮**他们解脱困难。"

"你**该**把全世界的老鼠都叫来啃你的骨头**才对**!"[②](郑达华:2005)

译文2:"**嘿**——我有**责任**帮他们摆脱困境。"

"你的**责任**就是邀请全世界的老鼠都来啃你的骨头。"

原文对话出自一对夫妻之口,丈夫乐善好施但惧怕老婆,妻子自私小气且尖酸刻薄。丈夫希望妻子接受自己救济穷人的想法,是乞求的言外行为,妻子毫无诚意的建议,充满了讽刺挖苦。译文1恰当地把副词"well"翻译成语气词"唉",名词"duty"分别译成请求句式"该帮帮"和建议句式"该……才对",使丈夫懦弱的性格和妻子强硬的情态跃然纸上。反之,译文2中的"嘿"和"责任"让译语读者感到丈夫是在向妻子做出帮助穷人的承诺,理直气壮、不容商量,从而歪曲了原著中丈夫的言外行为,歪曲了作者对丈夫软弱形象的真实刻画。

(3)句法层面

①黄胖子:(严重的沙眼,看不清楚,进门就请安)哥儿们,<u>都瞧我啦!</u> <u>我请安了!</u> 都是自己弟兄,别伤了和气呀!(老舍《茶馆》第一幕)

---

① 曹雪芹著.红楼梦.杨宪益,戴乃迭(Yang Hsien - yi & Gladys Yang)译.*A Dream of Red Mansions*[M]. Beijing: Foreign Languages Press, 1978.

② D.H.劳伦斯(Lawrence, D.H.)[英]著. Women in Love. 郑达华等译.恋爱中的女人[M].北京:中国戏剧出版社,2005.

英若诚译：Tubby Huang：…Now，now，folks，for my sake，please，I'm here greeting you all！ We're all brothers，ain't we？ Let's have none of them bad feelings！① （英若诚，1999：27）

霍华译：Fatso Huang：…Brothers，look at me. I'm paying my respects to you. We're all one big family —don't do anything to upset our friendship.②（霍华，2001：35）

流氓头子黄胖子作为纠纷调解人来到茶馆，自然会说出"都是自己弟兄，别伤了和气呀"之类市井语言，根据上下文提供的信息以及北京方言的特点，译者应了解到句子"都瞧我啦"不是字面意思，即黄胖子并非指令纠纷双方注意他（"look at me"），而是希望他们能看在他的面子上化解彼此矛盾，英若诚将其译为"for my sake，please"，才准确地传达了说话人的真实意图；黄胖子作为调停人，身份地位和纠纷双方平等，表达"我请安了！"不是向尊长询问安好（"I'm paying my respects to you."），其交际意图只不过是平常的打招呼，因此英若诚的译文"I'm here greeting you all！"更能贴切传达黄胖子的言外行为。

② "…" said Legree，"…Come，Tom，don't you think you'd better be reasonable？ — heave that ar old pack of trash in the fire，and join my church！" （Harriet Beecher Stowe：*Uncle Tom's Cabin*）

黄继忠译："得啦，汤姆，我看你还是放聪明点儿！ 把那本破书扔进火里去，改信我的教吧！"③（黄继忠，1982：521）

张培均译："来，托姆，你不觉得明白道理比较好些吗？ ——把这本尽是废话的老书丢在火里，来参加我的教会！"④（张培均，1982：657）

原文对话发生在奴隶主雷格里和黑人奴隶汤姆之间，雷格里威胁汤姆放弃自己的宗教信仰，决意压垮他。在译文 1 中，反问句译成了感叹句，直白地表露出奴隶主对待奴隶专横野蛮的态度；译文 2 虽然在句式上忠实原文，但是委婉的语气没

---

① 老舍著. 茶馆. 英若诚译. Teahouse［M］. 北京：中国对外翻译出版公司，1999.

② 老舍著. 茶馆. 霍华译. Teahouse［M］. 北京：外文出版社，2001.

③ 斯陀夫人（Harriet Beecher Stowe）［美］著. Uncle Tom's Cabin. 黄继忠译. 汤姆大伯的小屋［M］. 上海：上海译文出版社，1982.

④ 斯陀夫人（Harriet Beecher Stowe）［美］著. Uncle Tom's Cabin. 张培均译. 黑奴吁天录［M］. 桂林：漓江出版社，1982.

有清晰地传达出雷格里说话时的凶狠无赖。

2. 言后行为符合言外行为

根据言语行为理论，听话人只有领会说话人意图并按照说话人意图行事才发生言后行为，言后行为是听话人对说话人话语的积极反馈。所以，我们在翻译人物对话时，还必须分析原语中听话人对说话人话语做出的反馈是积极的还是消极的，如图 3 所示。如果是积极反馈，那么译语中听话人的言后行为要符合说话人的言外行为；如果是消极反馈，那么译语中听话人的反应与说话人言外行为相左。通过观察言后行为，我们可以使人物对话翻译得更加妥帖到位。

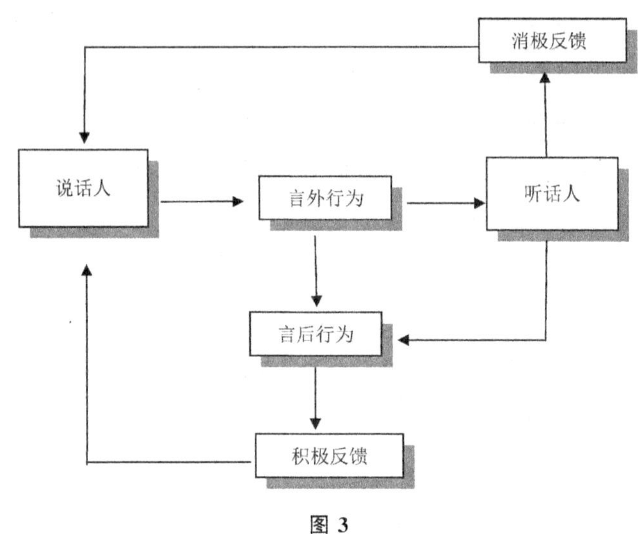

图 3

(1)译语中言后行为和言外行为相统一：

As is the Chinese cook's custom, my mother always made disparaging remarks about her own cooking. She chose to direct it toward her famous steamed pork and preserved vegetable dish, which she always served with special pride. "Ai! This dish not salty enough, no flavor," she **complained**, after tasting a small bite. "It is too bad to eat."

This was our family's cue to eat some and proclaim it the best she had ever made. But before we could do so, Rich said, "You know, all it needs is a little soy sauce." And he proceeded to pour a riverful of the salty black stuff on the platter, right before my mother's horrified eyes. (Amy Tan: *The Joy Luck Club*)

……妈端上了她拿手的清蒸排骨和腌菜,这从来是她的精心之作。尝了一小口后,她便**故意抱怨**着:"哎呀,这菜怕不够咸,淡而无味。"她不满地摇摇头,"简直做得太糟糕,无法入口。"

这从来是我们家的惯例:先吃上一口,然后称赞一番妈妈的手艺,但这次未及我们开始,里奇便道:"它所需要的,就是加点酱油。"然后便顺手从调味盆里拣出酱油瓶,于是,在妈妈的恐怖的注视下,一注黑色液体倒进了排骨。[①] (程乃珊,2006:162-163)

"妈"对自己烹饪手艺表示歉意其实是希望品尝人极力称赞她的精心之作,这是"中国式的谦虚"。里奇是美国女婿,没有领会"妈"说此番话的真实意图,"拣出酱油瓶","倒进了排骨",文化背景的差异造成了交际的失败,他的行为便是对"妈"话语的消极反馈;如果他能像"我们"惯常做的那样:"先吃上一口,然后称赞一番妈妈的手艺",才发生了言后行为。所以译者在原语引述动词"complain(抱怨)"前增加了"故意"一词,强调了"妈"说话时的语气,表明了说话人的真实意图,以便让译语读者理解里奇的举动不符合说话人的言外之意,不是言后行为,从而造成了饭桌上的尴尬。

(2)言后行为可以作为翻译对话的依据:

① 周朴园:(指窗)窗户谁叫打开的?

鲁侍萍:**哦**。(很自然地走到窗户前,关上窗户,慢慢地走向中门。)(曹禺《雷雨》第二幕)

译文1:ZHOU (indicating the open window): Who's opened that window?

MA: **Oh, yes.**(She strolls across to the window as if quite at home here, closes it, then goes slowly towards the centre door.)(王佐良,2001:148-149)

① 谭恩美(Amy Tan)[美]著. the Joy Luck Club. 程乃珊,贺培华,严映薇译. 喜福会[M]. 上海:上海译文出版社,2006.

译文 2：ZHOU：Why is the window open?

MA：**Oh.**(She goes to the window without thinking, closes it, then walks slowly up to the centre door.)

鲁侍萍不是周公馆的人，按理说对周家关窗户的习惯不熟悉，但是她"很自然地""关上窗户"的言后行为表明她充分领会周朴园的指令，了解他的用意，也暗示了她身世的不平常。所以鲁侍萍的回话翻译成"Oh, yes" 才能完整充分地表达她对周朴园命令的服从。

② "Mine is a long and sad **tale** !" said the Mouse, turning to Alice, and sighing.

"It is a long **tail** , certainly," said <u>Alice, looking down with wonder at the Mouse's tai l</u>, "but why do you call it sad?"(Lewis Carroll: *Alice's Adventures in Wonderland*)

译文 1：老鼠对着爱丽丝叹了口气道："唉，说来话长！真叫我**委屈**!"

"**尾曲?!** "爱丽丝听了，瞧着老鼠那光滑的尾巴问："你这尾巴明明又长又直，为什么说它曲呢?"

译文 2："我的**故事**说来真是又长又伤心!"耗子转身向阿丽思叹口气说。

"你的**尾巴**确实很长。"阿丽思惊奇地朝下看着耗子尾巴说。"可是你干吗说它伤心呢?"①(陈复庵，1981：39)

老鼠相信自己遭遇(tale)曲折，希望 Alice 用心聆听并给予同情。Alice 听了却对老鼠的尾巴(tail)发生了兴趣。可见 Alice 没有领会老鼠说话意图，没有发生言后行为的原因是她把"tale"误听成"tail"，所以我们翻译此段对话时，要注意同音异义现象造成交际失败的情况。译文 1 中的"委屈"与"尾曲"属同音异义词，较好地表达了这一幽默。译文 2 虽然译出了"tale"和"tail"的字面意义，但是译语读者会对 Alice 听老鼠提到"故事"却去瞧它"尾巴"的举动感到费解。

美国著名女作家韦尔蒂谈创作时曾说："发现对话成为最难写的部分……我需

---

① 路易斯·加乐尔(Lewis Carroll)［英］著. Alice's Adventures in Wonderland. 陈复庵译. 阿丽思漫游奇境记译［M］. 北京：中国对外翻译出版公司，1981.

要……表现人物的意思，同时又是他自以为是自己的意思，还要揭示他掩饰的意思，传达出别人心目中他所指的意思，以及……误解等等……而且这番话还必须能揭示出这个角色的本质，用高度凝练的方式呈现出他的全部独特面貌。"[①]（杨向荣，2007：122）翻译文学作品中的人物对话亦是如此：译者首先要把握原语中人物对话的言内外行为，尤其是要深入发掘他们的言外行为，并用译语中丰富的手段充分传达出来，使原著中人物的语言特色在译作中得以再现，人物的个性形象得以重塑；译者还要注意原语中言后行为是否预期发生，如果发生，翻译时要使听话人的言后行为符合说话人的言外行为，反之亦然，这样人物对话才能翻译得更加精当贴切。

---

① 杨向荣译．尤多拉·韦尔蒂访谈录[J]．青年文学，2007，(3)．

考古术语英译的接受美学观

摘　要：随着中外文化交流日益频繁，中国几千年优秀历史文化得到进一步发掘和传播。为了让世人更好地认识这个泱泱古国遗存的历史文物，妥帖到位的翻译显得尤为重要。接受美学的翻译理论扬弃了文本中心论，强调了翻译过程中读者的中心地位，读者的期待视野和审美意识决定了文本翻译的方向。从读者的语言习惯、文化背景和审美感受三个方面来分析考古术语英译的接受美学观，为今后的考古术语汉英翻译实践提供借鉴和参考。

关键词：考古术语；汉译英；接受美学翻译理论

引言

随着中外交流的进一步深入，中国几千年的优秀历史文化得到进一步发掘和传播，传世古物得到更多的搜集和整理，为了让世人更好地认识这个泱泱古国的遗存文明，更加妥帖、到位的翻译显得尤为重要。考古术语是在考古领域里，考古人员共同遵从、使用、交流、讨论的语言，很少在该领域以外使用，在日常生活中基本不用。考古术语翻译属于专业技术翻译的范畴，考古术语本身的难度，给翻译工作者提出了挑战，结合考古术语已有的汉译英翻译实践和构建考古动态术语数据库的经验，从接受美学的角度，探讨适应这个特殊领域的特有翻译原则，为今后的考古术语翻译实践提供借鉴和参考。

从2005年到2015年，中国考古术语的翻译研究不断深入，有从清代严复“信、达、雅”的普适翻译原则出发进行探讨的，2005年刘庆元在《文物翻译的“达”与“信”》一文指出，在处理文物翻译这种特殊的应用翻译时，在“信”与“达”产生矛盾时，要优先“达”，才能达到最佳的译文效果[①]；2007年师新民在《考古文物名词英译探讨》一文中将“信、达、雅”原则与考古翻译的文本特点相结合，提出民族性、简洁

① 刘庆元.文物翻译的“达”与“信”[J].中国科技翻译，2005，18(2)：41.

性、信息性、回译性等考古翻译的具体原则[①]。也有从直译与意译的角度探讨考古词汇翻译，2009 年吴敏焕在《论谈考古词汇的翻译——以汉阳陵遗址博物馆出土的文物为例》的文章中强调译者发挥创造性，直译或意译，在目的语中选择精确的词语[②]；2011 年吴敏焕在《奈达"功能对等"理论下考古发掘报告的翻译》一文中，又从语义对等、文体对等和读者反应对等三个方面，分析如何从语义到文体找到译语中最切近、最自然的对等语来再现原文信息，让读者更好地理解原文，从而产生较高品质的译文[③]。从这十年的研究文献资料里可以发现，考古翻译从对文本的细致探讨，逐渐发展到对译者角色的研究，对读者的关注也有所提及，但还不够深入。

关照读者的翻译视野

20 世纪 60 年代中后期，以德国康斯坦茨学派的姚斯和伊瑟尔为代表，创立了接受美学理论（Reception Aesthetics）。接受美学从以作者或作品为中心，转换到关照读者的视野，即充分考虑读者的语言习惯、背景文化和审美感受，使作品最大程度为读者接受，从而激发读者的想象，形成对作品最好的理解[④]。随着接受美学在中国的广泛传播，在接受美学的影响下，从接受美学理论的角度来探讨翻译理论与实践，成为中国翻译界新的动态和方向。接受美学的翻译理论扬弃了文本中心论，强调了翻译过程中读者的中心地位，读者的期待视野和审美意识决定了文本翻译的方向。接受美学的翻译理论不仅在文学翻译领域得到重视和发展，而且在如旅游、外宣、广告等应用翻译领域中也有研究成果，但是用接受美学翻译理论指导考古汉译英翻译的实践尚无先例，下面就从读者的语言习惯、文化背景和审美感受三个方面来分析考古术语汉译英翻译的接受美学观。

语言习惯

有人说，"如果亚里士多德会讲汉语，他就不会是亚里士多德；如果孔子会讲英语，他就不是孔子。"[⑤]不同民族的思维模式的确影响着语言的发展，汉语与英语在语言表达方面存在差异。在翻译过程中，应该充分考虑读者的民族的思维方式的

---

① 师新民.考古文物名词英译探讨[J].中国科技翻译，2007，20(3)：61-63.

② 吴敏焕.论谈考古词汇的翻译——以汉阳陵遗址博物馆出土的文物为例[J]. 考古与文物，2009，(4).

③ 吴敏焕.奈达"功能对等"理论下考古发掘报告的翻译[J].考古与文物，2011，(4)：111-112.

④ 姚斯. 接受美学与接受理论[M].沈阳：辽宁人民出版社，1987.

⑤ 高一虹.语言文化差异的认识与超越[M].北京：外语教学与研究出版社，2000，1.

特点，译文要符合读者语言表达的习惯。

修饰语的词序

汉语考古术语中心词一般放在最后，修饰语字数越多，越远离中心语，自左往右，依次为①表示领属关系的词语；②表示时间或处所的词语；③数量短语；④主谓、动词、介词短语；⑤双音节形容词或形容词短语；⑥不用“的”形容词（+中心语）。翻译时，修饰语词序会发生变化，英语修饰语的词序排列可以用一首口诀来记忆：美小圆旧黄，法国木书房，即自左往右，依次为①表示性质的词语；②表示大小的词语；③表示形状的词语；④表示新旧的词语；⑤表示颜色的词语；⑥表示产地的词语；⑦表示材质的词语；⑧表示功能的词语（+中心语），而且介词短语、非谓语动词短语、定语从句等较长修饰语往往放在中心语后面。例如在湖北枣阳九连墩发掘的战国时期文物“龙耳铜方壶”，曾经被错误翻译成“Bronze square pot with dragon-shaped ears”，这就违背了英语读者的表达习惯，即表示材质的修饰词 bronze 要紧跟中心词 pot，所以更好的翻译为：“Hu, square bronze pot with dragon-shaped ears”；再例如“中国古代建筑”被翻译成“Chinese ancient architecture”这也违背英语读者将“国名修饰语”放置在“时间修饰语”后的表达习惯，正确的翻译应该为：“ancient Chinese architecture”。

中心词的位置

汉语中心词多放在修饰语后面，而英语中心词的位置富于变化，可在修饰语之前，也可在修饰语之后或中间，如考古术语“鹿纹彩陶盆”的中心词“盆”放在了汉语短语的最后，翻译成英语时可以考虑英语读者的表达习惯，将它调整到短语的中间，即为：“Pen, painted pottery basin with deer designs”，英语中心词“basin”前面有分词形容词修饰语 painted，后面有介词短语修饰语 with deer designs，位置灵活。

文化背景

考古翻译不仅仅是语言问题，更是与文化背景有着很大的关系。王佐良先生曾经说过：“翻译里最大的困难是什么呢？就是两种文化不同。”“他（译者）处理的是个别词,他面对的则是两大片文化。"[①]文化背景是指特定文化下的人物物品、意识观念、风俗习惯、宗教信仰等。中国几千年优秀遗产文化要在世界范围内得到传承与发扬,必须充分考虑读者的接受程度,译文必须在原文与译文所涉及的两种不同的特定文化观念之间达到一种平衡,才不会引起读者的反感和抵制[②]。

人物物品/意识观念

中国古代建筑独特结构"枋",即两柱之间起联系作用的横木,断面一般为矩形,这种结构在西方建筑上很少见,如果采用 transliteration(音译法),使用汉语拼音简单地将它翻译为 "fang",这在英语读者中间很容易产生误解,甚至让他们对这种建筑结构心生厌恶,因为在英汉双解词典里,英语单词"fang"的解释是:"a long sharp tooth of an animal, such as a dog or a poisonous snake (犬、毒蛇等)的尖牙"。在这种情况下,增加阐释性文字来翻译中国古建筑结构"枋":"Fang, square timber connecting two pillars",才能够更好地为英语读者接受。再例如在大英博物馆里陈列的中国古物"元青花折枝牡丹孔雀大罐",被翻译成"Guan jar, porcelain with under-glaze cobalt-blue decoration of a peacock and peahen. 14th century AD"。在西方文化里,孔雀是狂妄傲气、爱慕虚荣的形象,人们经常说 as proud as a peacock (像孔雀一样高傲),牡丹只不过是一种普通花卉。但是在中国文化里,牡丹是百花之王,代表荣华富贵;孔雀是百鸟之王,代表吉凤呈祥,这些深刻寓意在译文中得不到传达,中国古物的内涵也就无法真正为英语读者体味。同样地,需要增加阐释性文字以添补文化之间的差异,即"Guan, under-glaze cobalt-blue porcelain jar, with the decoration of a peony and a peacock, a kind of glorious and auspicious design in Chinese culture.14th century AD"。

风俗习惯/宗教信仰

考古术语汉译英动态数据库的词条"南阳市万家园画像石墓由墓道、封门、墓门构成,并且发现 9 块画像石"里的"封门",是中国民间风俗里特有的概念,它是用来封闭墓室的厚木板,英语里没有与之对应的词语,不能简单地翻译为"a sealed door(封闭的门)"。为了让英语读者准确理解,需要增加文字进行阐释性翻译,即

---

① 王佐良.翻译中的文化比较[M].北京:中国对外翻译出版公司,2000:20.

② Andre Lefevere.翻译、历史与文化论集[M].上海:上海外语教育出版社,2010:35.

"Fengmen, a plank used for sealing the coffin chamber"。

审美感受

随着各个民族社会历史文化条件和生活环境,长期在不同民族心理深层进行沉淀,不同民族的读者在审美感受上,存在不同的差异。在考古术语汉译英时,我们要考虑英语读者的审美感受,不能一味将汉语的思维模式和审美标准强加于英语读者,在翻译时尽量避免不地道的中式英语。

词汇的审美感受

颜色词是对大自然和社会生活中颜色的描述,带有浓厚的文化色彩和寓意作用,折射出社会的生活特征和人物的心理活动。英汉两种不同文化背景下的读者对颜色词语的审美感受存在差异。中国古籍《说文解字》提道:"**青**,东方色也。木生火,从生、丹。"在中国古代社会里,"青"象征着庄重古朴,传统的器物和服饰上多为青色。"青"本义为蓝色(青天),《荀子·劝学》中有:"**青**,取之于蓝,而**青**于蓝";"青"也可以代表嫩绿色(青草),唐代诗人王维《送元二使安西》中有:"客舍**青青**柳色新";"青"还可以代表黑色(青丝),唐代李白古诗《将进酒》中有:"高堂明镜悲白发,朝如**青**丝暮成雪"。在西方文化中,蓝色象征着高雅端庄,圣母、天使的衣服和艺术徽章是蓝色①,而不是绿色。因此,在翻译考古术语中的颜色词,要充分考虑英语读者的审美判断。例如首都博物馆里陈列的"景德镇窑**青**白釉戏剧舞台人物纹枕",其英语词条是"greenish-white-glazed pillow with a play scene","青"被翻译成"greenish(淡绿色)",而忽略了实物的颜色,会引起英语读者审美上的困惑,翻译成 bluish 更为妥帖。

中国五千年的历史文化是精耕细作的内陆农业文化,而西方文化的主体是希腊、罗马文化,起源于四千年前以航海扩张拓展为生的腓尼基文化(Phoenician culture)②。中西文化生活方式的历史差异,决定了汉语读者对词汇的理解是聚焦思维模式的审美感受,而英语读者属于发散性思维模式的审美感受。汉语考古术语用字简短精练,却有着丰富内涵,往往用具体数字表达抽象概念,翻译时,应该充分考虑英语读者与之相反的审美感受。例如"'蚩尤受庐山之金(铜)而作**五兵**'是

---

① 刘长林.中国系统思维:文化基因探视[M].北京:社会科学文献出版社,2008.

② 彭秋荣.英汉颜色词的文化内涵及其翻译[J].中国科技翻译,2001,14(1):31.

江南地区最早用铜记载”,考古术语“五兵”用字凝练,字面上的含义是“五种兵器”,具体指哪几种兵器,也很难考证,其实是泛指各种兵器,翻译时应该考虑英语读者的发散思维,“types of ancient weapons”比“five weapons”的译文更妥帖。

句子结构的审美感受

汉语是一种意合的语言(parataxis),句子结构较为流散灵活,连接各部分靠的是语义与意境;而英语是一种形合的语言(hypotaxis),句子结构较为缜密严谨,用关联词连接各部分形成整体①。汉语句子的主语或者谓语可以省略,而英语句子必须有完整的主语和谓语。例如青铜矿冶文化考古词条“经考古发掘,共清理出打制石器88件,以及大量古生物化石。这处遗址的发现将矿冶文化的源头追溯到二、三十万年前的远古时代”被翻译为:“In archeological excavation, 88 chopping tools and a lot of paleontological fossils were cleaned out, **tracing** the source of mining industry culture back to 200,000 or 300,000 years ago”。译文中,tracing的主语是“...tools and...fossils”,英语读者会觉得莫名其妙,建议改为:“In archeological excavation, 88 chipped tools and a lot of paleontological fossils were cleaned out, **which traces** the source of mining and metallurgical culture back to 200,000 or 300,000 years ago.”关联词which引导的非限定定语从句,指代前面整句话,即定语从句的主语是“这处遗址的发现”。由此可见,考古术语汉译英翻译应该遵循英语句法的严密逻辑,才能满足英语读者严谨的审美感受。

接受美学翻译理论强调读者的主体性,翻译时以读者为中心,充分考虑读者的语言习惯、背景文化和审美感受。将接受美学的翻译观融入考古术语的英译实践中,这样才能让英语读者通过他们感受妥帖得体的译文,更好地认识和了解中国遗存的历史文明,领略和欣赏华夏千年文化博大精深的醇厚魅力,从而唤起他们心中对中国悠久历史文明的向往与敬重。

① 周芳珠.翻译多元论[M].北京:中国对外翻译出版公司,2004:15,38-39.

妙合之译及诗歌语法

龚　刚[1]

翻译是为了打破语言障碍，信是第一位的。要做到信，不光要还原本意，还要还原风格，当雅则雅，当俗则俗，当文则文，当白则白。兵无常势，水无常形，运用之妙，存乎一心。严复有信达雅说，钱锺书有化境论，顾彬（Kubin）有超越原文论，诺奖得主布罗茨基（Joseph Brodsky）有诗化论（Poetry is what is gained in translation），我之翻译观或可称为妙合论。

《暮光之城》（*Twilight*）有如下台词：

I only love three things in the world, the sun, the moon and you. The sun for the day, the moon for the night and you, forever.

试依诗化论和超越原文论翻译如下：

吾爱者三，日月与卿。
日存于昼，月存于夜。
汝存于心，至死不渝。

日暮惜落霞
晓来辞月华
吾意最怜卿
情深永无涯

诗与哲学都以创造性使用语法的方式表达特殊意涵。如美国诗人狄金森

① 澳门大学教授，博士生导师

(Emily Dickinson)的诗歌喜欢违反语法常规使用大写:

Experiment to me
Is every one I meet
If it contain a Kernel?
The Figure of a Nut

Presents upon a Tree
Equally plausibly
But Meat within, is requisite
To Squirrels and to Me

又如弗兰克·扎帕(Frank Zappa)的专辑名为 *You Are What You Is*,其中的 is 不合常规语法,但如果从存在主义哲学的角度看,is 对应 being(在),而你之在,是独一无二的,在此处,you 被客观化了。这是诗化的表达,突破了常规语法。

西外吴烨洲认为:"兰波的 je est un autre (I is an another)就是故意这样写,有自己独特的哲学意识在里面,按照目前我们学的语法,表面上看可能是错的,但深层次想表达的情感就是依靠这特殊的句式体现的。"

俄国形式主义又称语言诗学,主张突破常规表达与日常语言,令人发现习焉不察的常见事物的本真面目。什克洛夫斯基认为,奇异化的文学语言的功能就是让石头成为石头。雅各布·布森则进一步强调陌生化效果。

从中西诗歌与哲学的大量语用实例可见,个性化或诗化的表达常常有意突破语法常规。Garry 认为,如果你是 rap artist,"Then all rules go out the door, and 'you is' becomes acceptable"。

参考文献

[1] 程登吉.幼学琼林[M].长沙:岳麓书社,1986.

[2] (德)康德.纯粹理性批判(英文)[M].(英)米勒顿,译.上海:世界图书出版公司,2011.

[3] (德)康德.实践理性批判(英文)[M].(德)阿尔伯特,译.上海:世界图书出版公司,2011.

[4] (德)尼采.查拉图斯特拉如是说[M].南京:译林出版社,2016.

[5] (德)叔本华.作为意志和表象的世界[M].北京:商务印书馆,1982.

[6] 王国维.人间词话(汉英对照)[M].(美)李又安(Rickett, A.A.),译.南京:译林出版社,2010.

[7] 王国维.人间词话(汉英对照)[M].(台湾)涂经诒,译.北京:北京语言大学出版社,2016.

[8] 姚淦铭,王燕.王国维文集(上部、下部)[M].北京:中国文史出版社,2007.